# PASSING NOTES

TEACHERS' LOUNGE
BOOK 1

**NORA EVERLY**

# COPYRIGHT

# CHAPTER 1
# NICK

*Meet me at Daisy's Nut House after school. - Nick*

"Ethan, Sasha! It's time to go! Being late the first day is not how we want to get the school year started, okay?" And lord help me if their mother found out if we were. We'd been divorced almost as long as we were married and a lecture from her was the last thing I needed.

I heaved out a sigh and straightened my tie before pouring my third cup of coffee for the day. Was I addicted? Yes. At this point in my life, I was pretty sure I couldn't live without it. Hell, I could mainline caffeine straight into a vein and it wouldn't perk me up. Nothing motivated me lately, aside from being the best father I could be for my kids.

*Burnout, thy name is Nick.*

"All my friends are riding the bus," Sasha complained as she slunk down the hall and slid onto a barstool, all while furiously texting on her cell phone. "I'm the only one being dropped off," she huffed. "You can't walk me in. None of my friends' parents are walking them in. Please?"

Sasha was eleven going on forty-two. She was precocious, ran mental rings around my oldest, Ethan, and had me worried for my future sanity if her request last night for me to drive her to Daisy's Nut House after school and leave her there with her friends for the evening was any indicator of her budding social life. The answer to her request was an unequivocal *no*. As far as I was concerned, eleven was far too young for unsupervised fun with friends.

*As for me?* In addition to being perpetually exhausted, I was an English teacher and football coach at Green Valley High School, in my hometown of Green Valley, Tennessee. I also snapped up all the paid advisory positions I could manage, taught summer school, and ran a football camp. I couldn't afford to take time off. My divorce had ruined me financially. Going from two incomes to one with two kids to support, paying rent on my cheap apartment, and forking over enough to cover one-third of a mortgage payment could do that, especially on a teacher's salary.

But those days were finally over. After scrimping and saving every extra penny for the down payment, I was finally buying another house in town. My ex was still in the house we had bought together. I didn't begrudge her the place; the kids loved it, and it had been their home since Ethan was born. I would never try to take that away from them just to save a few bucks.

This coming weekend I would be moving into a house around the corner from their mother's place. Hopefully they would love it just as much, especially since we'd be close enough for them to walk between our houses—and ride the bus to school in the morning, which had apparently become a huge deal.

Every other week at Dad's would soon level up to include a corner lot with a huge backyard and a swimming pool, and I couldn't wait. The thought of mowing my own lawn and having a garage again would have made me smile if I wasn't so damn tired. Instead, all I could manage was a slight relaxation of the tense scowl that had become a permanent fixture on my face.

"Do we have any Pop-Tarts?" Sasha broke through my semi-conscious reverie with a put-upon sigh, and I snapped back to attention.

"Yes, we do. And hey, you'll be able to ride the bus next week. We'll be in the new house by then, okay? Everything you chose for your room is ordered and on the way."

"Okay, Dad." She hopped off the stool to rummage through the pantry.

"Ethan, come on!" I called. "Time for breakfast."

He appeared in the kitchen entrance, sleepy-eyed and dragging ass. "I need at least another week of summer vacation," he grumbled. "I'm not ready for school to start." He was almost thirteen but, in many ways, much younger than Sasha's eleven. He liked video games and skateboarding at the park, Marvel movies, and Minecraft. His friends were the same way. When they were here, it was nothing but Xbox, computer games, and pizza. Girls were not on his radar yet; boys weren't either for that matter, not that I cared either way. I just wanted my kids to be happy.

"You'll be fine. Once we get outside in the fresh air and get moving, you'll feel better."

*Yeah, right.*

He shot me a side-eye and a grin as he scrambled onto a barstool and took a Pop-Tart from Sasha. He didn't believe that any more than I did. "No, I won't."

I shrugged. I had lost the will to be encouraging. "Well, you can camp out on the couch and watch TV all you want when you get home. No time limit. How about that?"

"Can we go to Daisy's Nut House and have cheeseburgers for dinner?" His eyes lit up. "Oh! Can we stop there and get doughnuts on the way to school too?"

I gestured to the Pop-Tart in his hand with a sardonic smile but decided to give in, just a little bit. "How about we pick up burgers on the way home?" The day hadn't even truly started, and I already knew I'd be exhausted by the end of it.

"Deal. I feel a little bit better, but only like ten percent. I'd still rather go back to bed." He shoved half the Pop-Tart in his mouth and took a bite.

"Don't forget to chew." I shook my head. "Look, I'm tired too, but we've got this. We're Eastons and nothing keeps an Easton down, right?" They rolled their eyes in good-natured amusement at my attempt to rally them up. "Now, y'all finish your Pop-Tarts—don't forget to *not* tell your mother I still buy them for you—and let's get going."

"Yeah, and you know she'll be ticked off if we're late. Come on, Ethan." Sasha brushed the crumbs from her T-shirt, grabbed her new backpack from the table, and hoisted it over her shoulder. "I don't want to be late anyway. My friends are meeting me by the cafeteria." I could tell by the unconscious furrow of her brow and the tremor in her voice she was nervous.

"Whatever, my friends won't care." Ethan slipped his phone into his pocket and snagged his backpack off the back of the stool. "They're probably still half asleep too. We won't be fully awake until it's time for lunch."

"Are you sure you don't want me to walk you in, Sasha, honey? It's okay to be nervous on the first day. Or any day for that matter."

She shook her head and shot me a tremulous smile. "I'll be fine. But thanks, Daddy."

*Daddy.*

She'd made the switch to "Dad" soon after her last day of elementary school and it had broken my heart a little bit. Time was slipping away almost too fast to bear; each year, they became more independent and needed me less.

I ruffled her hair as I passed her to grab my keys and messenger bag from the table. "Let me know if you change your mind on the way."

Both kids would be attending Green Valley Middle School this year. The high school was just down the street. I liked the idea of being close to them all day. School should be the safest place for a kid, but unfortunately, that was not the world we lived in anymore.

The drive to school went quickly despite the morning traffic. After all my years teaching, I had perfected my timing. One minute off schedule would get us stuck in the rush of school buses, parents driving their kids to school, and people on their way to work.

After dropping them off with wishes for a great first day—and another refusal from Sasha to have me walk her in—I drove the few hundred feet down the street to the high school, swung into the teachers' parking lot, and found a spot. I had exactly five minutes to sit in the air-conditioned cab of my truck and attempt to find my focus for the day. I ran my hands into my hair and rested my forehead on the steering wheel. The temptation to take a nap was almost overwhelming.

*Just one minute.*

I closed my eyes and let out a breath. A headache was beginning to form at my temples, and the press of the steering wheel combined with the cold air blasting in my face eased it.

This would be my last year of taking on extra work—except for coaching football; I loved that. It reminded me of high school, when I used to play. Something about the evening air, the teamwork, and the competition kept me going. It gave me a sense of nostalgia and reminded me of a time when I felt like I had something to live for—aside from my kids—that was solely for myself. I wanted to keep that feeling; it gave me hope that I'd find something just for me again someday.

Knuckles tapping on my window jarred me awake. I jerked upright, blinking rapidly against the glare of the sun shining through my windshield.

*Shit.*

"I'm awake. I'm up."

Frantically, I checked the clock on my dashboard. I'd been out for four minutes. That wasn't so bad. I'd still be on time for first period.

I lowered the window to find one of my students, Gracie Hill, standing there. She was part of the student paper—which I was the faculty advisor for—and she would be a senior this year. She also sometimes babysat for Ethan and

Sasha, and if I recalled correctly, would be in my English 4 class this year. She watched me with her eyebrows up. A sideways smirk crossed her face and I winced. "It's only the first day, Mr. Easton. Burnt out already?"

I shook my head. "I'm okay. I, uh . . ." My voice trailed off when I caught sight of who stood glaring at me behind her, arms crossed over her chest, one hip leaning on the driver's side door of a hot little BMW parked a few empty spaces away.

My jaw dropped. Black leggings hugged every inch of her delectable curves, and her cropped hoodie told me she was still a fan of *Smash Girl* comics. Pale blond waves crowned her head in a messy bun as big cornflower-blue eyes flashed fire into mine. Her eyebrows dropped low into a V and she turned away with a sneer.

*It was her.*

Clara Hill.

The woman who had wrecked me for all others at the age of eighteen.

My first love, my first everything. She had broken my heart into pieces and ran off with most of them when she left Green Valley after we graduated. She was the biggest secret I had ever kept, and the only true regret I had in my life.

Damn, there were so many things I would have done differently back then if I had known better.

My heart thudded and my senses spun at her nearness. I was instantly wide-awake as the shock of seeing her after all these years hit me full force. She was beautiful. Even more so now that I understood what I had lost when she left me.

Of course I knew Gracie was her little sister. In a town as small as Green Valley, everyone knew at least a little bit of everyone's family history. Who was related to who, marriages, divorces, scandals . . .

Gossip spread through a small town like ours faster than a hot knife through butter. But even so, it was surprisingly easy to keep a secret when given the proper motivation. And Clara and me? Our history was buried so far deep in the past no one would ever find out about us, not unless we wanted them to. However, Gracie was clever enough to pick up a clue if Clara unleashed even half of that anger she was currently aiming my way.

I stroked a fingertip down the bridge of my nose, struggling to find something to say to Gracie as memories crashed into my brain and stole my train of thought.

*Why was she so angry when she was the one who ended everything?*

"Uh . . ."

Gracie turned to her sister, then back to me with a pitying laugh. "Have you met Clara before? You had to have gone to school with her, right? Don't worry, you're not the first man I've seen turn into an idiot around her. Anyway—"

"Oh, no, I—" I slammed my eyes shut with a cringe. *Busted.* "I'm just tired. I had a late night. Um, insomnia kicked my butt. Thanks for waking me up. Go on to class, Gracie. I'm on my way."

"You're welcome. Just so you know, I'll be running late for a while. I have a sprained ankle. I'll be in this boot with crutches for the next couple of weeks or so. Clara will be dropping me off and picking me up until it's better." She held up one of her crutches as evidence.

"No problem. I won't mark you tardy. Make sure the front office knows so they can spread the word."

"Thanks. See you in English." I watched her hobble off, then turned in time to see Clara shoot me one last glare before shutting her door with a vicious slam and speeding away.

# CHAPTER 2
# CLARA

*Hey there, quarterback. Just because I hang out under the bleachers doesn't mean I'm easy. Stay in your own habitat, try a cheerleader. I'm busy. - Clara*

**W**as there ever a time in my life when I had known what I wanted? Like, from the bottom of my soul knew how I wanted to spend the rest of my life? *No.*

*Liar . . .*

I pulled into my garage and cut the engine. The rest of the day loomed in front of me like a one of those nightmares you wake up from that lingers around in your subconscious all day to wreck your mood.

Had school always started in August? What utter bullshit. It was hot, way too bright outside, and far too early for my liking.

At least I had done something useful before the Nick sighting. My baby sister had sprained her ankle over the weekend, and I had been pathetically quick to volunteer to chauffer her around for the next few weeks. Why not? It wasn't like I had anything else going on in my life.

Leaving the garage door open, I wandered out to my driveway as my sister and brother-in-law pulled up to the curb to pick up his daughter, Lizzy, on their way to work at Monroe & Sons, a local contracting company. Barrett was an architect, and Sadie was an interior designer; together, they were adorable and nauseating. Barrett lived next door before they got married, but Lizzy and her husband rented the place now.

Gracie was the youngest of my three sisters. Sadie was the oldest, I was next, Willa was third. The three of us were all born within two years of each other and Gracie came almost ten years after Willa. She was the last hurrah of my parents' miserable marriage before my dad took off for parts unknown, never to be heard from again.

We grew up on a farm in the foothills above Green Valley called Lavender Hill. When we were kids, it was a run-down mess, but year by year my mother had grown it into something spectacular.

"How were the boys this morning? First day drop-off go okay?" The look on Sadie's face told the tale. My twin nephews could be *a lot* in the mornings.

"How do you think? It went by in a blur of exhausted chaos, whining, and complaints. Let's schedule a margarita patio night. I need to unwind." Barrett helped her out of his truck, the dang frickin' gentleman. I couldn't even hate him for taking my sister away—he was just too nice of a guy.

"So much yes to that. You're my soul mate, Sadie. Sorry, Barrett, she's mine and I'm never letting her go." For years it had been me and Sadie against the world; sharing her with Barrett had taken some getting used to.

We'd grown up hard. Our mother was not a warm person. In fact, she used to be downright cruel. Her disappointment in us was the one constant in our childhood we could always count on, and she had never been shy about expressing it.

He closed her door and met me on the porch with a grin. "Aw, Clara. You don't have to let her go—I'd never dare attempt to get between the two of you. Choose a night, I'll take the boys with me and pick up tacos for dinner while y'all relax."

"Damn it, I adore you, you sister-stealing punk ass."

"Right back at ya, sweetheart." His smile shifted to the side as he spotted Lizzy walking out of her house. He flicked two fingers out in a wave. "See you later." Hand in hand they went back to the truck and left with Lizzy.

I waved them off, then wandered through the garage into the kitchen. I had bought this dang house to help out Sadie after her dumbass ex-husband left her, and for a while it had been great. It was impossible to feel lonely with her here to talk to and my twin nephews running amok all over the place.

After years of living alone in Nashville it had felt great to be with family again. And then Sadie got married to Barrett, took the boys, and moved up to Bandit Lake, into the house they fell in love in while renovating it for Monroe & Sons.

I missed the closeness I had shared with Sadie and the boys when we were all together under my roof. Late nights and early mornings were the times you really got to know a person, when the masks you wore during the day came off and everyone became their true selves.

The house was too quiet now and the last thing I needed was to be alone with my thoughts.

The past couple years had been terrible. I'd lost out on a partnership at my law firm for not sleeping with the newest partner—who was also the founder's son—then quit in a fit of righteous fury. The HR complaints I'd filed were still "pending" and would probably be buried somewhere beneath a pile of proverbial papers for the rest of eternity. There's nothing that old rich white guys loved more than other old rich white guys, and my former law firm was as old money and established as you could get. I suspected someone had been bribed to squash my complaints. I knew I should push the issue, but I'd lost the will to fight.

I'd had a boyfriend, a breakup, a pregnancy scare, and a second chance with said boyfriend, only to be unceremoniously dumped about two months ago when he decided to take a job on an oil rig and leave town. According to Chris, I was a handful. It seemed I was both too much for him and not enough all at the same time.

Good riddance to bad rubbish. I was better off unemployed and alone anyway. At least that's what I was trying to convince myself of, though I didn't quite believe it just yet.

I needed to reevaluate my life and it had to be done on my own. Therefore, with the exception of my brothers-in-law—who had proved their worthiness of my sisters—I was on an indefinite break from all men.

Like my father, who left when life got hard and never looked back.

Like the creeper I had worked for, who felt like I owed him free access to my vagina and a BJ in exchange for a promotion to partner.

Or like my ex, Chris, who dumped me for requiring respect and basic human decency—like, why is a good morning text such a dang big deal? Was acknowledging my existence that hard?

I deserved to have a break from the stresses of life, which I found were almost always caused by an entitled, stupid man.

I deserved to have some Zen and inner peace, damn it.

I needed a fresh start.

*But how many "fresh starts" can one woman have?*

At what point should I pack it in and just commit to a lifetime of solitude? Maybe I should continue living off my savings and hide out in this house for the rest of my life. I mean, I could certainly afford to do so. It's not like there were men waiting around to hit on me in my pantry, dang it. I was safe from temptation in here.

I paced a circle around the kitchen island like a lion in a cage, growing more frustrated when I finally acknowledged what had really set me off.

It wasn't *men*.

I could handle *men*.

Hell, I'd been handling idiot men and the various messes they'd brought into my life since I was a kid.

It was *one man*.

The truth was my mood had shot to hell when Gracie stepped to the side and I saw Nick Easton's head pop up in the window of that stupid truck.

*Nick was different.*

He had always been the exception to every rule I had ever made for myself, the main one being to stay away from men.

He'd broken my heart a long time ago and I'd never quite managed to put it back together right. It pissed me off how much it hurt to see him after all this time. So far I'd managed to avoid running into him in town, and I had wanted to keep it that way.

My heart lurched in my chest, and I flung my keys across the kitchen as I slammed my eyes shut and tried to force out the memories his presence this morning had awakened in me.

He was my first love. My first *everything*. He had held me together after my dad left. Nick had loved me, comforted me, and treated me like a princess. When I was with him, for the first time in my life, I had felt like I was worth something. So in return I gave him my whole entire heart, along with my body and soul. I trusted him with everything I had to give and confided in him my deepest feelings. He was one of the few people I'd allowed to know the real me. I hadn't been the same since I lost him.

Mindlessly, I prepared a pot of coffee and continued pacing the kitchen as it brewed. Caffeination and distraction were the name of the game for me lately.

I found my favorite self-help podcast and mentally prepared to zone out. By now, I had it memorized; it always gave me a mood lift. It was either listen to this woo-woo bullshit or start plotting some murders.

*"Focus your breath and quiet your minds. Let us manifest a positive outlook together . . ."*

I inhaled a deep breath then let it out alongside a burst of rage as my thoughts swarmed with images of Nick and me together. How could I manifest anything when there was not a single speck of serotonin left rattling around in my brain and a dopamine hit was nothing but a distant memory?

I filled my huge travel mug with coffee, dressed it up with hazelnut creamer, and stalked outside. My favorite coping mechanism of late was to sit on my porch and watch the neighborhood as I worked on my knitting, took care of my plants, and performed a live reenactment of *Rear Window*—except my injuries were all mental, unlike good ol' Jimmy Stewart in his wheelchair. I felt like the captain of my own little ship, cruising along while I watched the world go by. Safe and sound—and alone—with all the comforts I needed right inside my house.

Watching everyone else's lives go by as I let mine fade into a lonely and boring oblivion was the only thing keeping my finger on the pulse of humanity. It was either this or embrace rock bottom and become a full-on hermit.

*This is how busybodies are made.*

Speaking of busybodies, I glanced down the block, waving at Mr. Neal as he got into his old Buick to drive to the high school. He was ancient and had been the librarian at Green Valley High for decades.

*Yeah, I see you, you bitchy little troll.*

He'd never liked me or any of my sisters, like it was our fault our circumstances were bad as kids. He used to call us trash whenever we went to check out books. He was judging me right now; I could see it in his holier-than-thou sneer as he waved back to me. Like, how dare I be able to afford a house better than his? But I didn't really care since I judged him back just as much for being mean to three girls who just wanted something to read to help them escape their shitty home life.

I shook the thought off. I did not need that kind of negativity at the moment, thank you very much. Not when I was barely hanging on by a thread.

Rationally, I knew I had options, but I was not in the mood to see reason. Logic was for people with motivation, goals, and the will to make life changes. I was fresh out of all that stuff. Chris had stolen most of it when he left, along with the bulk of my pride. And Nick had taken the few remaining shreds of that this morning.

Okay, I admit it. Being alone sucked.

I propped my feet on the porch railing, took a huge burning hot sip of coffee, and waited for something to happen.

*Bring on the freakin' inner peace.*

Even though it was empty now, I still loved my house. Two stories, four bedrooms, three bathrooms, and a huge backyard. The fact that I'd ended up in the middle of Green Valley, owning a house on Clearview Lane, was ridiculous. Especially considering the way I had blown out of town nearing on fifteen years ago, determined to never come back.

The image of Nick sitting there in his truck, all sexy and handsome with his adorable, floppy, dark hair and gorgeous square jawline—looking even better than I remembered, for Pete's sake—flashed through my mind and I forced it right back out. Thinking of him would be the opposite of peaceful. Seeing him had knocked the air out of my lungs and launched me straight back to the morning after high school graduation and the sad, pathetic hours I'd spent at the bus station waiting for him to meet me before finally being dumped with a note.

I remembered calling his house days later, desperate to find out how he was doing, only to have his mother tell me he was fine. He was happy, all moved into his new apartment at college, getting ready to start football practice, and living next to a cute girl with possibilities. She had hinted broadly that I should leave him alone. Something about her tone had made me wonder if she had somehow found out about us.

*Enough.*

His family would never accept me, no matter what I'd made myself into. I'd had nothing back then and he'd had everything to look forward to.

I picked up my knitting and watched as a moving truck backed into the corner lot next door. It had been empty since last weekend when the Middletons, my elderly next-door neighbors, had moved out to cruise the country in their RV. *Maybe I should buy an RV and get the hell out of here . . .*

Nah, I liked this porch too much and I had finally gotten my yard exactly the way I wanted it. Old lady porch life was the way to go. I just had to figure out exactly what that entailed, beyond being a busybody, of course.

I didn't think I was old enough yet for bird-watching; so far, I found it boring and I couldn't tell the different species apart. I perked up. Maybe I'd get an interesting new neighbor to observe, for science and boredom and my own amusement.

Maybe a lonely hot guy would move in, and we could start up an illicit friends-with-benefits affair. Or perhaps I could just surreptitiously watch from my balcony when he would inevitably take a skinny-dip in that awesome pool in the backyard.

*How convenient would that be?*

So far, the alone part of my life was terrible, but I felt it would ultimately become survivable. After all, I did have family and friends to hang out with, so I wasn't actually *alone*-alone, just lonely sometimes. It was the horny part that was becoming an issue.

The dry spell was real.

A man in a moving company polo shirt stepped out of the cab of the truck with a grin.

I smiled back as he slid open the garage and headed inside.

"Alexa, volume up!" I shouted through the open window behind me.

*"True inner peace begins when we allow ourselves to acknowledge our pain."*

"Oh, fuck off," I mumbled as I stabbed my knitting needles into the ball of yarn. "Alexa, stop!" My mood was too bleak for this crap today and it was all frickin' Nick's fault—as if I needed another reason to hate him. I'd been acknowledging my dang pain all morning. Maybe it was time for a new podcast.

*God, how I wished I really did hate Nick.*

I chucked my knitting across the porch with a low scream of frustration. "Damn it."

My across-the-street neighbor, Leonard, strolled outside through his open garage, gardening gloves on and hands full of supplies, at exactly the right time to see my outburst.

He was hot, and I watched him frequently. But he was also a total weirdo —not that I had room to judge when I was currently in the middle of my reign as the Wackadoodle Queen of Clearview Lane.

I couldn't decide if he was trying to have a better yard than mine, or if he was just very into gardening; either way, he wouldn't win. Mine would always be better.

He lived with his mom, Janice, who used to be the band director at the high school. I remembered her from when I went there. Janice was good people. Sometimes she brought me brownies and joined me on my porch for a chat. Being a lonely object of pity sometimes came with baked goods, which was a bonus I had never expected but one I could get behind.

"Mornin'," he called, lifting his chin in my direction as a knowing smirk slid across his face.

I narrowed my eyes and shot back a smirk of my own. "Hey."

*Was he judging me?*

So what if I was out here every day?

So what if I frequently yelled at my Echo Dot? I could do what I wanted on my own damn porch.

Sure, on occasion I wondered what my neighbors thought of me with my positivity podcasts blaring through my window, crystals lining my porch railing, and my mug of coffee constantly within reach as I sat out here all day clad in my various leggings and hoodie combinations as I spite-knitted in a straight line because I didn't know shit about knitting except what my mother had forced me and my sisters to learn as kids.

*Whatever.*

Leonard had no life either, aside from his obsessive gardening and bunco night with his mom and her friends—The Bunco Broads. They'd invited me to join them, but I was at least two-and-a-half decades younger, so I'd said no. It had felt like a pity invite. Anyway, Leonard could just fuck all the way off if he was judging me.

"Clara!" I was so far into my internal rant that I almost fell out of my chair at the sound of my name being called. My head whipped to the side as Sadie jumped out of Barrett's truck and came hauling ass my way, her face filled with concern.

"Oh crap." She carried a box of doughnuts from Daisy's Nut House and an iced mocha. "What is it?" Whatever she was about to tell me had to be bad if she came here armed with doughnuts. I mean, doughnuts were great. But also harbingers of doom. Why did everyone bring me treats with their bad news? Was I that easy to placate?

Her eyes darted to the moving truck next door as she barreled to a stop in front of me. "I have news," she announced. "And you're not going to like it. Take these, you're gonna need at least one of them first." She shoved the doughnuts my way and sat next to me on the porch swing. "Eat one. Go on, take a bite."

I opened the box and stuffed half a cream-filled into my mouth. "I'm ready," I murmured, covering my mouth with a hand as I chewed. "Tell me."

"The Middletons sold their house to Nick Easton. He's moving in this weekend. And yes, I do mean, *your* Nick Easton . . . that stupid ass, leaving you waiting at that damn bus stop all alone, dumping you with a damn note like a dang coward—frickin' Nick. I should march right over there when he moves in and—"

"Sadie." I slapped a palm on her thigh. "Focus, please."

"Fine," she grumbled, flinging a hand in the general direction of the place. "He bought it. We can't do anything—it's a done deal. It's happening and soon." She blurted the rest out quick. Like pulling off a Band-Aid.

She knew about me and Nick. She was the only one in the world aside from Nick himself who knew what had gone on between us, and that was because I always told Sadie everything. Well, almost everything. She still didn't know how I'd paid my way through college; no one knew about that.

"Nooooooo," I breathed. I took another huge bite. If I had to stuff my feelings, at least I had doughnuts.

"I'm afraid so. Becky Lee told me when we were going over plans for the day—at some point today someone from Monroe & Sons will be by to make some minor repairs on the deck. So I picked up the doughnuts and came straight here to break the news."

Becky Lee Monroe was Sadie's mother-in-law. She was also my sister Willa's mother-in-law, and my best friend Molly's. Her sons had basically infiltrated my entire life, which was fine because they were great. The only bad thing about them was they were all married and there wasn't one left for me to snap up to protect me from Nick and all the sucky, heartbreaking memories that were about to put the smackdown on me even harder once he moved in and I'd have to see his stupid gorgeous face every day.

"What the hell, Sadie?" I said with my mouth full.

"Listen. I know. This sucks, but it's true. She heard it from Janice at bunco night." She gestured across the street toward Leonard and Janice's house. "Janice heard it from Mari—what's it called when our grandfathers are brothers? Second cousins? Third?" She wrinkled her nose in confusion as I shook my head and gestured for her to get to the dang point. "Whatever, it doesn't matter. Mari took over for Janice years ago. She's the band director at the high school, so she knows Nick pretty well now." I stared at her blankly as she rambled away. "You know Nick teaches there too, right? And he coaches the football team. Anyway, they're friends and—"

"*Gah!* Stop." Mari was our cousin. We used to play together at all the Hill family functions but drifted apart when my father left and my mother cut off his side of the family. We'd reconnected after I came back to town to stay.

Sadie's mouth slammed shut. She stabbed a straw into the mocha and took a huge slurp, watching me carefully as my mind slowly unraveled. "I'm sorry," she murmured. "I don't know what to say and you're kind of freaking me out right now. I've never seen you this quiet. Usually news like this would have you enraged, plotting—*Gah!* At least get up and pace. This silence is scaring me."

"I saw him this morning at the high school when I dropped Gracie off. It was like an omen. I thought it then and I was right. This day is shit. My life is worse." I half groaned, half whined, "I can't move. Can I? I mean, I like it here, my yard is awesome, and what would I do without my porch, Sadie? It's all I have, damn it."

"Hell no, you aren't moving. We'll deal with this. I'm here for you, okay? I promise you'll be fine." She rubbed a hand across her forehead. "Maybe we could do something to make him think the place is haunted or something. Maybe important things could start 'accidentally' breaking, like his toilets, or his garage door opener, and he'll get frustrated and move away." She air-quoted the word *accidentally* and I laughed in spite of myself. "Oh my god! I know!" She stood up, hands in the air. "We could put a bunch of red Jell-O powder in the pool. Boom! Instant creepy murder scene. *Redrum,* amirite?" Her grin was infectious and I smiled back, but it didn't last.

"No, we can't do any of that. We're apparently adults now." I scoffed. "Damn, I've been a wreck all morning and I only saw him for less than a minute sitting in his truck." I tossed the doughnut into the box and dropped my head into my hands. "He's one of Gracie's teachers, for the love of god. Does he have kids? Is he married? Holy crap, how am I going to deal with this?"

The thought of him with another woman made me want to vomit. I had deliberately never asked around about him. The thought of knowing where he'd been and what he'd done without me over all these years was simply too much to bear, so I'd kept my head in the sand when it came to him.

Eyes soft with sympathy met mine as Sadie sat back down and took my hands. "He's divorced and he has two kids, a boy and a girl. Both go to the middle school in town. His ex-wife lives around the corner, in that big house with that yard full of daffodils you've been coveting, and he's been living in one of those crappy apartments across town. Now he's moving in next door."

My eyebrows rose as I reached for another doughnut. "Kids?" I wanted to cry but somehow managed to avoid it.

"I asked Mari about him, okay? I knew you'd want to know. Look, what happened between the two of y'all was almost fifteen years ago. You don't have to talk to him. You don't have to acknowledge he even exists." She dropped her chin and looked me in the eye, her tone much more serious when she said, "You've come a long way and you don't have to do anything that makes you uncomfortable. You have the power now, right?"

I nodded. "You're right. I have the power." I chucked my doughnut back into the box and grabbed her by the shoulders. "I have the freaking power. Damn straight I do. Alexa, play!" I shrieked. I needed my podcast to confirm it.

*"Only you have the power to make positive changes in your life."*

"See?" Sadie let out a laugh and pulled me close. "You have this. Ice him out. And if you're into getting a little bit of petty revenge, you know who to call. Jell-O is on sale at the Piggly Wiggly. I got your back, sister."

# CHAPTER 3
# NICK

*You're a little heartbreaker, aren't you? Give me a chance. I'm not trying to get in your pants. Not yet, anyway. JK. I heard you talking to Molly about your dad in English class, okay? Hit me up if you ever want to talk. I think we can relate to each other. Friends, that's it. - Nick*

Finally, I'd made it to my prep period. In a daze, I wandered from my classroom to the teachers' lounge, heading directly to my favorite Keurig on the battered old table in the corner. There were three, but I only had the mental capacity to maintain one of them. I had no idea what went on with the other two, but some of my co-workers were slobs.

The dim light and dingy décor felt familiar, almost comforting. I shoved a mug under the machine and waited for it to do its thing as I contemplated all the choices I'd made that led me here.

Damn, I did not have time for an existential crisis right now. I had an entire day of classes to get through.

My stomach rumbled and my head pounded. I inhaled a deep breath to get myself together and almost gagged as that familiar musty odor from the fridge assailed my olfactory senses. Of course no one had cleaned it over the summer —gross.

There were a few first day of school celebratory boxes of doughnuts from Daisy's Nut House next to the K-Cups and other coffee accoutrements. Starving, I snagged a cream-filled and had it halfway to my mouth before turning to my fellow English teacher, Clay—known to the students as Mr. Meadows— who grinned knowingly as he watched me from his seat at the long table that bisected the room. "Are they safe?" I asked.

Clay was also from Green Valley and had been a few years ahead of me in school. He had become a good friend over the years.

"Pin Dick brought them in this morning, they're fresh." Principal Pindich, not so lovingly called "Pin Dick" by ninety percent of the faculty and staff behind his back, had become the bane of our collective existence. Hiring him after the former principal, Kip Sylvester, had done nothing for the morale around here. One would have thought any person who replaced a lying, cheat- ing, secretary-banging, criminal asshole would be an improvement, but here we were, stuck with his numbskull successor.

"Good, I'm starving. I skipped breakfast." Grinning, I took a huge bite as I waited for the coffee to finish brewing. I'd brought a breakfast burrito with me this morning, but my perpetual exhaustion coupled with the Clara sighting had caused me to lose my appetite, so I'd tossed it.

"You were almost late today. Is everything okay?" Clay asked just before he took a huge bite of his own doughnut.

"Yeah, I'm fine. The kids didn't want to get up this morning." I'd never been late before. Ever. Blaming them for my four-minute nap in my truck felt wrong, but the truth was a secret. The thought of spilling it felt like a betrayal, even though it had been well over a decade since I'd even seen Clara.

"That's relatable. And hey, first day is almost half down. Only a hundred eighty or so to go. I will not get specific until we're under three digits." He looked as tired as I was.

"That would be depressing. Weird how we can love this job so much and dread it at the same time."

"You got that right," he affirmed with a sardonic smile.

I grew quiet as my mind pathetically wandered back to Clara. I laughed to myself because *back* was not the right descriptor. I had been fixated on her ever since I saw her this morning.

"Your coffee is done. You okay there, Nick? You seem distracted."
*Shit.*

"Sorry, yeah. I'm good." He was right. I was hopelessly distracted and nowhere near okay. If I didn't get my shit together, my students would run all over me, which was not the way I wanted to start the school year off.

I had to get Clara out of my head again.

*How had I done it last time?* I cringed as the haze of memories of myself drunk or hungover in my dorm room infiltrated my thoughts. Going off to college and spending nearly every day wasted was not an option anymore, and I never should have done it in the first place. I'd have to forget about her sober this time.

*Who was I trying to kid?* I'd never forgotten about her. She had been lurking somewhere in the back of my mind ever since I lost her. Right or wrong, she was the standard I had compared every woman I'd ever been with to, and they all came out lacking.

Was it because she was my first love? Or was it more than that?

I had yet to figure it out.

The rest of the day went by in a blur. I'd managed to keep control of my classes only because I made it a point to always be thoroughly prepared and the first day was no exception. I was also able to coast by on my reputation as firm but fair. Friendly but not to be messed with. However, I knew the goodwill would not last if I didn't bring my A game tomorrow.

Damn her for showing up when my life was so close to being settled again.

I'd often felt like my life was divided into a series of boxes: my father's death and how it had destroyed my family, my losing Clara, then my failed marriage and having to share my kids' time with my ex-wife, leaving me a part-time dad, which was never the type of father I'd set out to be. I coped by labeling my shit and packing it away to deal with later.

The problem was, later never came and my boxes had been stacking up for years.

*She left me.*

*After all the plans we'd made, she fucking left me and never looked back, not even once.*

The weight of my life hit me hard as I walked through the crowded halls at the end of the day to leave. The only thing I'd never regretted, not even for a second, was having my kids. They were the silver lining to everything I'd ever been through. Having them in my life meant at least some of my choices hadn't been terrible.

Students milled about at their lockers, chatting and taking their time on their way to the buses or the parent pick-up area. I was in no rush; the sound of the kids drowned out the thoughts pounding around in my head.

*Why couldn't I get her out of my damn mind?*

Seeing Clara was like having Pandora's box blown wide open, my memories of her scattering across the forefront of my thoughts instead of staying where they belonged: packed up, neat, and put away somewhere hidden in the back of my mind.

The sun blinded me as I crossed the parking lot and I squinted against the glare, keeping my head low until I reached my truck. I tossed my messenger bag into the back and looked up.

She was parked in the same spot as this morning, hip resting against her car as she waited for Gracie. My mood veered away from the cloud of confused melancholy I'd been stuck in all day to anger. Why would she park here again? Right by my truck.

*Was she taunting me?*

"Hey, heartbreaker." I tried to be impassive, to keep my simmering anger at bay. But a wry, twisted smile crossed my face despite my efforts, and gave me away.

Her eyes flared as her hip came off her car and she faced me, standing tall and just as angry as I was. "Heartbreaker? Really?" she sputtered in surprise. "You have some nerve, Nick."

My eyebrows shot up. "I—"

Her eyes flashed and her brow furrowed. "After all these years, that is what you choose to say to me? *Heartbreaker?*"

"I—"

"I have no patience left for men who don't stick around and can't keep their promises, so let's pretend we don't know each other, okay?" she hissed. "Kind of like the last fifteen or so years, right?"

I reared back, completely at a loss. "What are you talking about?"

"Hey, Mr. Easton, you look peeved. Did she shoot you down?"

I spun to find Gracie hobbling toward us on her crutches with a huge smirk on her face. "What? No."

*Had she heard?*

She couldn't have. Not when I'd barely heard Clara's almost-inaudible whispers myself.

"Clara is not in a dating frame of mind right now. I'd steer clear if I were you—"

As she spoke, I noticed her T-shirt was stained with partially dried-up food. My eyes narrowed as I interrupted her. "What happened to your shirt, Gracie?"

Clara rushed to her side. "Who did this? It looks like someone threw a few pudding cups at you. Is that chocolate?"

"I don't want to talk about it."

"Does Pindich know?" I prodded. "Did the cafeteria staff report it? If someone is bothering you, you can tell me, and I'll help you. I hope you know that." Even though Clara was still right there, I managed to turn my focus to Gracie.

"Thanks, I know. But I'm fine. Nothing happened. I got clumsy with a Snack Pack. It happens."

"Pindich?" Clara butted in. "Who's that? That name sounds familiar. What's going to be done about this?" She gestured to Gracie in her pudding-covered shirt.

I already knew Pindich would do nothing. He was the type to engage as little as possible with the students and staff beyond making demands and acting like a self-important, pompous ass.

"He won't do shit." Gracie confirmed the thoughts I hadn't said out loud. "Pudding bombing someone isn't really something you can hide, right? Everyone in the cafeteria saw what happened. *'Kids will be kids,'*" she air-quoted, her voice rising in obvious frustration. "A little pudding is no big deal, right? Clara, can we go now? Please?"

"Of course." Clara opened her door and took the crutches as Gracie folded herself inside.

Gracie's voice was softer when she said, "To your house, please. Can I borrow some clothes? And maybe take a shower? I'm sticky."

"What's mine is yours. Anything you want."

This situation wasn't okay. "I'll look into this, Gracie. No one deserves—"

"Thanks," she muttered before Clara shut her door with a slam.

Clara's glare for me was ice-cold. "Don't worry about Gracie. *I* will handle this."

"She's a good kid," I argued. "And I won't stand by and allow one of my students—*any* student at this school—to be bullied. I'm not that kind of teacher." I dragged a hand over my beard. Except for today, apparently, when I had almost drowned in the riptide of memories I'd been swirling in since seeing her. My students could have gotten into a knock-down, drag-out fight in the middle of my classroom and I don't think I would have noticed.

She huffed and rolled her eyes. "Fine. If it's to help Gracie, then step in all you want. Just leave me out of it."

I took a half step in her direction. "I can't help but think there's something I'm missing here—"

"Don't think about me at all." She cut me off with a sneer. "I don't exist for you. A fact you made abundantly clear about fifteen years ago when I rode out of Green Valley on that bus alone. Goodbye, Nick." She spun on her heel and marched around to the driver's side, casting one last glare as she climbed in the car and slammed the door.

# CHAPTER 4
# CLARA

*I'm sorry about your dad, Nick. Meet me behind the library during fourth period. I don't feel like going to English class today. Friends, huh? Of course. Whatever was I thinking? - HB*

Unbelievable. Men were on an entirely different level of idiocy.

*Heartbreaker.*

I threw the car into gear and backed out of my spot. Nick was lucky I didn't run his ass over. I'd think about him later—or not. Gracie needed me now.

I glanced at Gracie. "Okay, that principal of yours is a useless idiot, right?"

"Pretty much," she scoffed.

I couldn't help myself. "And, what about uh, the teacher from the parking lot. How's he?"

"Mr. Easton is cool. Everyone likes him. Did he ask you out? And you turned him down? Is that why there was such a chill in the air? You seemed pissed. You still do."

*Crap. Crap, crap, crap.* "No, I'm fine. Uh, we were just talking about you and your ankle. It doesn't matter. Pindich is on my shit list, and I'll deal with him later. Forget about Mr. Easton, that's nothing. Who did this to you? Pudding, right?"

She shut her eyes as her head hit the back of her seat. "Yeah. I got doused at lunch."

"Give me a name. I'll—"

Gracie held a hand up to stop my tirade. "No names. I got this. I'll clean up at your place, then go home."

"Fine, but at least tell me why," I demanded. Names could come later. Plus, the *why* often led straight to the *who*.

"*Fine*, since obviously you're not going to drop this. So, you know, um . . ." She let out a huge sigh. "Look, Ruby and I aren't the most popular or well-liked girls at Green Valley High, okay?" Ruby was Gracie's best friend and had been for years. "Ruby has that whole overachiever, pushy, know-it-all nerd thing going and I'm, um . . ."

"Let me guess, a trashy hillbilly Hill?" I looked away from the road to raise my eyebrows in her direction, and she huffed a laugh.

"Yup, that."

"Sounds familiar. Been there done that. Want me to go down to the school and raise hell? 'Cause I will. I can make life very unpleasant for Pindich and anyone else who gives you a hard time. You know, I taught you how to throw a punch. No one in the family will be pissed if you get detention. What's the problem? Is it the crutches? Is balance an issue? You could always start a food fight or put a few cockroaches in their lockers."

"No, I can't hit any of them. And damn, Clara, remind me never to mess with you." She laughed, then got more serious. "Forget about detention, I could get expelled or suspended. Pindich has instituted a zero-tolerance violence policy—"

I stopped at the red light and turned to her. I couldn't help the fact that my voice rose in time with my indignation. "Oh, but people can throw pudding at you at lunch? How is *that* okay? It's bullshit. No, uh-uh, nope." I shook my head, getting more heated with each passing second. "How else are you supposed to keep assholes from picking on you if you can't beat the shit out of them? I do *not* understand kids today. Do I need to buy a few cases of pudding to arm you with? What do I do? Give me some names, Gracie. I need somewhere to channel this rage."

She shrugged.

"Tell me everything so I can take care of it for you. I'm gonna figure this out, Gracie." Her eyes glinted with hesitation, so I pushed her. "I can handle it. Don't worry about Willa or Everett or Sadie." I tapped my chest with my pointer finger. "I'm the one who takes care of shit like this." The only response I got was a weighty sigh. I hit the gas once the light turned green.

After a few moments, she said, "Fine. After Weston graduated and left for college no one has any reason to not treat us like shit anymore." Gracie's boyfriend, who was also Ruby's older brother, had been the quarterback on the football team, homecoming king, and senior class president. You name it, and he did it—he was exactly like Nick, now that I think of it, damn it. Weston had been the walking definition of popular his junior and senior years and now he was off to become a football star at UT—the University of Tennessee—just like frickin' Nick. "Remember Ruby's friend Marianne?"

"Yeah . . . ?" I pulled into my garage and cut the engine. "Let's get you cleaned up. I have a stack of clean shirts in the laundry room—well, more like a pile since I don't fold—so help yourself." She followed me inside, heading into the laundry room while I fixed us drinks. "Keep talking!" I shouted as she changed.

"They used to be close but then it became all about Weston. Turns out she was just hanging around and being nice to us to get close to him." She entered the kitchen, and I handed her an icy Dr Pepper. "Thanks."

"To the porch."

She snagged a bag of popcorn with an amused grin. "Are you ever not sitting out on that dang porch?"

"That would be a no. Come on." We settled on the swing, and I took a huge sip of coffee—iced, of course, since it was afternoon. I raised my eyebrows and waited for her to continue.

"So, she'd been crushing on him, and was like, waiting for an opening or something. Now that he's away at college and she found out he broke up with me, she's become an unsufferable bitch. It started a few weeks before school, mostly on social media—starting rumors about me and stuff like that. But she ramped her shit up today." She looked like she was on the verge of tears. "First day of school, no Weston around, and with a sprained ankle so I couldn't even run away? Boom, I get covered in pudding. Ugh, could it get any worse?"

My head reared back in shock. "Back up—you and Weston broke up? What the heck happened, Gracie? Why didn't you tell me? And was Ruby there when the pudding thing happened? I can't imagine her not defending you, or at least sticking by you."

She shot me a look. "She has no idea what happened today, and don't you go telling her. She's not like us. She can't handle shit like this. I mean physical shit—direct confrontations, fights, or whatever. I saw Marianne coming and I knew it would be bad, so I sent Ruby to get something out of my locker."

"I could see that about her. She's kind of innocent, right? And Weston?"

"He broke up with me so I could have a fun senior year without having to like, wait around for him or whatever." She threw her hands in the air, letting me know exactly what she thought of that idea. "He still texts me every morning. He still loves me, and I still love him. It's the stupid distance that has him all worked up. He doesn't want to hold me back."

"So, this is more like a break than a breakup? What a noble little idiot man-boy he is." That earned me a smile. "I think y'all will be okay. If the two of you are meant to be, it will work out in the end, right?" *Says the woman who was dumped hard by the teenage love of her life . . .*

"I guess so. I mean, probably. It still sucks for now though."

Hating seeing her so sad, I switched the subject. "Let's put a pin in the Weston thing. We'll talk that through later. Give me some names, Gracie. Tell me everything."

She shook her head. "I ratted out Marianne, that's enough. And you can't say anything to anyone about any of this. Promise me."

I held my hands up. "I'm not making any promises. Secrets are bad." *Said the woman who was hiding an entire past relationship with her sister's teacher . . .*

I was sensing a theme here. *Was I destined to keep providing advice I would never, ever take?*

Why was I being so encouraging when life so rarely worked out the way you wanted it to? Damn, I was such a hypocrite.

"I don't want Weston driving back here to protect me. And don't get me started on Everett and Willa—they have their own crap to deal with. I don't want them going to prison for murdering my bully bitch trio, okay? Plus, they're exhausted because no one ever sleeps over there. Toddlers are insane." Our mother had given Willa and Everett custody of Gracie after they got married, and she lived with them a few streets over from mine.

Did it piss me off that she refused to let me or Sadie take her to live with one of us years ago? Hell yes it did. But now I was just happy that Gracie was with Willa and her hubby, Everett, and that my mother was finally in therapy and trying to atone for how she'd treated us over the years.

I nudged her shoulder with mine. "Oh, but it's fine if *I* go to prison? Real nice, Gracie."

She huffed a laugh and leaned into my side. "We both know you'd never get caught. Besides, I can handle myself. I'll be fine. I just needed someone to talk this through with. Dealing with stupid boys at school is easy. Marianne and her little minions are not. For whatever reason, they are determined to make me miserable. I am not looking forward to the rest of the year."

"Mean girls are insidious," I agreed. "Trust me, I know. You hold tight. I'll come up with a way to fix this without resorting to murder or violence. I promise. Stealth mode is my best mode."

"I'll be fine, Clara. I swear."

"Yeah, you sure as hell will be. I'm going to make sure of it. You deserve to have an enjoyable senior year. At least one of us Hills is going to have a positive teen experience, damn it. I know you're missing Weston. You don't need a bunch of rotten little bitches adding to it."

Tears filled her eyes. "I love you, Clara." Her lower lip trembled; she bit it and looked away.

Forget my promise. I was ready to commit murder. All I needed were the names of the other two little *Mean Girls'* Plastics wannabes and I'd find a spot in the backyard to bury them in. Metaphorically, of course.

"I love you back. Come here." I wrapped my arms around her and pushed the swing with my foot. "You tell me everything from now on. I'm fine with no names—for now, anyway. Promise me, Gracie." I felt her nod against my shoulder, and I relaxed.

*It was on.*

Sadie, Willa, and I had a miserable time back in high school. Our dad had left, our mom was fully ensconced in her verbally abusive bitch era, and the three of us had acted out in every way a teenage girl could. Cutting school, drinking under the bleachers, running around with boys, and doing all the things we shouldn't.

Sadie got pregnant and married her dumbass ex-husband straight out of high school. Willa ran away from home to marry her loser boyfriend and had stayed gone for almost a decade. And I had ended up in Nashville secretly stripping at various burlesque clubs to pay my way through college and law school.

*Lavender Lane*, indeed. That name had died when I stopped stripping. Nobody knew about it, not even Sadie. It was the only secret I'd ever kept from her. A purple bobbed wig, creative stage makeup, and lavender-tinted cat-eye glasses had kept my face disguised. And who would ever recognize me in Nashville, anyway?

I had majored in pre-law and minored in finance. Every penny I made—and stripping had made me a lot—was invested into my education and the stock market so I could ensure that the Hill sisters would never be treated like shit again and we'd always have what we needed.

But one look at Nick this morning had sent me back to feeling like I was curled up in a ball under the bleachers, half-drunk and crying about my dad being gone and my mom being a bitch, and I resented it.

Nick had never been part of my delinquent friend group, which was probably why it had been so easy for us to keep our relationship a secret. Even though he had been working through the loss of his dad and his mother's quick remarriage, he had put his focus on his grades and the football team and all the other extracurricular crap he did.

He hadn't wanted his mother to find out about me, about how much trouble I was always in. He said she'd never allow him to date me if she knew. But the bottom line was I just wasn't good enough for him.

A car sped around the corner, shaking me out of my thoughts. I watched as it pulled into the garage next to Janice and Leonard's place and Curt Pindich stepped out. I only ever referred to him by his first name. He was your garden-variety man on a power trip. Mediocre in every way but determined to rise above it by stepping on others on his way up.

"Oh, crap." I gestured across the street as my mind connected the dots that Nick had distracted me from earlier. "That's him. Pindich, right? I knew that name sounded familiar." He had a huge, unkempt pine tree next to the driveway that drove Leonard nuts because the dried-up needles and little branches constantly dropped off and littered his yard. It was hilarious to watch Leonard mumbling curses as he swept them up, but infuriating that Pindich insisted on being such a dick about it. It was a blight on the entire street, the jerk.

Gracie glared in his direction. "Yup. The one and only."

"Hmm, okay. All right." A plan began percolating in my brain. I had to get into that school somehow to keep an eye on Gracie. She needed a bodyguard. Once Marianne and her little buddies realized I would absolutely make their lives a living hell on earth if they didn't back off, they'd leave her alone. I was sure of it.

Maybe I could volunteer? Or perhaps become a substitute teacher?

I refused to let Gracie suffer the way we had. I refused to let her suffer *at all*. Especially not after I'd spent most of my adult life in therapy, making money, gaining knowledge, and working hard to make it so I could protect myself and my sisters.

No one would take advantage of or look down on us ever again—not on my watch. I decided to give our cousin Mari a call and ask her to keep an eye on Gracie while I solidified my plans to infiltrate the school and watch over her myself. Mari was family, she'd keep this hush-hush. And Nick had already offered to help. Even though he'd left me high and dry after high school, I didn't think he'd let anyone pick on Gracie. She'd be okay until I could take care of the situation once and for all.

A pickup truck with the Monroe & Sons Construction logo emblazoned across the side pulled up to the curb in front of Nick's future house. Gracie and I exchanged a look when Everett stepped out, waving to us with a huge smile across his face. "Hey!" he called as he started walking over. "You missed spaghetti night. Is everything okay?" He stopped at my porch railing with his eyebrows raised as he waited for my explanation.

"Hey," I muttered, feeling guilty for missing dinner as I spied the huge cooler bag with a loaf of bread sticking out of the top.

"Busted." Gracie laughed. "I forgot to tell you he'd be coming by with leftovers."

After he married Willa, my sisters and I met at their house once a week for dinner. It was always spaghetti and Everett always cooked for us. He was sweet as could be, like the brother I never knew I needed. But last night I had been in no mood to be anywhere near my sisters, who were all living the dream with their hubbies and their kids and their happy bunch of bullshit. Though, if I'd known Gracie was as miserable as me, I might have reconsidered. "Yeah, I had a headache." I had not had a headache; I'd spent the evening binge-watching *Bob's Burgers* and stuffing my face with a bag of Cheetos.

His face softened. "Aw, I'm sorry to hear that. I have to work on the deck next door, so I figured I'd bring you some leftovers. I know you aren't fond of cooking."

"Thanks." I stood and took the bag.

He let out a laugh when my stomach growled. "What have you had to eat today?"

I shrugged. "Coffee and angst."

At that moment, Nick pulled into the driveway next door, and it was all I could do not to visibly react when two adorable middle school–aged kids popped out of the truck's back seat carrying Daisy's Nut House takeout bags. They stood in the driveway excitedly taking in their new house and my heart melted a bit—a very tiny little bit.

Gracie sat up, watching them just like I was. "Mr. Easton is going to be your neighbor?"

"I guess so."

"He is," Everett confirmed. "You know he was on the football team with Wyatt back in high school," he informed Gracie as he waved at Nick. Wyatt was the only Monroe brother not married to one of my sisters or besties.

I already knew Nick had been on the football team. I used to know everything about him. Since this morning, the impulse to ask around town and find out what he'd been up to since high school was a huge temptation and it pissed me off. I was over him. *Wasn't I?*

Everett turned to me. "You remember Nick, right? He's a good guy, always has been. He's been divorced for years—maybe the two of you could go out. I think he could be good for you." He waggled his eyebrows at me, and I froze.

My mouth dropped open with a panicked gasp. "Uhhh . . ."

*Shit. Shit. Shit.*

"What an awesome idea. His kids are cool. I babysit for them sometimes and he's super nice." Gracie nudged my shoulder, unwittingly saving me from answering Everett. I closed my mouth and plastered a smile on my face. "Now you don't have to worry about another dickhead like Pindich moving in next door. One jerk on the block is enough." Gracie called out with a wave and a huge grin, "Hi, Mr. Easton!"

"Hi, y'all." Nick's face was deliberately impassive as he took in the sight of us on the porch.

Clearly, he'd had no idea I lived here. The laws of small-town living had failed us both. Normally, information like where your exes lived and what they'd been up to since your breakup was easily obtainable, as people loved butting their heads in with helpful warnings about such things.

"Dad, it's Gracie!" The little girl grinned at Gracie then introduced herself to me with a smile and wave. "I'm Sasha, and this is Ethan."

His daughter was gorgeous. She was the spitting image of Nick; his son was too. All three had wavy dark brown hair, big golden-brown eyes, and perfectly matching noses—straight and slightly upturned at the tip. It was uncanny. I could tell they were both tall for their ages. Nick had hit six feet in middle school, and had finally topped out at six-foot-four.

"This is Clara and Everett," Gracie introduced us.

"Nice to meet y'all." Sasha's huge grin and friendly, wide-open expression were unmistakable indicators she was an extrovert. "Do all of you live there?"

Gracie was already off the porch swing and halfway to their driveway. "No, just my sister, Clara. But I'm here all the time—"

"We know Everett already too," Ethan interrupted. "He's our dad's friend." He turned and looked at me. "You're the only one we don't know." Probably because I'd made avoiding Nick an art form since I got back to town.

"I'd better get to work on y'all's deck," Everett chimed in. "Eat that spaghetti, Clara." His head dipped in my direction. "You can't live off coffee and angst," he said under his breath.

"I will. Thank you for bringing it over."

"I'll drive Gracie home when I'm done. I shouldn't be too long. Thanks for picking her up from school."

"Of course," I murmured.

He lifted his chin with a grin and headed to his truck.

He was more of a father to Gracie than our own father had ever been. I almost felt bad for keeping the pudding incident from him, but not quite. I'd been her sister since she was born, and I had been protecting her the entire time, which meant I'd take her secrets to the grave with me if she wanted me to.

The kids' voices blended into background noise as they chatted about Gracie's ankle and their new house. Nick and I locked eyes, his hands shoved into his pockets and his shoulders hunched forward as he took a step toward me. I stared wordlessly across at him with my heart pounding.

*Those should be my kids.*

Startled, I flinched at the unexpected thought.

*We should be moving into that house together.*

Maybe then I would have been happy all these years. I bit my lip as intrusive thoughts anchored me to the porch swing. The shock of the images running through my mind rendered me helpless to escape them, so they just kept coming: me and Nick married, having babies, laughing together, just being together out in the open like we had intended to be after graduation.

I swallowed the lump of despair in my throat, choking it down before it obliterated my ability to disguise my feelings and I ended up bursting into sloppy tears in front of everybody. I had to get away from him.

"It was nice to meet you all." I held up the cooler bag from Everett and smiled at Nick's beautiful kids. "I have to get this put away." My fingers twisted anxiously around the handle as I stood, yet I didn't move from my spot in front of the porch swing. I couldn't seem to look away from Nick.

The tenderness in his expression had me entranced; it was how he had always looked at me. It belied the hostility in his expression when he'd called me heartbreaker before. Confused, I took a step back as mixed feelings surged through me.

*Was he thinking the same things about me?*

I was so close to saying something to him. Waving him over so we could talk. Anything to make that look on his face stay.

But it didn't last. I opened my mouth to speak right as his face emptied and turned cold. Only then was I able to break the spell and enter the safety of my house.

# CHAPTER 5
# NICK

*Hey, heartbreaker, come to my window tonight. I have something for you. No, it's not what you're thinking. - Nick*

"Can we go see Clara?" Sasha asked—again—as she slid onto a barstool on the other side of the kitchen island from where I was preparing dinner. "We can bring her cookies, or brownies, or banana bread, like new neighbors do? She's pretty, don't you think? I love her hair, it sparkles in the sun. Can I dye mine like that? How does she get it so shiny?"

I slammed my eyes shut and set my wooden spoon on the counter, trying to get the sudden surge of memories of having my hands wrapped up in Clara's hair out of my head. I used to love burying my face in her neck and holding her in my arms with those soft, thick waves tickling my nose and their sweet floral scent filling my senses until all I could feel was her.

I let out a frustrated sigh and tried to adjust my attitude. None of how I was feeling was Sasha's fault. She didn't deserve to bear the brunt of my irritation. I plastered on a smile and tried to keep my tone light. "First of all, we're the new people on the block. If anyone's bringing baked goods, it will be people bringing them to us—that's the tradition. And second, no. You have beautiful hair, honey. Maybe when you're older, if you still want to."

"Fine, okay. Thank you. But don't you think she's pretty?" she pushed.

"Uh, I guess so." Pretty was not the right word, not when Clara was still the most beautiful woman I'd ever seen. We'd been here for a little over a week and Sasha's preoccupation with Clara was glaringly obvious.

As was my own, unfortunately.

"She's so nice. She always says hi and talks to me and Ethan when we're walking home from the bus or Mom's house. I like her."

I grunted in answer and resumed sautéing the asparagus for our dinner. My own preoccupation with Clara was hidden, like it had always been, and her nearness was driving me to distraction.

A few nights back I discovered our bedrooms were separated by nothing but a few feet of empty air, windows, and two sets of fucking curtains. When I saw her sexy silhouette changing clothes through her sheers, I'd installed blackout blinds and gave up on ever seeing natural light in my room again.

After the way she'd broken me when she left town, I found it infuriating she still had the power to occupy my mind. It was constant. It was torture. It had to stop.

"I wonder if she's on her porch. She's always out there. We should decorate our porch like hers. Then you could go outside and sit there and drink coffee or whatever, and maybe talk to her. Or ask her on a date, or something."

*Little did she know . . .*

"Decorating the porch is a great idea. You can be in charge of it." Anything to distract her from talking about Clara worked for me.

Her eyes lit up. "I know! I could do my homework out there. Ethan is always hogging the backyard with his football crap and his dumb friends. And you too, with all your barbeque stuff. I want a pretty porch, just like Clara's."

"Great idea. Go online and pick out a few things for me to buy. But stick to the sales, okay?"

She hopped off the stool, buzzing with excitement. "Yes! Thank you, Dad."

I loved seeing her happy. "You're welcome. I want you to love it here, and if having a pretty porch is what it takes, then that's what you'll have."

She beamed at me. "I already love it here. You picked the perfect house. My room slays."

"I'm happy to hear that—"

"But I still want a pretty porch."

I laughed. "Of course you do." I watched as she ran off to the living room to the computer. "I'll try to have it ready for you before you come back from your mom's place."

"Yay! I love you! I'll make a list."

"Love you too." My every other week was almost up. But we were within walking distance now, so I anticipated seeing them much more throughout the week. They'd had dinner at Morgan's house a couple of nights during my turn and I was happy that she'd been willing to loosen her stringent adherence to our custody agreement. The kids were already more relaxed now that they could go back and forth between our two houses without lots of planning and a car ride across town.

In fact, Ethan was there right now raiding her pantry because I was out of chips. Speak of the devil . . . I looked up as he appeared in the doorway carrying a bag of Doritos.

"It's official. Sasha's lost her mind over Clara. Check out what they're wearing. They match." He tipped his head toward the kitchen window, which I studiously avoided since it had the perfect view of Clara's porch from the side of the house. "She wants to be her clone or something. They're both wearing purple. What's for dinner? It smells good."

"Garlic-rubbed baked potatoes, asparagus, and steaks on the grill." I pointed to the bag in his hands. "Maybe save those for later. You'll spoil your dinner."

"Nice. Can we eat on the patio?"

"Sure." Eating outside always ran the risk of a Clara sighting. But half the reason I'd bought this damn house was for the yard, and the kids knew it.

"Can we go in the pool after?"

"I guess so."

Sasha shouted from the living room, "Can we invite Clara to swim with us?"

"Not this time," I answered.

*Or ever.*

I knew what Clara looked like in a bathing suit. And out of one, too. The thought of seeing all that gorgeous, soft alabaster skin again was too much for me. I got hard and immediately stepped into the corner of the counter to hide it.

I thought about the times we'd snuck up to Sky Lake together. We'd skinny-dipped when we we'd been lucky enough to be alone, and if people had been around, I'd pulled my truck into the trees, and we'd spent our time there instead. We used to make out for hours in the cab, or if it was dark, in the bed under a blanket.

My eyes drifted to the side window. Sure enough, she was out there on her porch using her foot to rock the swing while she knitted and sang along with the Foo Fighters. Nostalgia hit me straight in the gut. My erection died and my eyes turned glassy with unshed tears as *Everlong* floated lightly over the air between our houses. I mouthed the last line along with her as it faded away. I'd been ignoring her music as I cooked but seeing her made it real.

*We'd been real.*

If I couldn't make peace with these memories, I would never be able to live in this house. I had to talk to her at some point. The look on her face each time we caught even the slightest glimpse of each other told me it would be nearly impossible to get her to listen to me. And what could I possibly say?

I pulled the potatoes out of the oven and put them on a tray along with the fixings. "Let's eat! Come on, y'all."

* * *

*Beep*

   *Beep*

   *Beep*

"Shit." With a scowl, I slammed a hand on my cheap, old-school alarm clock. Mornings were not my thing. I needed clocks like this so whenever I ended up breaking one, I didn't have to feel too bad about it.

"Are you awake, Dad? Can we have Toaster Strudel for breakfast?" Sasha had always been a morning person. She was up and raring to go every day, even on the weekends, which I hadn't been a fan of when she was little. But now that she could get breakfast and settle into the day on her own, I didn't mind so much. She could get up at the crack of dawn all she wanted, so long as I could sleep in.

"Yeah," I answered with a grunt.

*Had I remembered to lock the door?*

I shoved a pillow over my hard-on to be safe. Images of Clara's naked body with my hands and mouth all over it had played like a dirty movie behind my eyes as I slept. To say I'd tossed and turned all night in a horny, fitful slumber would be the understatement of the year. I was hard as a rock, and it was painful.

She burst through the door, and I turned to my side, and tucked the pillow tight against me.

"You're always so grumpy in the morning." She popped one hip and put a hand on the other. "You need daylight. That's what Mom always says. These curtains suck." She crossed the room and swept open my blackout shades.

"Ahh! No sun, I'll melt," I teased, hissing like a vampire as I yanked my quilt over my face.

"Oh hey, look. Clara's outside. She's asleep on her balcony."

My eyes shot open under my covers. *Was she okay?*

At that moment, Ethan entered, because of course he did. "Why is she out there?" he asked Sasha who, naturally, opened my window and asked her.

*Shit.*

"Miss Clara! Why are you sleeping on your balcony?" she yelled.

Clara's faint voice hit my ears as she said hello, and I almost lost my mind with the need to find out what the problem was.

"Oh, I'm fine. Don't y'all worry about me. There's a bug in my room. It's probably gone now."

"I'll get my dad."

"No! No, I'm okay."

"Dad!" Ethan hollered as if I wasn't right here in hearing distance. "Miss Clara needs you. She can't go inside her house."

Luckily, my morning wood situation had, by now, gone away. Having my kids burst into the room would do that. I made my way to the window, bleary-eyed and scratching my bare chest, as per usual.

"Morning, Clara." I squinted into the sunlight to find her sitting on the edge of a lounge chair with a sheepish expression dancing across her face. She was delectably mussed up with messy hair and sleepy eyes. We were only a few feet apart and I wanted nothing more than to climb through my window and join her on her balcony, climb on top of her in that lounge chair and do all the naked things we used to love to do together.

"Hi," she answered with a sheepish little wave.

"So, there's a bug in your bedroom, and you came out here to sleep where all the rest of them live?" I teased.

Two adorable scarlet circles appeared on her cheeks. "It made sense at the time. I was tired and all out of logic, okay? This bug meant business. It had facial expressions, Nick. It wants something from me."

"Is your house locked?"

"Yeah, I mean, I could just go inside, but I really don't want to. If it was a spider, I'd have just caught it and put it outside, but this was a big bug, Nick—huge. I have no idea what kind it is, but it's on a mission. I know it." She threw a hand over her eyes. "God, I'm being such a baby about this."

I caught a glimpse of Sasha and Ethan watching me as I spoke to Clara as though I knew her—which obviously I did, but had been pretending not to.

*Damn.*

"Uh, we went to high school together," I muttered while trying to figure out the best way to help her.

Sasha wasn't buying it. "Sure, Dad. Get the ladder and climb up there. You can go inside, find the bug, and like, save her life or whatever." She bit her lip to hide a laugh.

"Can I go too?" Ethan asked. "I'll catch it."

"No," Sasha answered him before I could. "We have to get ready for school."

"You're not climbing up there, Ethan," I confirmed. "Good idea, Sash."

"Hang tight," I told Clara. "I'm coming over with my ladder."

"This is so stupid. You don't have to do this." She stood, putting a hesitant hand on the knob of her French door. "Okay, never mind. Come up, please. I can't. I—"

"Shh, I got this." I held up a finger. "Don't worry." I turned back to Sasha and Ethan, who were watching me with rapt attention. "Y'all get ready for school now or you'll miss the bus."

Sasha grabbed Ethan by the arm. She was making connections in her brain. I could see it in her eyes. "Come on, Eath."

Whether she was figuring out Clara and I had a past together or she was making plans to meddle in the future, I couldn't tell. But one thing was clear: she was about to start running mental rings around me too.

I dashed down to the garage, grabbed the ladder, and walked through the gate in the low fence that led to Clara's backyard.

Crystal-blue eyes met mine as I extended the ladder up to her balcony. "It's okay, Clara. I'm coming."

The time that had passed between us somehow ceased to exist as, rung by rung, the years between us vanished.

"Thank you," she murmured as I threw a leg over the rail and landed in front of her.

I didn't answer her. I couldn't find the words. I reached out, trailing a fingertip down her soft cheek before brushing her hair over her shoulder. My god, she was beautiful. Her face was delicate and lovely, but strength had always shone through in her expression. Her full lips parted, and she let out a tremulous sigh.

The barrier of anger and confusion that had formed between us was gone, at least for the moment. My heart thumped wildly in my chest and a fresh rush of pink stained her cheeks as we moved closer, pulled together like magnets, unable to resist the attraction that still, after all these years, drew us to each other.

My face lowered inch by slow inch as past and present collided and instinct took over. "Look at you," I choked, swallowing the lump in my throat. "You're right here. God, how I've missed you."

"Nick, it's been so long . . ." Her sweet voice, barely a whisper, faded away into the hushed stillness of the morning. Her tongue darted out to wet her lips as her dark lashes swept down across her cheekbones.

"Dad!" Ethan yelled from below. "Can I come up and help?" Startled, I spun around to see him about to climb the ladder.

"Ethan!" Sasha hissed as she ran up behind him. "Ugh, you're such a dumbass. Come on. The bus will be here in five minutes. Forget we were here, Dad. See you later."

*Too late.*

The moment was broken. "Bye, be good. Love you!" I called out as I watched them walk to the corner to meet the bus.

I turned back to Clara. She'd shut down. "Thank you for coming up here," she muttered, gesturing toward the door.

"Yeah, no problem." I went inside. A giant black bug—I thought it was a stag beetle, but I wasn't sure—sat plumb in the middle of her bed. Those things freaked me out; I didn't blame her for sleeping outside.

Was it planning something? Perhaps it was. Its beady little eyes tracked my movements as I spotted a glass on the bedside table to trap it with. I grabbed the glass and chugged the water inside before carefully lowering it over the bug's shiny black body.

I called out to Clara, "You can come in now. I need something to slide under your glass. I don't want to squash it on your bed."

"Oh god, oh god, ew, ew, ew," she chanted as she crept along the wall toward the hallway. "I'll get a piece of cardboard or something."

Once she got near the bedroom door, she wasted no time running through it. The sound of her feet dashing down the stairs made me laugh as I pressed the glass deeper into the bed. "You're not going anywhere." The little shit glared up at me from beneath it. If this fucker were any bigger, we'd all be dead.

She returned with a few pieces of junk mail. I snagged one and carefully slid it under what had become our mutual enemy.

"I have to get going or I'll be late," I muttered as I lifted the glass.

"Yeah. I appreciate this. I'd offer to bake you some cookies or something as a thank you, but I don't do that. Maybe I'll buy you a plant. Sasha told me your yard is boring."

I let out a chuckle. "That would actually be perfect. Sasha is determined to have a porch just like yours. She would love that."

"She's a sweet kid. They both are, Nick." Her eyes drifted to the floor. "I'm happy for you."

"Thanks. I—can we talk? Not right now," I clarified. "I have to get to work." She turned toward the hallway, and I trailed behind. "But can we, um, maybe be friends at some point? I don't like this feeling between us. I feel like I'm missing something—"

I followed her downstairs, keeping my eyes on the bug in the glass and not her perfect ass in her purple silk pajama shorts that did nothing to hide the luscious bounce after each step.

When we reached the bottom of the staircase, she whirled on me. "Friends?" she snapped. "Okay, sure, we can be *friends*. Have your people call my people and we'll schedule a lunch meeting or a Zoom call or something."

"Clara, please, I didn't mean—"

"The door is over there." She threw out an arm in the direction of her foyer. "I'll give Sasha her plant next time I see her. Or better yet, I'll have it delivered." Her eyes were as hollow as her voice sounded.

Regret burned through me like acid. Somehow, I'd fucked up. "Clara, I—"

"I don't feel like talking." She threw the door open.

The spark of hope that had unexpectedly started to blaze in my heart extinguished in an instant. I crossed the threshold and tossed the bug into the bed of flowers that lined the edge of her front steps. "I understand and I'm sorr—" I tried to catch her eyes again after I turned back to her, but she was not having it.

"Goodbye, Nick. Thanks for . . ." She gestured to the flower bed, snatched the glass out of my hand, then slammed the door in my face.

I turned around just in time to see Mr. Neal, the cranky old librarian at the school, back out of his driveway. He waved to me when he passed with a knowing smirk on his face as I headed home in what looked exactly like a walk of shame—shirtless, wearing only my pajama pants.

*Shit.*

# CHAPTER 6
# CLARA



The. *Audacity.*

He had made me feel stuff—mushy stuff, nostalgic stuff. I was having *feelings* for him when the only thing I should be feeling for Nicholas Andrew Easton right now was rage. *Frickin' Nick.*

He hurt me.

He broke my damn heart.

So what if it was a long time ago? A woman doesn't forget her first real heartbreak that easily. Even after a decade and a half, damn it.

I wish I had kept that damn note so I could find it and read it again. Apparently, I needed a reminder of how he had broken my heart.

We'd planned out an entire future together, and he'd thrown it away like it was nothing.

And like a fool, I had almost allowed him to do it again. We'd almost kissed on my balcony, for eff's sake.

*Damn him.*

Maybe I *should* talk to him.

We could have lunch together. I could let him attempt to explain what the hell he had been thinking back then, and then I could yell at him and throw a drink in his face or smack him around a little bit.

He deserved to be given a piece of my mind. He deserved to be as broken up about seeing me as I was by seeing him . . .

with his cute kids . . .

in his beautiful house . . .

all happy and content and living his life like—

*UGH!*

*Friends*, he had said.

He wanted to be my *friend?*

After all we had been through together?

After all we had meant to each other?

No frickin' way.

He was living over there with a family and all I had was a freaking bug to keep me company.

After spending the better part of my morning simmering and sulking and showering, I threw on my best leggings and sports bra combo. I fluffed up my boobs, then added a silky robe over the ensemble and pulled my hair up in a bun. If I was going to be miserable, I was going to look hot doing it. I grabbed a deep berry lipstick and slicked it on.

*Frickin' Nick.*

Freaking stupid dumb feelings.

I was in a spiral. I hadn't been this pissed off since my old boss grabbed my ass and I broke his fucking nose.

Nick had better watch out. He was lucky I liked his kids. He seemed like a good dad, too. And there was the whole bug rescue thing, damn it.

*No breaking Nick's nose.*

After heading down to my kitchen, I switched on my coffee maker to make a fresh pot and paced around the kitchen island, muttering to myself as it brewed.

I fixed my mug and stalked to my front door and threw it open dramatically, because that's the kind of mood I was in.

"Damnnnn, Clara. Look at that face. What's wrong?" My lifelong best friend Molly stood there with her hand formed into a fist ready to knock on the door. Leo—my other bestie, ever since grade school—was with her. They were not just my friends; they were also my high school companions in delinquency. They used to be as messed up as I was, but now I was the only one left rotting in misery now that they were both loved up and each part of a healthy marriage, the jerks.

We'd spent our days cutting school, usually drunk, as we commiserated over our problems.

When Molly's dad had passed from cancer, her mother had mentally checked out, and shortly after, remarried and left the family. Her oldest brother —who was now Leo's husband—had taken his siblings under his wing and was now essentially a father figure to Molly and her other two brothers.

Leo's parents had kicked him out when he told them he was gay, and he'd moved in with his grandparents.

Sadie had joined us on occasion, whether it be under the bleachers at the football field, or behind the library, but she'd usually been too wrapped up in her stupid boyfriend to hang with us.

"Who put this tragic look on your face? Tell us who to maim." Leo placed the cooler bag he was carrying on the porch, shoved his way around Molly, and tugged me into his arms. "We got you, sweetie."

"Yeah, give us a name," Molly insisted. "Say the word, and we're off. Is it your ex-boss? Is something finally happening with that situation?"

My voice was muffled against Leo's chest when I said, "No, I've given up on that, it's going nowhere."

Molly balked. "The hell you're giving up! His ass needs to be nailed to the wall. Sue him or file a complaint outside of the HR department. Report him to the bar or whatever. Do all that stuff you were talking about after you quit that place and were freshly pissed off. Don't let him get away with it."

I stepped out of Leo's embrace and shook my head. "No, I just want it to be over. I'm letting it go." The thought of having my own past dredged up was inconceivable. Why would I put myself through that? No, thank you.

She nodded and backed off. "Okay, I understand. It will dredge it all up again and that would suck. If you change your mind, we're here to support you. Did you hear from Chris again? Is that it?"

"No, and I'm over him."

"Then what's with the rage fest?"

"Let's settle in," Leo tutted. "I brought you a summer squash and prosciutto quiche, with all the extra Gruyère your heart could ever desire." Gently he pushed at my shoulders until the back of my knees hit the swing and I sat. "Let us take care of you. You need a good breakfast. You need emergency cheese, and old friends. When your mood is this bleak, it's essential to keep yourself fed, so it doesn't devolve into anything worse, trust me. The last thing you need is a prison sentence for killing"—he waved a hand around— "whoever."

Molly's family owned the Smoky Mountain Inn. It was uber fancy. Like, if you had a special event to plan, you'd have it there—weddings, birthday parties, baby showers, girls' trips, you name it. Leo was their chef, which meant this quiche was going to taste like heaven in a pie plate. I was almost distracted enough to forget about Nick for a minute and simply stuff my face.

"Why can't I be like you, Leo? All grown up and settled, cooking for yourself and other people, just like a real adult." I sighed, the quiche no longer enough to make me forget about my troubles. "I tried so hard to make it work with Chris. I tried hard to make it work with all my relationships, but no. I failed every single time. I've spent all these years adding to my red flag collection and look at you two," I said, gesturing towards them. "You have Landon, and Molly has Garrett. Even my sisters are happy—Sadie has Barrett and Willa has Everett." I wrinkled my nose. "What the hell is up with those names?"

Molly shrugged. "Mrs. Becky Lee Monroe is a bit compulsive. Two *t*'s for all of them. But back to you and names. Chrises are cursed, but I won't say I told you so, even though I did, like, so many times. I could write an entire book about it, for eff's sake." Molly had four exes named Chris, so she should know.

Leo rolled his eyes. "Molly, now is not the time—" Molly was fond of a good rant and once you got her going it was hard for her to stop. But she was great at making me laugh and gave the best soft squishy hugs, so I scooted next to her on the swing and put my head on her shoulder.

"*Gah!* Leo is right." She pulled me into her side and kissed the top of my head. "I'm sorry. You deserved so much better than him. You deserve the world, Clara. We're here to take care of you." She pulled a small, credit card–sized envelope out of her bra and tossed it on my little wicker end table. "For the new spa. It's a gift card for an entire day of pampering—mani, pedi, massage, facial, the works." The inn's spa was new, and I couldn't wait to try it. My eyes lit up in spite of my bad mood.

"Y'all! This is too much. I can't—"

"Shh. Nope." She pointed to the cooler bag next to Leo, who was nestled in my little pink Adirondack chair in the corner. "There's no such thing as too much when it comes to friends. Leo brought you food for the week and there's more where that came from. We will not allow you to subsist on coffee and angst. No way."

I couldn't help the laugh that burst out. "Coffee and angst, huh? Everett has a big mouth, y'all. I can't accept all this."

"Shut up. You can, and you will. We love you. You are always, *always* there for us and you have been since we were kids. It's our turn to be here for you."

"Don't act like you weren't there for me too back then. We helped each other. I don't know what I would have done without y'all—"

"Back then we were three disasters figuring out how to cope with our problems, darling," Leo said. "Now we're two happily-ever-afters and a friend in need."

"I'm so stupid, Leo. Why did I waste so much time on a dumbass like Chris?" *But more importantly, why, after all these years, am I still hung up on Nick?*

He held up a hand to shush me. "No. First of all, you are not stupid. Wanting to find love, trusting people, and giving second chances are all beautiful things. But my second point is that unfortunately, people who grew up like we did tend to waste a lot of our time trying to make people who don't deserve our efforts treat us better, instead of just walking away from them and moving on. Forgive yourself for that, Clara."

"I'll try. I promise I will." I contemplated telling them about Nick. I needed to get it out of me. "I want to tell you something. I feel like I have to get this off my chest. But you have to keep it to yourselves, okay?" I pulled out of Molly's arms and sat straight, scooting to the edge of the swing so I could watch their faces.

They exchanged a glance. "All right . . . ," Leo drawled as his eyebrows shot up.

"Of course. These lips will remain sealed, just like always." Molly mimed turning a lock with a key and I grinned at her. "Spill it."

"Remember Nick Easton? From back in high school?"

Molly's eyes got big. "You mean hot quarterback Nick who now comes to the inn to play touch football with Garrett and Wyatt and all the rest of their superhot friends who me and Leo totally do not spy on from the kitchen window? The football coach at the high school? *That* Nick Easton?"

I grimaced. "Yep, that's the one. So, uh, anyway, we were a thing back in high school, starting the end of junior year and through the entire time we were seniors. We were in love. We were going to run off to Knoxville together after graduation." Their eyes were wide; their mouths too. "Leo, remember when you dropped me off at the bus station?"

He nodded and was able to pull himself together enough to answer. "Yes, of course I remember that. You didn't want me to wait with you. I'd always thought it was weird."

I shrugged. "I was supposed to meet Nick there. He had a football scholarship to UT. We'd been saving up our money. We were going to buy tickets out of town, find a place to rent together, get jobs, and I was going to go to junior college. But he never showed up, so instead of going to Knoxville, I went to Nashville. I left alone."

Leo's face fell. "Oh sugar, you should have called me. I would have come back and sat with you or drove you home. I would have been there for you—"

"I'm sorry. I know you would have. I just couldn't face it. I had to get far away, and Nashville was as far as I could afford to go and still make it back home if I couldn't hack it there—"

He took my hand and squeezed. "No apologies. You buried everything, didn't you?"

I nodded.

"I get it. You buried it deep and moved on, as we three were wont to do at that age. And as you still are." He was sympathetic even though he was calling me out.

"But I can't seem to do that now for some reason." My voice was small, I hated how weak I sounded. I let out a huge sigh and reached for the cooler bag full of food. I unearthed the quiche and dug straight into it with the fork Leo had so thoughtfully included. "Probably because he moved in right next door."

Leo's eyes bulged. "Oh shit."

"I know." I practically wailed, hand over my mouth, through a huge bite of quiche.

"What the heck, Clara?" Molly stared at me stunned, her mouth hanging wide open and her head shaking side to side. "You're telling me you hid an entire relationship. With Nick Easton? Hot quarterback Nick? With the great hair and the big shoulders and that spectacular football player ass?!"

"Not the point, Molls," Leo playfully scolded her.

"Right. So, you hid it? For all these years? Damn, girl. He's a nice guy. I like him. He always buys a crap load of Leo's brownies for his kids before he leaves. You and Nick Easton. Damn, girl."

I chewed and swallowed before answering. "Yeah, that frickin' Nick."

"I'm so sorry. I wish you had told me so I could have been there for you." Her head tilted toward Nick's place. "And now he lives right there?"

I nodded.

"And we're the only ones who know?" she continued.

"Yeah, and Sadie. She's always known."

They nodded in unison. "Obviously."

I flopped back against the swing. "It's like, I want to punch him in his stupid face, but I also want to find out what happened to make him not want me anymore. I kind of want to kiss him, too. I almost did this morning when he saved me from a huge-ass demon bug on my bed. It's stressful. I'm confused and mad and sad and there's more."

"Oh crap, what is it?" She reached in the bag and pulled out a muffin to take a huge bite.

"I'm about to become a substitute down at the high school. Once my background check goes through, it will be official."

"What?" Leo's head drew back on his neck. "Why would you do that? That seems a bit out of left field. You were an attorney."

"Uhhh . . ." I couldn't tell them about Gracie; that was not my secret to spill. "I guess I need a change. I can't spend the rest of my life out on this porch *Rear Window*-ing my neighbors and puttering around in my yard."

"But-but—substitute teaching? Kids? Like, actual children?" Molly sputtered. "The only thing you've ever taught is a pole class down at Suzie Samuels's studio."

"That's hardly what I'd call teaching experience, sugar." Leo turned his attention from Molly to me. "What's really going on?"

"Hey! It counts, okay? Plus, there's a nationwide teacher shortage, you know. I'm doing my part to help out the youth of America. I'm college educated and I'm fully qualified."

Molly huffed a laugh. "Okay, sure. We can wait. You'll tell us the real reason sooner or later. We all know that. Even if it takes fifteen years," she added with an eye roll.

"I'm sorry, I should have told you about Nick ages ago."

"No, it's okay." Her face softened. "You don't have to apologize to us. None of us were in our right minds back in high school. Didn't his dad die? And his mom got married right away to her boss, right? Damn, that must have been hard for him."

"Yeah, it was. Plus, he thought she'd be pissed about him dating me. She was pushing him hard to go to college, constantly nagging him about his grades and extracurricular activities, his SATs and GPA or whatever, and, as you know, I was not exactly a good influence back then."

"Oh, hell no," Leo snapped. "You're torturing yourself over someone who wouldn't even stick up for you?"

I lifted one shoulder in a resigned half shrug. "He had problems too. His family was a mess after his dad died, and he didn't want to drag me into it. He didn't want me getting hurt by her."

"*Hmph,*" Leo scoffed. "I don't know about all that. Sounds pretty weak to me."

"It wasn't like that. Or at least it hadn't felt that way, not until the end. When we were together it was—" My eyes filled with tears. I brushed them away with a mini wail of frustration, but to my chagrin, they kept right on coming. "He loved me, he really did. Remember his family used to live in the trailer park down the hill from me?"

Molly pulled me close again and dried my cheeks with a soft napkin from the bag. "Yeah, I remember that. Then after his dad died, they moved into that big-ass house up at Bandit Lake." Bandit Lake was exclusive. Only the richest of the rich lived up there. I would have bought a house there when I moved back to town, but they could only be passed down through inheritance, or shared within families.

"He used to let me climb through his window whenever Momma was being extra mean. Sometimes Sadie and Willa would come too. We'd make sure Gracie was asleep, then sneak out of the house and camp out on his bedroom floor. Willa had no clue, but Sadie knew about us. She was the only one."

"Oh, Clara. I'm so sorry. I wish I had known too."

"I know. I should have—"

"No, no," she soothed. "No apologies. We all did the best we could back then. None of us were capable of making wise decisions when we were going through so much. Kids do the best they can, right Leo?" she hinted not-so-subtly.

He shrugged his shoulders and his eyes lit with sympathy as he thought it over. "The main thing is we're here for you today. What's happening with him now?" he asked. "Why are you so upset? Besides the memories, of course."

"I'm about to start subbing at Green Valley High—his school. Aaaand, he's one of Gracie's teachers."

"Clara!" Molly was aghast. She pulled away and lifted my chin to study my face. Suspicion was etched all over her expression as her eyes narrowed on mine. "I defended your teenage choices, but this is crazy. Unless you want to end up banging him somewhere in that school, of course. Is that your end goal? Because if it is, I'll help you get him back. I love a good second chance love story. I'm here for you no matter what."

"I'm not going to bang him anywhere." I backed out of her grasp with a defensive laugh. "He hurt me, and I hate him." Even I couldn't sell that lie. My feelings were written all over my face. The last thing I felt for Nicholas Andrew Easton was hate.

"Sure you do. You hate him *so* bad." Molly's head tipped to the side as she watched me. "This is why you're so upset. You still care about him. The opposite of love isn't hate. It's indifference. And you are an obsessy Nickoholic right now. Do not even try to deny it to us."

"I am not obsessed with him. I'm mad at him. I'm upset."

"Well, duh. But he's going to come up with some totally understandable explanation for what happened at the bus station, and then y'all are going to forgive each other. You obviously still have a lot of feelings for him. It's written clear as day on your face, and I don't blame you. First love can last forever if it's real and the timing is right."

"Yup. She's right and you know it." Leo nodded his agreement.

"I do not know that. I know no such thing." I was a total liar. What Nick and I had was real and I did know it. That's why seeing him had hurt so much. But I wasn't ready for them to know it too.

Molly held up a hand. "Let's talk about something else, something fun, to cheer you up. Your bridal shower will be a hot-for-teacher theme and I'm calling it right now. It's mine to plan, not one of your sisters'. I declare dibs on the shower and we'll have it at the inn. The rest of them can battle it out for maid of honor duty."

"You have lost your damn mind." I was indignant. "I'm telling you about my rage, about my abandonment issues and my tragic first love, and you're talking about bridal showers."

"I'll make the cake!" Leo burst out. "The topper can be a little chalkboard with two hot nerds kissing in front of it. Or two houses side by side."

"Oh my god, that's perfect." They high-fived in front of my face.

*What the . . . ?* "Y'all! Quit it!"

"Nick is a nice guy," Molly stated matter-of-factly. "He has great kids. Garrett wouldn't be friends with him if he was an asshole. Something happened back then—a misunderstanding, a youthful error of judgement, maybe cold feet or his mother got to him somehow. Bet on it. Y'all were kids. Kids are dumb."

The thought struck me that maybe this is why none of my relationships had ever worked out. I'd always gone for men who were the opposite of Nick. Nick was careful, caring, even downright methodical when faced with making a decision. He had also been so sweet and romantic, thoughtful and loving.

Maybe he hadn't been faking that shocked, hurt look on his face when he saw me in the parking lot with Gracie. Maybe something really had happened to make him think I didn't want him, and that's what caused everything to fall apart.

Maybe we could have another chance.

*What the hell, Clara?*

No.

Molly and her wild theories were getting into my head. I had to be smart about this. I couldn't let him hurt me again, I'd never recover.

"Oh, lookie there." Molly clapped her hands together. "Here he comes now. How fortuitous."

Our eyes followed the path of his truck as it drove up the street and pulled into his driveway.

She stood, waving wildly over the porch railing as he drove up his driveway into his garage.

"Stop it," I hissed. "He'll see you."

"That's the point. The only way to feel better is to talk this out with him. Otherwise, you're going to be a seething mess of anger and stress every time you see him, and that's not healthy." She took a big breath, and I knew she was getting ready to serve me up a dose of reality slash tough love. "Look, I was mostly teasing about all the bridal shower stuff. But I'm not joking about this. Make peace with him. It's the only way to be okay with having him live next door."

"Quit being smart," I shot back. "I still want to be mad and irrational."

"It's weird when the shoe is on the other foot, isn't it?" she mused. "I remember you giving me all kinds of smart advice when it came to me and Garrett. And look at me now." She threw her hands out at her sides and smirked at me.

"Fine," I grumbled.

"Let's go, Molls," Leo took her hand and pulled her up off the swing.

Panicked, I hopped up and attempted to block their escape. "Wait! I need buffers. Y'all can't leave now."

"You don't need us," Leo insisted. "You got this. But definitely call us after and tell us all about it. Better yet, come to the inn and we'll have a BFF night. I'll bake your favorite chocolate chip blondies."

I smiled through my annoyance. "I love your chocolate chip blondies."

They were right. Being an adult and facing my issues head-on was the best thing to do, I'd had enough therapy to know that. Plus, it's the advice I would have given them if they needed it, damn it. Advice was more fun when you were the one giving it. Receiving it was bullshit.

Nick stepped out of his open garage with a hesitant smile on his face.

"Hey, Nick," Molly waved him over. "You're off early today."

"It's an early release day for the high school."

"We're about to go back to work. It was good seeing you." They headed to Leo's car and took off.

"We have to talk," he informed me without preamble. "Can I come over?"

# CHAPTER 7
# CLARA

*You're the only one I want. I can't imagine being with someone else. - Nick*

"Sure, come on over. I guess we should clear the air. We are neighbors, after all. What about the kids? Will they be home soon?"

I met him at the edge of where our lawns met. For some dumb reason, having that dividing line between us made me feel safe, as if my emotions could be contained within the border of purple pansies and petunias I had planted the other day as long as we stayed on our separate sides.

"They're going to their mother's house after school. It's her turn with them."

"Ahh, I see. That must be tough. Sadie still struggles sharing the boys with her ex."

"It's not what I imagined when I pictured having kids, as you may recall."

*I did recall.*

We used to talk all the time about what it would be like to have a family together and all the things we'd do differently than our parents. "I'm so sorry, Nick."

"It is what it is. Anyway, it's going to be a lot easier now that I live here. My ex lives around the corner. They've already started coming and going between our houses. I see them a lot more."

"Good. Do y'all get along, or . . . ?" I couldn't believe we were standing here making innocuous small talk like this when we had once been able to share everything. It felt strange. It felt wrong. I didn't like it one bit.

His hesitant smile turned to a frown when a brand-new Range Rover pulled up to the curb. "Shit," he mumbled under his breath.

"That's her, isn't it?" I hissed.

A resigned nod was his only answer.

He looked beat down and exhausted. I decided to stay put.

Intrigued, I watched as a gorgeous, flashy brunette exited the vehicle. "Nicky, we have to talk. The kids want you to come to the wedding. They wouldn't let up, so I agreed." I didn't like the way she said his name. It wasn't an endearment. The way she said it was condescending, like she was trying to diminish him in order to get her way.

"That is the last thing I want to do. No thanks." He crossed his arms over his chest and stepped away from her. He was now in my yard, on my turf. My hands hit my hips as I took in the snotty look on her face.

"That is neither here nor there." She whipped an expensive-looking envelope from her Louis Vuitton Speedy and waved it in his face. "The kids want this to happen. So, here's my personal invitation to you, hand delivered. Don't disappoint them, okay?"

He snatched it, folded it roughly, and stuffed it into the pocket of his jeans. "I'll think about it."

She went on, dismissing his concerns with a roll of her eyes. "Feel free to bring a date, Nick. I mean, if you can get one, that is. How long has it been? You must be positively dying. How's the hand?" She snickered.

*Why wouldn't he be able to get a date?*

Was she nuts? Could she not see how sexy he was?

He was hotter than ever, and I remembered lusting after him extensively in high school.

I had sat behind him in history class during our senior year—when I was there anyway. He was the quarterback, and I was usually drunk under the bleachers with my friends, but it didn't make me blind, for eff's sake.

My eyes roved over his broad-shouldered, wide-chested form, noting the way his biceps were about to bulge right through the sleeves of the blue Green Valley High polo shirt he was wearing. It was tight around his pecs too, and don't even get me started on his ass in those jeans.

*Thank you very much, casual Friday.*

Also, what a witch, talking down to him like that. The look on her face triggered me. I flashed back to my mom, waving her pointy finger in the air as she berated me and my sisters.

*Nuh-uh.* Nope. My protective hackles rose. Damn my constant compulsion to stick up for an underdog.

He heaved out a sigh. "I'm not currently dating anyone, Morgan. You know I've been busy working every hour I can get to afford the down payment on this place."

"Nicky, my god," she snapped and held up a hand. "You're impossible."

I watched, fascinated as he mentally and physically retreated at what had to be a familiar gesture from her. His eyes dimmed and he shrank back.

*Hell no.*

"Let's not get this started again—"

She wasn't going to stop, I could tell. She was getting warmed up for a fight.

"You wouldn't have had to do that if you'd taken the job with your stepfather after we got married like you said you were going to do."

*Ha! She wanted a fight. I knew it. What a cow.*

"I never, not ever, said that. Not once. How you got that idea into your head is beyond me," he protested. But it was half-hearted, like he was compelled to defend himself, but his first instinct was to walk away.

"Well, why you'd want to struggle like you do will always be beyond me, especially when you could have gone so much farther and made so much more out of your life."

"That's enough. I'm not discussing this with you anymore. We're divorced, remember? I can do what I want now without your input."

Her haughty huff was obnoxious as all get out. "Fine. Have it your way."

*Was she a gold digger? Maybe she'd found out about his stepdad and staked her claim on him back whenever they first got together.*

I had to be right. She wasn't even hiding it. It was blatant. She was dressed designer, head to toe. Her engagement ring had to be at least five carats, and her Range Rover was brand-new. I took a glance at her shoes—red soles. Louboutin. Yup.

*Eff this and eff her.* I stepped closer to Nick and slid my hand from his shoulder to the center of his chest.

Nick was more than good enough, for anyone. He was a teacher, for eff's sake. It was the most noble profession of them all.

"He has a date," I burst out. "Don't you worry about that."

*Whoa, stop it. Back up. Frick!*

She sneered, "And who might you be?" She lowered her Fendi sunglasses down her nose and squinted at me over the rim.

"I'm Clara Hill. Nick's neighbor. We started seeing each other after he moved in. It's new, but—" I shrugged and tilted my head as I shifted my eyes up to Nick's with a flutter of my lashes. "We went to high school together. He's an old friend with new possibilities."

He bit his lip, hiding a grin as I slid my hand down his arm and took his hand in both of mine. I pressed my boobs into his big biceps and leaned my head against his shoulder.

"I see. Well, it's nice to meet you."

I held out a hand, making sure my tennis bracelet flashed in the sun. "You too. Your kids are wonderful. I always knew Nick would make such a good dad."

"Thank you. They are wonderful, my pride and joy." Her face pinched and I grinned harder as the smugness left her expression.

"One more thing." She turned back to Nick, completely dismissive of me. "I wanted to ask if you could keep the kids for the next few days while I finish up the last-minute wedding details at the country club." Her eyes drifted back to mine, making sure I understood she was part of the country club.

I rolled my eyes. Big whoop. That place was full of snobs. I was only a member on paper just so I could say I belonged.

"No problem. I would love to have them more often; you already know that."

Her smile turned genuine—how weird.

"I had a feeling you would. This living arrangement is going to suit us both just fine. Of course, they can come on by whenever I'm there. It's just been so hectic lately with all the running around for the wedding and such. I'd much rather they get quality time at home with you than having to tag along all over town running errands with me. I appreciate this."

"I'm happy to do it." His smile for her was genuine too.

They both loved their kids, that much was certain. *Good.*

"Once we're settled and you need time with"—she waved a hand in my direction as she eyed me up and down—"your flavor of the month, I'll be happy to return the favor."

I bit my lip as I hid a laugh. She was entirely too obvious. "Well, bless your heart. Look how generous she is, *Nicky*. Now we can have alone time whenever we want. Isn't she sweet?" I nipped at his neck and wrapped my arms around his waist.

"Uh, yeah." He cleared his throat. "Thanks, Morgan."

Was she jealous or just a bitch?

Did she want him back?

What was her deal? I couldn't read her, which both fascinated and irritated me in equal measure. But the bottom line was, I didn't like her. I added her to my shit list. No one got away with being unkind when I was around.

She gave me one last derisive look up and down. "I have to go."

"Bye now." I waggled my fingers in a wave as obnoxious as she was as Nick stared down at me. I could feel the confused brain waves emanating from him.

He raised an eyebrow and said, "So, I guess I have a date for her wedding?"

I dropped his arm like a hot potato and stepped away.

"You sure as hell do and you can bet your ass I'll be dressed to kill. But I hope you realize that this has nothing to do with you. I do not like her one bit. I don't like how she talked down to you. None of that was okay. I hope she's not like that with Ethan and Sasha—"

His eyes softened. He knew about my mother's old ways and how I grew up. "She not. I would never allow that. Wedding planning has her stressed out lately, is all."

"Good. I didn't really think you would. But you shouldn't let her get away with talking to *you* that way either. It doesn't matter what it is that's stressing her out, it's rude and uncalled for. How'd you end up with a moody little witch like that?" I gave him the side-eye and crossed my arms. "You used to have much better taste in women."

He let out a bitter laugh. "She was your opposite in every way, and I had to do something to forget about you. She got pregnant with Ethan, so I married her. We tried to save the marriage with Sasha—which I don't recommend— and got divorced a few years after that. She's great with the kids, it's me she has a problem with. And you too now, apparently."

"Uh, okay, well that was brutally honest."

He shrugged. His mood had shifted into one I'd never experienced with him in the past. He was dejected, cynical, cold.

I didn't know how to react, so I kept quiet.

"Lying is pointless," he added.

"Ironic, isn't it? Considering the situation we just found ourselves in." I tried to catch his eyes and failed.

"Secrets aren't the same as lies," he insisted. "Who would we be hurting?"

"You mean besides ourselves, potentially?"

A small grin tipped up the corner of his mouth, but it didn't reach his eyes. "So what about you?" he asked. "Married? Divorced? I assume you're single right now, yes?"

"Obviously, I'm single." His attitude was getting to me. *Was he trying to accuse me of something?* "*I'm* not a liar, and I *always* do what I say I'm going to do. And no, I've never been married."

"Just out there breaking hearts then?"

"You know it." I scowled as my mood flipped from feeling protective of him to angry at what he had implied about me. As if I'd volunteer to be his date if I was seeing someone. "It's my favorite pastime."

"I guess me joining you on the porch for a chat right now is not gonna happen."

"You're smart for a man."

He placed his hand over his heart. "Ouch."

"Don't worry, *Nicky*. Unlike your ex, I rarely shoot to kill. I think you'll survive."

"I'm sorry, okay? Morgan pushes my buttons. I'm exhausted, and you're getting to me. You left Green Valley and didn't look back and I—" He ran a hand over the back of his neck, leaving it there as his mouth twisted into a frown. "I don't know how to feel about it is all. First, we almost kissed on the balcony, then you kicked me out. You defended me just now and then pushed me away. You're confusing as hell, Clara."

"It's fine. It's whatever." I took a page from his ex's playbook and waved a hand in dismissal. "Feel whatever you want to feel."

"I—never mind. This isn't the time. I need a damn nap."

I watched his fine ass as he headed up his walkway to his own porch where he sat in the cute wicker rocking chair I had been admiring ever since it had been delivered. He pulled out his phone, then put his feet on the railing as he pretended to peruse whatever was on the screen as he watched me from the corner of his eye, the big hot stupid jerk.

*Were we playing games now?*

I couldn't figure him out. But then again, how could I when I wasn't even sure about my own feelings? Well, at least one feeling was clear: I was mad at him again. We definitely needed to talk, but now I didn't want to. Again. *Damn it.*

He had no idea who he was messing with. The sweet little Clara he used to know was buried so deep beneath the pieces of the heart he had broken that I doubted she'd ever find her way out again. And *this* Clara only played to win.

I, *Lavender Lane* stripper, walked up the steps and slid out of my robe. Never had I been more grateful for Lululemon's vast array of sexy athleisure wear. I blew him a kiss as I sat down, lifting a foot up to the railing to push the swing while glaring at him from the corner of my eye.

I reached for my phone and scrolled to the local nursery's web page to order an entire buttload of plants for Sasha to enjoy on her porch. She was sweet, she deserved to be surrounded by pretty things, and Nick deserved to take care of them all.

*Figure out how to keep a fiddle-leaf fig and a few Alocasia alive, you arrogant asshat.*

I glanced up. He was waving me over. "I'm sorry," he called. "I mean it."

*As if.*

"I'm busy," I hollered back at his grumpy ass. "Take a nap and maybe I'll reconsider talking to you at some point."

I scrolled back to the page and added a watering can, a Boston fern, and a pothos. It was hard not to *muah ha ha ha* out loud, but I managed. My eyes drifted over the ever-growing collection of greenery on my porch and throughout my yard. Plants could be persnickety; keeping them alive took time and knowledge. He'd find out.

Shots fired. *Bang.*

Yeah, so it was plants and not something truly mean. He had kids and they were nice. And damn, the man looked exhausted. I couldn't bring myself to do anything truly hurtful.

But no one messes with Clara Jean Hill and gets away with it. Not anymore. And never again.

# CHAPTER 8
# NICK

*When I think of you, it makes me smile. When I'm with you, you touch my heart. We're in our own little world together and I never want to leave it. - Clara*

Sasha was brilliant. This rocking chair was comfortable, and the view from my porch was spectacular.

I felt like shit for how I'd behaved. Morgan knew how to get under my skin, and she'd been in rare form today. I shut down so I wouldn't fall into our usual argument over her disapproval of my career choice. It wasn't fair to Clara. I'd acted like an ass. And oh my god, I was so damn tired.

I'd never seen her angry like that before and I was only slightly ashamed that I found it hot. She had always been sarcastic and mouthy when she was mad, but it had never been directed at me. And before, she had an underlying sorrow and vulnerability I had always done my best to protect. Now that she was just pissed, it was sexy as hell. The years had made her strong. She was bold, she was beautiful, and she'd stuck up for me even though we had yet to clear the air between us.

I wanted to know her again. I wanted to know everything that had put that glint of steel in her eyes.

I would figure out how to make it up to her. And I would find a way to make her talk to me about our past too.

After that, who knew? If the feelings she aroused in me were any indicator, we'd end up being a lot more than neighbors.

*Did I want another chance with her?*

Maybe? Probably.

Okay, yes, I did. But I was nowhere near ready to face the reality of it, of how it would feel to have her be part of my life again. At least not now, when it was so obvious there was some kind of misunderstanding between us. But I had time, proximity, and chemistry on my side. I knew I could fix whatever it was.

She was hurt about the past but interested in me at the same time—that much was clear.

Our almost-kiss this morning on her balcony and the soft press of her body against my arm when Morgan was giving me shit told that tale. She could have stepped in with Morgan without moving so close to me. She didn't need to get physical to defend my honor. And why had she bothered to defend me at all?

Even if I didn't get a chance to be with her again, I'd fix it. She had meant the world to me. I had loved her more than anything, and I didn't want her to think what we'd had together wasn't real. Because it was, she was everything to me when I had needed her the most. I was lost after my dad died, and Clara had been the one to pull me through it. I sat rocking in the chair, remembering many of the small moments we shared.

I must have fallen asleep, because my text notification went off, waking me from my slumber. I sat forward to pull out my cell, heaving out a sigh when I saw it was Morgan.

MORGAN: I'm so sorry for being such a bitch to you. The wedding plans are overwhelming me and I'm exhausted. I got into it with Mal this morning and I took it out on you. I was horrible. Forgive me?

NICK: I know you're stressed out. Sasha told me. I get it. It's okay.

MORGAN: I'm sorry about being rude to your . . . girlfriend? Or is it too soon for labels? Clara, right?

NICK: Yep

. . .

MORGAN: Tell her I'm sorry, and don't forget we agreed to keep our dating lives away from the kids unless it's serious. Okay?

NICK: Will do. I won't forget.

MORGAN: I mean, bring her to the wedding, of course. But tell the kids it's a friend/neighbor thing unless/if you get serious about her and you know it's going somewhere. Are you two serious?

NICK: Don't worry.

MORGAN: Again. I feel terrible. Should I send her flowers or a plant? A bottle of wine?

I glanced at the collection of lush greenery on her porch and throughout her yard. She caught me looking so I gave her a wave.

NICK: Send a plant.

MORGAN: A plant it is. FYI, it's date night. I'll be incommunicado. The kids already know. Thanks again for keeping them during my time.

NICK: Yep

The slam of Clara's front door sent a smile unfurling across my face. For the first time in years I felt alive. Anticipation sparked inside me—for what, I didn't know, but I couldn't wait to find out.

Maybe I should just ask her out, take her on a date like nothing had happened to make her leave me all those years ago. I didn't even care what it was anymore. We were young, she had to have been scared. I could forgive her for anything. I wanted her in my life again, that much was clear to me. She didn't want to talk about what had happened between us, that much had also been made clear—abundantly.

*Was moving forward without looking back possible?*

My lips shifted into a grin as a truck from the local nursery parked in my driveway and the driver began filling a small dolly with a bunch of plants that could have only come from one person.

"Afternoon," he greeted. "Sasha Easton live here?"

"Yup."

"Dad! We get to stay with you extra days!" I smiled as Ethan hauled ass up the street, followed by Sasha who also began running once she caught sight of the plants being delivered.

She gasped, "Is that all for me?"

"Are you Sasha Easton?" the delivery driver asked with a smile.

"Yes!" she squealed.

"Then yes, little lady, these are for you."

"This is so awesome!" She tossed her backpack on the lawn and helped him carry the plants to the grassy area in front of the porch.

"Can we get pizza for dinner?" Ethan sank onto the padded wicker sofa adjacent to my rocker. "I'm so happy it's Friday. I'm going to sleep all day tomorrow."

"You and me both. And yes to pizza." Pizza meant no cooking, which also meant no cleaning up after dinner—which I was a huge fan of, especially on the weekends.

*Why were Fridays always so exhausting?*

My phone went off again. It was my mother. *Great.*

"Go inside, y'all. We'll sort all of this out later."

The delivery driver took off with a wave, the kids ran inside, and I swiped to answer the call. "Nicky! I'm calling to see how the kids' first day of school went."

"You're a bit late for that, Mom."

"I'm at the house in Hawaii. Island time has me all out of sorts. You know how I get."

"It's okay. I know." But I didn't really know. I didn't know her anymore.

We were probably seventy percent no contact by now. Then she'd call me or send gifts to the kids, and I'd feel bad about never talking to her. We'd find a time to have dinner and fight about me being a teacher and divorcing

Morgan, only to rinse and repeat the cycle a few months later. It was exhausting.

My therapist called it a soft boundary. I'd checked out of my relationship with her and had no expectations left. I should cut off contact completely, but it was hard to let go of that shred of hope, no matter how small it now was. I was still holding on to the idea that someday she would change back to the way she'd been when my dad was alive.

"So, I won't keep you. Tell the kids hi for me, or should I call Morgan at her place? Is it her week with the kids?"

"No—"

"Why you'd want to get a divorce from a woman like her is beyond me. She comes from a wonderful family, she's educated, goal oriented, has a good job . . . It's never too late for a second chance, Nicky—"

"We were never right for each other, you know that. I told you everything after we got the divorce. We wanted different things out of life—"

"She's beautiful, Nicky. You could have given her everything she wanted. You still can, if you'd quit being so stubborn and take the job with your stepfather. Phil says it's yours whenever you decide to give your children what they deserve. Think of how you'll be able to pay for their college when the time comes. Think of their future—"

"Is there anything else you needed? I'll give the kids your regards."

She let out a beleaguered sigh, as if every word out of her mouth wasn't an insult to me and everything I'd chosen to do with my life. "Yes, honey. Sam is heading to Green Valley sometime around Thanksgiving week to open the Bandit Lake house up and get everything ready before we come back to town for Christmas. Invite him for dinner, will you? I don't want him to be alone on the holiday and I want you to talk to him about his troubles with Ivy. It isn't looking good for his marriage, Nick. We can't have another divorce in the family. What will people think?"

"Sure thing. I'll talk to him." My older brother had used every advantage my stepfather had offered him. I didn't hold it against him, but we were no longer as close as we had been before our father died. And as for his marriage? From what I could tell, he was as happy with his wife as I'd been with mine. If they ended up divorcing, it wouldn't be a surprise.

Sam worked for my stepfather. He vacationed with him and my mother, too. In fact, he was in Hawaii with them right now. If my mother had accepted my choices without badgering and pushing me to do what she wanted, we'd all probably still be close.

"Talk soon, darling." She hung up before I could tell her goodbye or that I loved her, or any of the other things we would have said to each other before my father died and she had traded up. The fact that she didn't ask to talk to the kids had not escaped me; it never did.

Sasha, dressed in her bathing suit, poked her head out the front door. "Dad! Let's go swimming! Come on!"

"Be there in a minute. Wait for me to get back there before you get in the pool."

"I know!" she hollered.

I didn't need to take a job with my stepfather to take care of my kids and I'd never trade my integrity for a few bucks.

Being a teacher was what my dad had always wanted to do, but he went to work at the Payton Mill straight out of high school and never got to live out his dream. He transferred that dream to me through our shared love of literature. Our trailer had always been full of books, full of imagination, full of love.

A car accident took his life when I was in high school. It also took my mother's peace of mind. Over the years, I had forgiven a lot when it came to her. She had been left alone with two teenage boys to support on her secretary's salary. I could hardly blame her when she remarried right away. Phil was her boss and had been infatuated with her for years. He wasted no time; he asked her out a few months after the funeral, proposed not long after that, she'd said yes, and life as we'd known it had ended.

After changing into my swim trunks, I found Sasha and Ethan out back. "Cannonball!" I ran around them and jumped into the pool with a huge splash.

"Throw me!" Ethan yelled as he jumped into the pool to land next to me.

I grinned and grabbed him under the arms to throw him into the deep end, glad that at almost thirteen, he wasn't too cool to still have fun with his dad.

"Do not get my hair wet," Sasha told us. She was lounging on a huge pink floatie with a Dr Pepper in her hand. "I'm not in the playing mood today. School is exhausting and I'm tired. I want to float."

"You heard her, Eath. Don't even think about splashing her. What are the rules of the pool?"

"Um, don't go in without you and don't be a jerk," he answered. "Oh! Hey, Miss Clara, come over and swim with us!"

I almost drowned myself spinning around to find her on the other side of the fence, watering the multitude of plants she had on her back deck.

"I'm good over here, sweetheart, but thank you."

"We have more floaties and Dr Peppers," Sasha informed her. "I can get you one. It's nice and cool in here and I need you to tell me how to take care of all those pretty plants you sent me. I also need to say thank you."

"You're welcome, honey. I'm happy you like them."

It was hot out—one of those sunny, late-summer Tennessee days where all you wanted to do was jump in a pool or relax inside with the AC running. Not putter around the yard with a watering can. A droplet of sweat trickled down her temple and she bit her lip.

"Come on over, Clara. My pool is your pool. Ethan, run inside and grab Miss Clara a Diet Coke with way too much ice and a slice of lemon from the fridge. Grab me one too, while you're in there."

Clara's eyebrows shot up. Yeah, I remembered what she liked to drink because we had always liked a lot of the same things.

"Just like you, huh, Dad? How interesting." Sasha sent me a smirk from her floatie. "Come on, Miss Clara, you have to at least tell me about that one with the shiny pink and green leaves. Please?"

I could almost see Clara's wheels turning as she struggled for an answer. "The rex begonia. It's one of my favorites. You know what? I think I will join you and we can talk plants. It's so dang hot today." She set the watering can down. "I'll go change."

Ethan ran into the house for the drinks, and I floated on my back, doing my best to avoid looking at a smug Sasha.

"You like her, Dad. Don't bother telling me you don't, because then you'll have to ground yourself for lying, right?"

I dove under the water and swam across the pool to the deep end, chagrined because my eleven-year-old daughter had my number and I didn't know how to deny my feelings for Clara without looking like an ass or a liar.

I popped up in time to watch Clara gingerly open the side gate and tiptoe rapidly across the hot cement. My eyes bulged as they traveled up her long, slim legs, over the deep swell of her hips, up her taut stomach, and across her gorgeous tits to end up on her stunning face. Her bathing suit was a modest one-piece—deep purple with white trim—but it did nothing to prevent my mind from running wild. Not when I knew the stunning paradise under it. I'd touched and tasted every square inch of her body inside and out and it was all I could do to keep my composure and prevent my dick from getting hard.

"I should have worn my flip-flops, y'all." She rushed to the steps at the shallow end and sat on the first one. "Much better."

"I'll get you a floatie." Sasha climbed out and headed to the small shed at the side of the house where I kept the pool supplies.

"Got your pants caught on your pitchfork a bit, didn't you?" I decided to tease her. Flirting was out of the question and reminiscing was dangerous.

She rolled her eyes and waded into the shallow end. "I have no idea what you mean. And in case you didn't notice, I'm not wearing pants right now." She did a little jump before going under the water to swim up to my side with a smirk.

"Believe me, I noticed." I mock-glared at her through squinted eyes. "You wanted me to have to figure out how to deal with that jungle you bought for Sasha on my porch. But you can't help yourself. You're stepping in."

"Whatever. Sasha is a nice kid. I don't really mind." She backstroked away from me. "The water feels so good. Thanks, Nick."

"Anytime. I'm sorry. About before, I mean. I was a jerk."

"Eh, I guess it's okay. We'll call it a truce for now. This dip in your pool makes up for a lot. Being around an ex can be stressful, right?"

I let out a laugh. "Right."

She was in my pool, and she had a smile on her face—but I couldn't help but think this truce was temporary.

# CHAPTER 9
# CLARA



It was my first official day of work as Green Valley High's newest substitute teacher.

Once the news had spread to my family about my new job, Willa had let it slip that a group of high school teachers had become regulars at our Aunt Genie's eponymously named Genie's Country Western Bar, where Willa was a server. And since I had no intention of working at the elementary or middle schools, I had hauled my booty up there to make friends and ensure they knew to request me if they ever needed a sub.

I'd successfully managed to avoid Nick for the last couple of weeks while I waited for my background check to clear by only going outside when I knew he'd be at work. I missed evenings on my porch and his amazing pool, but it was a sacrifice I had to make to keep my heart safe. I had to protect myself, but most of all, I had to forget how he looked wearing only a pair of swim trunks. He'd grown up—a lot. The cute boy I had loved in high school was now a big, broody hunk of a man. I didn't know him anymore, but I wanted to.

As was the thought of being Gracie's unofficial bodyguard, the threat of potentially running into Nick throughout the day was as thrilling as it was terrifying.

I was no fool; just because I hadn't seen him except for across the yard or through the window didn't mean he hadn't been on my mind. I missed him, and our history was complicated and fraught, but that hadn't kept the chemistry from buzzing in the air between us every time we ran into each other, however briefly.

*Did I want another chance with him?*

I was not known for choosing what was good for me. So, like always, I was craving what I shouldn't and fighting it every step of the way. I'd do my best to avoid him today, but it would probably be impossible.

I finished fastening my lucky necklace then stepped into the pair of spiked black Louboutin slingbacks I'd laid out the night before. I'd raided the attorney section of my closet and found this little number. It was a professional yet feminine black A-line skirt with a matching silk blouse.

"Clara! I'm here." Gracie had used her key to get in. Everett had started dropping her off on the way to work every day so I didn't have to cross town twice to pick her up and take her to school.

"I'm coming down." I slipped on a few bracelets, grabbed my bag, and took one last look in the mirror.

I found Gracie rummaging through my pantry. "There's nothing in here but old bread and like, a million bags of coffee. How are you an adult?"

"Check the freezer. Nuke one of Leo's breakfast burritos." Leo had been keeping my freezer stocked up. Between bumming leftovers from Sadie, and Everett's weekly supply of spaghetti, I was no longer at risk of getting hangry and losing my shit with Nick. I should probably learn to cook, but sadly, that was a life skill that had remained permanently low on my priority list.

Sliding around her, I made it to the coffee pot. I had set the timer last night; if I had to be up this early, waiting for my first dose was not something I was willing to do. I reached for a travel mug and filled it.

"You're wearing that?" Her eyes flicked up and down my body. "Are you trying to declare this National Boner Day or something?"

"What?" I looked down at myself. "This is perfectly acceptable."

She scoffed. "Sure. But not on a human Barbie doll like you."

"Don't be sexist, Gracie. Didn't I teach you better? I'm totally covered up —neck to knees. This skirt isn't even tight, but if it was, would it really matter? You of all people should know better since you look just like me. We are not sex objects, we're human beings." I fastened the lid on my mug and waved it in the air. "Fuck the patriarchy."

"You're right, I'm sorry. It's sad how much this shit is ingrained in me.

You look pretty and professional, you really do. You're going to be great today."

"Thanks." I beamed at her. "And you look ready to kick someone's ass." Gracie was fond of Doc Martens and dark makeup, and lately she'd been begging to get a tattoo.

"Hey, I might just do it if Marianne keeps up her shit. The only thing keeping my foot out of her butt is my sprained ankle and the fact that she's backed off a bit. But if she starts with me when I can balance again, it's on—and I don't care about Pindich's zero tolerance crap." She put her hands on her hips and nodded once in my direction. "Beating someone's ass in self-defense is legit, dang it."

"Stand in line for the boot in the butt thing. You're looking at your official bodyguard. I have no shame and am not above terrorizing a few teenage girls for the sake of your inner peace. You will have a good senior year no matter what I have to do to make it happen. This is the official start of my villain era."

She bit her lip, hesitating before asking, "Do you ever wish we could have been normal? Without the hillbilly reputation? You know, with a dad and a mom who actually loved each other. And a home where no one had to run away, or get married at eighteen years old to escape it, or become a hard-as-nails, rich lawyer to protect all of us . . ." The edge of cynicism that usually filled her voice faded away as her eyes drifted to the floor.

"I think about that whenever I'm in a therapy appointment or spying on the neighborhood from my porch like a totally normal person." I grinned her way.

Her eyes raised to mine, flashing as her humor came back. "Thanks for paying for Dr. Simon, by the way."

I shrugged. "It's why I had to make the big bucks. I knew we'd all need buttloads of therapy. And yes, I do wish that we'd been brought up better, so much. But we can't go back in time, can we? Look, we Hill sisters are finally back together, all of us back in Green Valley like we're supposed to be. We have Dr. Simon to talk things through with, Momma is getting better every day, and I think we're going to end up being just fine. I mean, our family dinners have at least ninety percent less screaming and fighting now, and hardly anyone bursts into tears or storms off anymore, right?"

"You make good points."

I pulled her close and kissed her temple. "I've got you. I will do anything for you."

"By the way, I know you had Mari—I mean, Miss Mitchell—keep an eye on me. She's not very stealthy, you know."

"I needed eyes on the inside until I could be there myself to watch out for you, and I'm not sorry. Mari is family, she knows how it is. Maybe she's not stealthy, but she is discreet."

Her answering smile was grateful. "Thank you."

"Always, Gracie."

*Bing.* A cymbal crash rang out along with the timer on the microwave and we both jumped.

"What the hell?" I shoved the curtains aside. Dawn was rising in a haze of pink-tinted sunlight as what looked like a small portion of the high school band marched their way up the street.

"It sounds like the band." She grabbed her burrito from the microwave then joined me at the window. "What the hell?"

"What are they doing out this early in the morning? School hasn't even started yet."

"It's the seniors. They have zero hour practice, remember? That's why Ruby couldn't be the one to drive me to school."

"You mean, this isn't in my honor? To welcome me on my first day?" I joked.

"Yeah, right. Let's go see what's going on. They usually practice on the football field or in the parking lot." She hobbled toward the front door. Her ankle was getting better; the crutches were no longer necessary, just the boot.

We headed to the porch and watched Mari lead the band straight into Leonard and Janice's yard across the street. I flinched when a row of horn players marched right through his gorgeous bed of dahlias.

Janice had been the band director before she retired. Maybe this was something for her?

"Leonard is going to freak the eff out when he sees them." I nudged Gracie's arm. "This is going to be great. Watch."

"Hey!" Leonard came barreling outside dressed in one of Janice's silk robes and a pair of boxers with his floppy curls blowing in the morning breeze.

"Damn, he really pulls that off," I observed. Yes, we were one-sided yard rivals, but I could admit he looked oddly hot in Janice's pretty paisley caftan. I made a mental note to ask her where she'd bought it. Leonard wasn't the only one who could rock that look.

"Your neighborhood is weird as hell," Gracie mumbled through a bite of her breakfast.

I peeked at her over my shoulder. "Why do you think I'm outside all day? It's better than TV."

"Sing, Sing, Sing" blasted through the air as Sasha and Ethan wandered into my yard to watch the impromptu concert with us. "Hi, y'all." Gracie greeted them while I raised my mug with a grin.

"Oh, come on!" Leonard yelled, cursing under his breath as kids filled his pristine, freshly mowed lawn, trampling the neat lines he had oh-so-carefully created in the grass yesterday with his lawn mower.

I let out a laugh as Ruby stepped directly into his echinacea.

*Now who has the better yard?*

"Mornin', Clara." I spun to the side. Nick's voice drowned out the band, drowned out the kids' chatter, drowned out everything as I took him in, trying to stay mad as he stood in the early morning light looking way too gorgeous for my own good. "It's been a while. You look stunning. Where are you off to today?"

"He doesn't know?" Gracie laughed. "Clara's subbing for Miss Dalbotten today. She's got herself a new job as a substitute teacher."

A slow grin spread across his face. "Is that so? We'll be co-workers then. I'll show you around."

"I used to go there, remember?" I laughed to soften the rejection in front of his kids. "I can find my own way around campus, thanks though."

"Then let me take you out to dinner tonight to celebrate."

I reared back and shook my head to clear it. "What did you just say?" *He'd lost his dang mind.*

"Dinner." He grinned. "You and me. I'll buy you a steak at The Front Porch to celebrate." The Front Porch was fancy and had the best steaks in town. I loved it there.

My jaw lowered as I tried to gather my wits. I was too startled to offer an immediate objection.

"Yes!" Sasha pumped her fist in the air.

"You're asking Miss Clara out on a date?" Ethan questioned.

"She would love to," Gracie answered for me.

"Hey! I can answer for myself." I really couldn't, not when I desperately wanted both to go with him and also to run off and hide from him under my bed at the same time.

*No, no, a billion times NO!*

*Shut up. Say yes. Nick's hot.*

I caught sight of Sasha's big, brown, hope-filled eyes and before I could think too hard about it, the word "*Yes*" came tumbling out of my mouth, followed by, "Thanks, Nick. Dinner would be nice."

"Great. Six o'clock it is." He beamed at me, and it was all I could do not to throw myself into his arms. "Gracie, I'll pay you double your usual rate since it's last minute. Will that work?"

"Heck yes." Gracie was somewhat of an entrepreneur, at my influence. She was licensed, bonded, trained in CPR and first aid, and had her own website offering services for anything from grocery shopping, to driving the elderly to appointments, to babysitting. Apparently, Nick was one of her customers.

"Maybe we shouldn't," I hedged. "Uh, it's a school night . . ." So much irony floated in the air between us, it was ridiculous. Luckily none of the kids noticed the subtext-filled looks we were shooting at each other.

School nights had meant nothing to us in the past. We'd snuck around doing whatever we felt like with no regard for time, or propriety, or anything our mothers had to say about curfews.

But now? I had a whole entire list of rules forming in my brain for our dinner together. He never used to be a troublemaker like this. Asking me out in front of his kids and Gracie and putting our secret at risk? Who was this guy?

"Aw, you're right. We'll aim for Friday night instead, and I won't keep you out past your bedtime. I swear I'm a responsible adult now."

"Ohh, Friday is date night!" Sasha squealed. "You can stay out as late as you want."

"Dial it down, Sash. I'm being neighborly is all. New jobs deserve celebrating. Right, Clara?"

I bit my lip and gave him my best *what the hell are you thinking* glare. He shrugged it off with that devastating and adorably toothy grin I used to love before herding his kids back home to finish getting ready for school.

"Sash, Eath! Say goodbye, grab your backpacks, and get to the bus."

"Bye, y'all." I waved, trying to act normal, like I wasn't freaking out inside about Nick and whatever he was planning, or the way I was saying yes to everything he wanted and *not* telling him to go screw himself like I should.

Good lord, I should have tried harder to avoid him this morning. But the stupid marching band had wrecked my plans to hightail it out of here before he left for the day.

"I have to get my stuff too." Gracie headed to the house, stopping on the porch before she went in. "Oh, I'm free Friday, if you need me. But I'm still charging you double," she added with a smirk. "Supply and demand. It's only fair."

"You got it. Thanks, Gracie." Nick paused at the edge of my lawn and waited until I finally turned to face him.

"*Gah!* What now?" I burst out. "I'm supposed to be mad at you, remember? I mean, I am mad. Totally pissed, okay? We have issues, Nick. Big ones.

Big honking past issues that make whatever this is"—I swung my hand back and forth between us—"very complicated. I've been avoiding you for a reason, okay?"

"I know that. And I have to say, you're a master at it. We're neighbors and I hardly ever see you. I remember you being sneaky, but obviously I liked it a lot better when I was the one you were sneaking around with."

My nostrils flared at the amused twinkle in his eyes. He wasn't taking this nearly serious enough for my liking. *"Hmph."*

"Why do you think I asked you out?" he pushed. "We have to talk this through. We have to clear the air. I want to be on the same page as you."

I shoved a finger in one of his impressive pecs. "We're not even in the same freaking book anymore, Nick," I huffed. "What if I don't feel like talking about any of this? What then? What if all I want to do is eat a free steak and glare at you from across the table?" I took a step back and crossed my arms. *Take that.*

He shrugged as if it was all the same to him. "I don't care. I just want to be near you. And being your neighbor is not enough for me. From the moment I laid eyes on you in the parking lot, you're all I can think about. I want to know you again, Clara. That's it." As if it would be that simple.

Have dinner.

Know each other again.

*That's it.*

Warning bells went off in my head, bing-bonging all the ways I could end up getting hurt if I let him into my heart again.

Picking a fight was the only way to get him to back off. I saw how he had shut down with his ex the other day when she was being all bitchy and I needed him to do it with me.

*Shut it down.*

The emotion in his eyes was too much for me to handle; the nostalgia was killing me. He was too sexy, too determined, too damn engaged in this conversation and I was about to give in to anything he asked me.

"So, you tricked me into going out with you?" I accused.

His eyes flashed fire before he threw his head back and laughed, showing no sign of relenting. "How is me asking you a direct question tricking you?" This was the exact opposite of shutting down. *What the hell?* His eyes blazed into mine as his lips quirked up at the corner. "I invited you to dinner. You said yes. Could I be any more blatant with my intentions?"

"You're confusing me, and I think you're doing it on purpose." This was a lie; I was not confused. Not one bit. I was no fool—I knew when a man was interested, and Nick definitely wanted another piece of me. I was halfway tempted to yank him into my garage, shove him up against the wall, and give it to us both—conversation and clarity about our past be damned. "You're infuriating, quit it." Instead of jumping him on the lawn and having my way with him, I shoved a finger in his chest again. "Don't think you're gonna get away without hearing about this at dinner. I think I might have a lot to say after all."

He bowed forward until we were eye to eye with our foreheads almost touching. "I can't fucking wait," he growled, the sound of it sending goosebumps across my skin. Then, ever so gently, he removed my hand from his pec and kissed the tip of my pokey finger. "I want you to talk to me. I don't care if you're yelling, screaming, glaring at me across a table, or poking this cute little finger of yours in my chest. I'll take anything I can get from you. See you in the teachers' lounge, heartbreaker."

My hands hit my hips as I stood there sputtering as he walked off, mad at myself for letting him get the last word. And even more mad at myself for still wanting him so damn bad.

# CHAPTER 10
# NICK

*I wish I had a cell phone. All this note writing is exhausting. I'm not as good at words as you are. But I love you more than the entire world. - HB*

E*avesdropping is wrong.*

Clara and Mari were across from each other at the big table in the middle of the lounge and I'd been lurking at the door like a creeper for the last few minutes, listening in as they bonded over their collective feminist rage, complained about men, and ogled my buddy Court after he passed me going in.

"Heeeey," they greeted in unison when he cleared the doorway.

Like Clara, Court was a sub. Sometimes he joined us at the Smoky Mountain Inn's huge back lawn area for touch football with Clay, the Monroe brothers, and a few of the other guys I had played ball with back in high school. He was a good guy, but he'd better not even think about trying anything with Clara.

Since I was busted anyway, I headed inside, making a beeline for my favorite Keurig as I tried to catch Clara's eye.

She patted my shoulder on her way to the door as Mari darted past me toward the band room with a wave. "Later, neighbor. Maybe I'll see you around the block sometime."

"Hey, wait up a sec," I called, gratified when she came to an immediate stop and spun to face me. "Maybe I'll catch you at Genie's tonight instead. Mari invited you, right?" A couple times a month a varying group of teachers met at Genie's Country Western Bar to commiserate about our job complaints over margaritas and nachos. Tonight was one of those nights.

"She mentioned something about it, but no. I can't make it."

I took one step closer. "I think you should come. I'll drive you."

Old man Neal shoved around me on his way to the cursed couch that sat along the back wall. "She's not invited, of course," he muttered without looking up. "Midweek margarita night is not for subs. What could she possibly have to complain about?"

"Don't talk to her like that," I snapped. "Show some respect."

"Oh, like you were *respecting* her the other morning?" he hissed under his breath.

"Shut your fucking mouth," I hissed back. "If you say one word about that to anyone, I'll make you more miserable than you already are. Do you hear me? Clara is off limits."

He nodded once as he passed, glaring at me as he sat his mean ass down on the sofa along the back wall. If the rumors were true, it was one of the preferred spots our illustrious former principal and his secretary liked to conduct their extracurricular activities on. No one told old man Neal though. Quite a few of us teachers had been subjected to his judgmental bullshit when we were here as students. Suffice it to say he was not well-liked.

"Don't worry about it, I'm used to him. Whatever he said, it's fine. He's been talking behind my back for years because he's too scared to say anything to my face. Isn't that right, Geoffrey?"

"It's Mr. Neal," he corrected her as Court returned. He shoved a pod in the Keurig and shot Clara a grin.

"Whatever you say, Geoff," she bit out with a hostile grin. "Guess what, my schedule suddenly opened up. I'll see y'all tonight at Genie's wearing my best hillbilly trash outfit just for Geoffypoo's grumpy ass. Y'all be sure to save me a seat at the bar."

Mr. Neal sputtered and got up from the couch. "Miss Hill, you're impossible and you always have been. Good day."

Clara glared at him before breezing through the door with a little wave aimed his way. He followed behind, then turned down the hall toward the library.

"I like her—" Court started.

"Don't." My voice was a low grunt. Could I have acted any more like a possessive neanderthal? Shit, I was going to give everything away on her first day here if I wasn't careful.

"Not where I was going with that." He laughed. "But I get you loud and clear. Clara is off limits."

Clay breezed in, bag of takeout in his hand. "Who's off limits? The new sub?"

"No one," I bit out and Clay laughed.

"Gotcha." He took a seat at the table and dug into his lunch. "Don't ask the hot new sub out."

"I'm not available anyway," Court deadpanned. "No worries, Nick, seriously. We won't say a word about your massive crush on Miss Hill."

I heaved out a sigh. "Thanks, I know you won't. I just . . . She just . . . Fuck." Better to let them think I was crushing on her rather than dredge up all the history we shared.

"Look, we've all been there. In fact, I might be there too, right now," Clay added.

"Sorry, man."

"It is what it is." I knew he wouldn't talk about it with me. None of us were the type to share our feelings, at least not with each other. We were more prone to zone out while playing football in silent sympathy or by exchanging knowing looks over the pool table at Genie's.

Was that a problem? Probably.

"Later." I took my now-filled mug of coffee from beneath the Keurig and decided to finish out my prep period alone in my classroom and try to clear my head.

Clara was here.

In this building.

Driving me crazy.

*Again.*

Memories of how I'd felt passing her in the halls, running into her at her locker or the cafeteria, or seeing her under the bleachers with her friends while I was in PE or at football practice running the track assaulted me as I walked. Just like back then, she was *mine* and I couldn't say a word about it. She belonged with me, and I was the idiot who'd let her go without a fight all those years ago.

Instead of going directly to my classroom, I took a detour and wound up in front of her old locker. We'd always passed notes back and forth. I used to slip them inside her locker at lunch. Her mother wouldn't let her have a cell phone, so we didn't text like most of our classmates did.

I inhaled a sharp breath, stuttering to a stop when I saw her standing there, like something straight out of a memory or the dream I sometimes had.

"Remember when you used to slip notes through the side right here?" Her finger traced gently over the small opening. "That always used to be the best part of my day."

"I remember."

"I still have them," she whispered. Her eyes were lit with from within. The Clara I used to know shone through more and more each time I got the chance to be around her. It took everything in me not to yank her into my arms and kiss the hell out of her.

Every time I had seen her reading one of my notes from afar, I'd wanted to run to her and pull her close. Back then she would have let me do it; she hadn't cared about secrets like I had. She would have melted into me with kisses and smiles like she had done whenever we were alone. But she wasn't mine anymore, no matter how much it still felt like she should be, so I took a step away from her instead.

"I have yours too," I confessed.

"Really? Does your ex know about that?" The light in her eyes had died, leaving a dim melancholy glow in its place.

"No. There's a lot she never knew about me."

She smiled but it didn't reach her eyes. "Why do I like hearing that?"

"I'm not ready to give you that answer, probably as much as you're not ready to hear it."

"You're right about that." She laughed lightly. "I'm not ready for any of this. I didn't realize being here would feel this way. So nostalgic and sad. How can you stand it?"

"It's weird sometimes," I admitted. *Weird.* Right. Working myself to the bone and being too tired to think seemed to have been my coping mechanism after I'd quit binge drinking in college.

"It's like we're stuck in a stinky time machine full of old gym socks and Tater Tots. Why does it smell the same?" She gave a choked laugh, desperate to lighten the mood.

"You nailed it. The place reeks."

"Also, Mr. Neal is still a total dick. I mean, I knew it from him being in the neighborhood, but why did it have to hurt so much when he talked down to me here?"

The quiver in her voice nearly split my heart in two. "God, Clara—"

"Never mind." She managed a trembling smile, holding up a hand as if to wave off her emotions. "I know better than to let anyone get to me anymore. I have to go back to my class."

The bell rang. Students swarmed the hallway, and a few aimed curious glances our way as we lingered in front of her locker.

I took another step back. Old habits die hard and, apparently, keeping our relationship secret was still second nature to me.

"Will I see you at Genie's tonight?" Our eyes met and an old gleam of understanding flashed between us. "If old man Neal is there, I'll protect you, I mean it."

"Like when you told him he was wrong for being so mean all the time? That there are ways to teach lessons without being cruel?"

"That was kid stuff. I could probably do better now."

"It sounded pretty grown up to me. Anyway, spite has always been a great motivator for me. We'll see what happens." I watched her walk away as my heart thudded a painfully familiar beat in my chest.

My anxiety had returned. I used to be so keyed up when I was a student here. Years had tamed it, time had done its best to erase the way I had felt as a kid—after my dad died, after my mom changed, after my brother went off to college, and I was left swirling in the toxicity of what was left of my family.

Clara had held me together back then. Being with her—someone who could relate to the fucked-up mess my life had become—was the only thing that had kept me going. No one had ever understood me the way she had, not even my own brother.

I felt like I'd lost her all over again today and I didn't know how to cope with it.

The rest of the day went by quickly, but I was oblivious to everything. I was lost in my thoughts, trying to figure out how I could make things right when I still couldn't understand what had gone wrong in the first place.

Maybe I could take a shot tonight—get her to talk to me, buy her a drink, ask her to dance. Anything to force a reaction out of her, something beyond the cagey sarcasm she seemed comfortable hiding behind. It was cute, but I'd had enough of it.

I was ready for something real. Like that morning on her balcony, or when we first saw each other. She'd been pissed at me, but at least it was honest.

It felt like I was wound up in a string she was yanking around but I couldn't find it in me to care. Not when my past and present were tied up in memories of her and all I wanted was the truth.

# CHAPTER 11
# NICK



*One day we'll be able to do what we want, go where we want, and no one can say a word about it. I can't wait. - HB*

As usual, the gravel parking lot of Genie's Country Western Bar was full when I pulled in. This was Green Valley's place to go when you wanted a mellow night to unwind with friends over a beer or a game of darts. Genie kept the place classy, for a bar anyway. Line dancing and pool were big here, rather than fights and indecent hookups in the parking lot.

My boots crunching through the lot kept me anchored against the swirling river of hope threatening to drown me. I wanted to see her so bad, the thought that she wouldn't be here felt inconceivable.

Squinting against the dim light, I made my way through the small lobby area and onto the wooden dance floor. I tried scanning the sea of people as I made my way to the bar, but the winding strings of bulbs around the ceiling beams were the only illumination above the crowd of dancers and I couldn't make out any faces.

"Hey, Nick! Over here." Mari waved me over from her spot at the edge of the corner booth near the bar. "It's just the three of us for now. Everyone else is in that line, dancing their booties off."

She scooted over, patting the wooden bench so I could slide in next to her.

"Hey there, frickin' Nick," Clara slurred. I'd almost missed her, slumped in the corner of the booth. "It rhymes. You're an English teacher and I'm a poet, don't you know it. *Ugh*. That was dumb."

I had known Mari for years, the way you would know anyone you grew up going to school with in a small town, but we became better acquainted when became co-workers.

Ally Dalbotten, the art teacher Clara had subbed for today, was on the other side of the booth. "Shh, I'm not here. I needed a mental health day."

I chuckled. "These lips are sealed." She probably needed a day away from Pin Dick. Ally was not shy about going toe to toe with that jackass.

"She's a little bit tipsy," Mari leaned in close to whisper. "Drunk Clara is grumpy. I ordered some fried pickles and Diet Coke, that should probably help. She's fond of tequila shooters. I had no idea until a few minutes ago, when she had five."

"Ahh, I see. Are you okay there, Clara?"

"Dandy and fine. Keen and peachy. Don't you worry your little ol' self about me now. Where's Court? He drove us over here, that means we're kind of on a date, frickin' Nick, and I wanna dance."

"He's in the middle of that line dance over there, see?" Mari pointed him out. "He's surrounded by all those PTA ladies." Court was not a ladies' man, but he could be if he wanted to. Somehow, he found himself surrounded by women everywhere he went.

"Maybe she should dance?" Ally suggested. "It might burn some of the alcohol off. Um, so is Clay coming tonight?"

"I'm not sure. We didn't talk about it."

"Okay, dang." I had my suspicions; I would bet money that they had a thing for each other. We'd all grown up together. Ally was my age, but Clay was a few years older. Her older brother was Clay's best friend and they'd always been close.

"I'll dance with her." I gestured to the dance floor. "Come on, Clara. It will make you feel better."

"Let's all go dance," Mari agreed. "I need to burn off some of my excess energy or I'll never sleep tonight." She slid out and reached for Ally's hand. "Come with me."

With a laugh, Ally took her hand, and they were off.

I reached for Clara. "Let's go, my tipsy little heartbreaker."

"Mmmm-kay." She took both of my hands and let me pull her along the smooth wooden seat until she was on her feet. "I'm not a big drinker anymore—those shots hit me like a ton of bricks. This sucks. Where's Court? He promised me a dance. Maybe I'll ask him out—what do you think? Or maybe we're already dating? He did pick me up at my house, you know."

"That Court?" I pointed him out in the crowd of middle-aged line-dancing ladies he'd found himself in. He smiled and waved.

"Yup, that's the one." She giggled and blew him a kiss, shooting me a look from the corner of her eye to make sure I was watching.

I laughed. "You mean my buddy Court who I play touch football with, who wouldn't dare make a move on what he knows is mine? *That* Court?"

"Ugh, damn it, frickin' Nick." She threw her hands up in the air. "I'm so bad at lying when I'm drunk, and I'm not *yours*. I'm nowhere near yours."

"As I recall, you're bad at lying when you are sober, too. Remember when you bought me Foo Fighters tickets for my eighteenth birthday and tried to convince me we were driving to Nashville to tour some random college? And you know what I meant about you being mine—we have history."

"Fine, I knew what you meant. Lying is hard. I'm much better at secrets, aren't I?" She gave me a sarcastic smile.

"I suppose."

"Anyhoo, you look nice tonight. I like your arms in that shirt." She ran a hand up my forearm, stopping on the rolled-up sleeve of my plaid shirt. Her touch sent a burst of goosebumps shooting over my skin in its wake, and I shivered as I grew greedy for more. "You're bigger than you used to be."

"Thanks." I couldn't help but smile as I noted that drunk Clara was chatty. Maybe I'd invite her over for pool cocktails so I could speak to her every day. "But let's talk about you, beautiful. That dress should be illegal." It was bright red and hit at her knees, and it fit like it was made for her body: snug, with a scooped neckline and thin straps. Her heels were high enough to put us almost at eye level.

"Aww." Her full rosy lips pursed in an adorable pout. "You don't approve?"

"That's not anywhere near what I said, baby." I bit my lip and eyed her up and down. "You're fucking gorgeous, and I would never dare tell a lady how to dress. But I will tell you I'm ready to knock a few heads together if anyone gets any ideas where you're concerned."

"Chivalry isn't dead after all—how nice." She leaned in close with a hand on my chest and her voice dropped low so only I could hear it. "I bet you thought about me after I left, didn't you?" Her eyes turned briefly shrewd through the drunken haze.

She stumbled into me and for one split second I was seventeen again. I inhaled deeply, the familiar scent of her perfume transporting me to the front seat of my truck with her sitting in my lap. She was flowers and sunshine, love and light, and I wanted nothing more than to kiss her again.

"Of course I did." I pulled back to look in her eyes, taking her hand in mine to kiss the back. "For a long time you were all I thought about."

"I did too. I missed you, Nick."

I raised an eyebrow. "Admitting you had a real feeling? How unexpected."

"I'd never felt with anyone how I felt with you. Then you took it away."

"*I* took it? That's not what I remember."

"Dance with me, Nick. I don't want to talk about this anymore. It hurts too much." She threw her arms around my neck and pressed her body into mine.

She tucked her forehead against the side of my neck. The soft warmth of her sigh tickled my collarbone, and it was all I could do not to get hard.

Damn fucking right I'd thought about her when she was gone. I'd have to get drunker than she was right now in order to handle the memories.

Like I'd wanted to do all day, I yanked her into my chest. My hands on her waist in a polite dance weren't enough. I wrapped my arms around her and buried my face in her neck to breathe in the sweetly scented memories that were torturing me by holding her like this.

I could fall for her again. All I had to do was let it happen, and I'd be under her spell once more.

I held her close as we swayed to the music; closer than I should but not as close as I wanted. We'd never danced. We didn't have a song. Our relationship had been a secret at my insistence. I'd thought it would protect her from my mother, but in retrospect I realized it was a mistake to have kept it that way. There were so many memories we'd never had a chance to make together.

Her hair rustled against my chin as her lips moved to whisper in my ear. "Take me to Sky Lake. I want to remember how we were together. I want to feel it."

"Anything you want. I'll text Mari and let her know we're leaving."

"'Kay . . ."

I offered my hand to guide her out of the bar. She gripped it tight in hers, looking up at me with a soft smile.

"We never got the chance to dance together back then, did we?" she asked.

"No, we didn't," I confirmed. Secrets prevented us from attending any of the dances at school together. No homecoming, no prom—nothing that could give us away. We reached my truck, and I helped her climb into the cab, then hurried around to the driver's side with my heart racing out of control.

"I liked dancing with you tonight, Nick," she murmured into the dark as the lights of Green Valley disappeared into the background. I turned onto the rural county road that led up to the lake, wondering if I was doing the right thing.

"I liked it too. A lot." I glanced her way as I turned down the road to Sky Lake. Her temple pressed against the passenger window created a confusing duality in my mind. Her reflection in the glass, so much like the faded images of her face that had haunted me throughout the years, was now eclipsed by the real woman sitting at my side.

I didn't know how to be with her right now. Years of pent-up feelings simmered at the surface of my consciousness—the hurt I had thought I had long since buried, the many nights I'd spent wondering what had gone wrong, the pain of her loss—and felt like knives in my heart. And they were twisting deeper with each mile I drove.

*What was I doing?*

She was going to destroy me again, and I was going to let it happen. Was it her I really wanted? Or did I want to recreate the time in my life when I'd last felt happy?

"We were too young, weren't we, Nick?" The sad sound of her voice startled me out of my thoughts. "It never would have worked between us."

"Maybe not. Or maybe it could have been amazing. There's no way to know now. But maybe we can be something else together instead. Why do we have to look back to move forward? It was so long ago—we're different people now."

"Do you want that?"

"I think I do. I want to try, at least."

The lake was deserted. I drove my truck down to the edge and cut the engine, thankful for my all-wheel drive.

Her reflection in the window blended into the starlight dancing across the surface of the water. Somehow it was easier to see her that way, as if this were a dream I'd found myself inside of again, rather than a decade and a half of subconscious yearning suddenly come to life right next to me.

The safety of the illusion disappeared when she turned to face me fully. "I want you to kiss me. Right here in this spot, just like we used to do."

Her words plunged me out of the dream and into the deep end. I reached out a shaking hand to sift it through the soft flaxen hair flowing over her shoulder. "We can't relive the past," I murmured. "You know that right?"

"I know. I just want to feel it again."

"Feel what?" I whispered, desperate to know what was on her mind.

She closed her eyes. "Safe."

My heart shattered in my chest as I realized I would do anything for her. Whatever it took to make her feel happy, secure, loved, *safe* . . .

Was this my mission now? Was I risking my emotional safety for hers?

"Clara—"

"Please, Nick, one last time so I never forget what it felt like to have what I wanted."

"You're breaking my heart right now. I don't want to take advantage of you."

"I'm not that drunk anymore, and who says I'm not the one taking advantage of you? Maybe I want a piece of the past I can hold on to. Maybe I want closure. Or maybe I have no idea what I want and I'm a selfish bitch for bringing you out here." Tears glistened on her pale, moonlit face. I never was very good at saying no to her.

My heart turned over in my chest as I wiped her cheeks with my thumbs and drew her closer. Her eyelids fluttered as she dropped her lashes to hide the hurt that seemed to live inside of her; it was always there, every time I looked at her.

"Shh," I soothed as I shifted closer and drew her face to mine. "It's okay. You are in no way selfish, and don't insult yourself using cuss words like that. Are you sure?"

"Yes," she whispered, her trembling lips parting on a sigh. "Please, Nick . . ."

I pressed my lips to hers, a featherlight touch at first, but I needed more. We both did. Gently, I covered her mouth with mine. I devoured her softness as each and every kiss we had ever shared exploded in my mind like a bomb, fragmenting into pieces as all the pent-up longing I'd buried scattered through my body like shrapnel.

The pain of losing her shimmered at the edges of my vision, and I slammed my eyes shut before the hurt overpowered the longing. I didn't want the pain, not when she was finally here in my arms after all this time.

Burying my face in her neck, I breathed a kiss there before pulling away. I had to let her go now or I wouldn't be able to stop. And I had to stop. There was no way we were ready for anything more. Not now—not yet.

She might think this was only a one-time thing, one last kiss, a way to revisit the past or a way to feel a sense of closure. But I knew better. The chemistry we shared was a once-in-a-lifetime gift and I refused to squander it again. I was beginning to believe she was meant to be mine. But she wasn't ready yet, that much was obvious, and I wasn't either.

"God, Nick. Drunk or not, I don't know what the hell I'm doing out here with you." She covered her face with her hands.

"Getting lost in the past and questioning the future, same as me."

"I don't know why I made you come all the way out here when I feel so hopeless all the time."

"Because you're just as curious about me as I am about you, and you're sick of tiptoeing around our mutual feelings. And hopeless? No, baby. We have all the time in the world to let this unfold. There's always hope."

"Quit being so direct. I'm sobering up and you're making it hard to get back into denial."

I huffed out a laugh. "Denial, huh?"

"It's my preferred state. Life is hard enough without the past coming back to haunt me every time I leave my house and see you in your yard."

"We should talk about that."

"There's that word again."

"What word? Talk?"

"That's the one. I don't think I can do this with you. It hurts too much. This thing between us feels too big, and I can't let myself get hurt that way again. I just can't do it." She reached over and pushed the button to start up the truck. "Take me home. I'm sorry."

"What if I don't want to give up on you? What if we never talk about it and just start over?"

She looked at me, her doubt clear on her face. "Do you really think that will work?"

"Why not?"

"Sure, Nick. *Not* talking has solved so many problems in my life." Her laugh was bitter, and I decided to let it go—for now.

"I'll take you home. Expect me to stop by in the morning. I'll bring you breakfast and a hangover smoothie."

"You don't have to do that—"

"I'll drop it off and leave, if that's what you want."

"Okay, I appreciate it and will return the favor somehow. Thank you."

The bubble of nostalgia was gone now, and we were back to . . . whatever we had become after I moved in next door.

Pushing for something as big as a second chance would have to wait until I got to know her again. There was too much history between us to force the issue.

# CHAPTER 12
# CLARA

*I can't wait to tell everyone how much I love you. Graduation is soon, then we'll be free. - Nick*

*W*hat made him change his mind?

*Why couldn't he talk to me about his concerns?*

The questions that had haunted me in the past and wouldn't let me be with him now were the ones I was terrified to ask, because deep down, I already knew the answer to both:

*I wasn't good enough.*

Maybe things would be different now, like he'd said. We'd grown up, after all. We were on our own, no longer bound to the rules of our mothers. Their opinions held no weight now; we were free. I'd made something out of myself and so had he. If we had another chance to be together out in the open, without all the secrecy, would that really make a difference?

I turned, burying my face in my pillow. Sleep was out of the question when I was being bombarded with all these out-of-control thoughts.

Sunlight streamed through my window, and I pulled my covers over my face with a groan.

*It will never work with him. We'd hurt each other too much to ever move past it.*

The feeling of being small and powerless, the knowledge that I would never truly be accepted for who I was and where I had come from, was at the core of all my problems and, intentional or not, he had been a huge part of creating them. It was the wound that would not heal, no matter how many bandages I covered it with.

I was a broken girl from a broken home who had clawed her way up to make herself seem better than she was. The way I had been treated ever since childhood was part of me, ingrained in me, and no matter what I did—the years of therapy, my job as an attorney, my house, my money—nothing completely got rid of it.

What if he found out how I'd put myself through college?

What would he think of me then?

How would he explain to his sweet, beautiful, innocent children that he was dating a woman who stripped to pay her way through college and law school? He wouldn't, he couldn't, and I refused to consider letting him, no matter what he said if he ever found out the truth. He was a good guy. He'd say all the right things and I'd be so tempted to take what I wanted without a care.

A knock at my door had me frozen in my bed.

Shit.

It had to be Nick. With breakfast and some kind of hangover cure.

*Gah!* What I really needed was coffee and maybe a bubble bath. Combine the two and we'd have a winner.

Nick at my door was the opposite of what I needed.

*Or maybe he's everything you need?* Shut up, brain.

I threw the covers back, determined to snatch whatever he'd brought me, thank him for being neighborly, then slam the door in his face. It was the best thing for both of us.

A clean break.

No more wondering *what if?*

No more questioning if we could start over.

None of it.

He had kids to consider, and I was bad news, bad at love, just bad— everyone said so.

I had to be the strong one for both of us. *Story of my damn life.*

I grabbed the robe off the footboard of my bed and slipped into it.

*Why was I so angry?* He'd done nothing to deserve all the shit going around in my brain. Nothing recent, anyway.

*Deep breath. In with the good, out with the wackadoodle bullcrap that usually fills your head.*

"Alexa, play!" I shrieked as I ran down the stairs.

*"The past has no bearing on your present. It exists as lessons to learn, nothing more . . ."*

"Freakin' hell, are you serious with this right now?" I yelled to the room. "Alexa, stop!"

I threw open the door. Damn, he looked good. Dark gray joggers, white T-shirt, tight in all the right places, and a pair of sneakers. He was like a walking, talking buffet of all my favorite man parts. Big biceps, wide chest, messy morning hair—he'd better not turn around or I might take a bite out of his ass.

"Good morning, heartbreaker."

*"Heartbreaker?* Really?"

"The look on your face is ominous. You're a walking, talking thundercloud, aren't you? Heartbreaker seemed apropos. Perhaps even prophetic."

I had to make him understand. "This isn't going to work. I can't be your friend—or anything else—when I can't let anything go. I can't try for more when I know we'll end up breaking each other's hearts again somehow. It's too complicated."

He held up a plastic bag filled with a bunch of that fancy glass storage container crap I kept meaning to buy. "I made breakfast, baby. Let me in. You look" —I glared at him, hard—"as gorgeous as ever, of course. And also, uh, like you might need what I brought you." He held a travel mug under my nose. One sniff told me it was coffee. *Good* coffee. Score one for Nick.

*Damn it.*

I took it and turned toward my kitchen, leaving the door open. He could follow me inside, or not. I'd leave that up to him.

"Come in, if you want," I tossed over my shoulder. "But know I can't guarantee your safety. I woke up in a mood."

"Hungover?" The door closed behind him, and I heaved out a sigh. I guess we were doing this.

I growled in answer as I swung open my fridge in search of my hazelnut creamer.

I could hear his smirk when he said, "I'd say I don't want to fight with you, but it would be a lie. This is kind of fun."

"Shut up," I huffed. "You're way too cheerful. It's too early and I'm miserable. I'm trying not to be rude, but it's impossible. I apologize in advance for every mean thing I will inevitably end up saying to you. I'll only mean about one percent of it. Probably."

He let out a chuckle. "And I forgive you in advance for all if it. Five tequila shots are a lot for a lightweight like you."

I spun to treat him to another of my signature glares over the top of the refrigerator door—this one was number three on my *don't fuck with me* rotation. Snarly, with just a bit of teeth thrown in for good measure.

His return grin was as infuriating as it was hot.

I was both confused and turned on and now at a complete loss as to what to say to him because I, too, was now having fun. "You are aggravating me right now," I finally muttered.

"Really? I couldn't tell. It seems like bringing you food and pissing you off is the way to your heart. Not gonna lie, I'm totally into it."

I rolled my eyes. "Whatever, Nick."

"Keep it up. None of this is a turnoff, *heartbreaker*."

"You can't call me that anymore. It makes me feel things I don't want to feel. I'm a mess right now."

"And?"

"I have turned into a difficult woman, Nick. Ask around, you'll find out."

"Why would I give a shit what anyone else thinks about you? I think you're amazing. You're sexy as hell, you make me laugh, but best of all you make me feel alive again. Fuck what anyone else says about you."

I dropped into one of the chairs at the kitchen table. "*Argh!* I am damaged goods, okay? I carry baggage from so many different things that I am collapsing beneath the weight of it. I am not the same. I can't be that girl you used to know. I am grown now, and I am fucking unhinged. I'm trying my best to keep my head above water, and I am not ready for this thing—whatever it is—with you." Well, that ought to do it. After he turned tail and ran off, I could relax with this awesome-looking breakfast I was about to stuff my face with. Maybe I'd even keep the containers too. Payment for my pain and suffering.

"There's something still between us and ready or not, it's happening."

I blinked. He was still here, and he was incensed.

Angry Nick was sexy. His broad chest heaved with determination, and his jaw was clenched tight. I'd never seen him mad at me before and it was even hotter than when he was cheerful and teasing me. *Damn it.*

"It doesn't matter if we're ready," he insisted. "Me and you explode when we're together, Clara. It's out of control. You're beyond any temptation I've ever felt in my entire life, and I don't want it to stop. If you were honest with yourself, you'd admit you don't want it to stop either."

I threw my arms in the air. "It doesn't matter what I want. I'm no good for you. I'm not in a healthy place right now. I just went through a breakup. I'm not ready to jump into anything new. Or old as the case may be, okay?"

"Did he break your heart?"

I thought for a minute. "Not really. I think I've been living with a broken heart ever since my father left. It never repaired itself. Maybe it never will."

"Consider this—maybe I'm the one who's supposed to heal it for you."

I shook my head. "It's been too long. This is too much for me . . ."

"I'll drop it for now. I get it," he conceded. "I promise I do, and we'll talk everything out—"

My head hit my arms on the table, and I shook my head. "Not ready for that," I managed to mumble.

What I didn't tell him was I didn't even need to hear his explanation. It didn't matter—why wouldn't I forgive him for whatever it was that drove him away when we were both too young to know any better?

What I really wasn't ready for was to be near him with no excuse to push him away.

*How horrible did that make me?*

He dropped into the seat across from me and rubbed comforting strokes over the top of my head. "I know, baby, shh . . ." The deep soothing quality in his voice hit me like a ton of bricks. "I won't say a word until you're ready to hear it. But listen, you don't know me anymore, either. Please think about that. You have no idea how I felt when I lost you. Not one fucking clue about how much it broke me. I wasn't a man back then, I was a stupid eighteen-year-old kid, just like you were."

*I hadn't thought of that. Why?*

*How selfish was I?*

He had feelings too, and here I was, trampling all over them, too lost in my own shit to listen to him.

"I'm listening," I said into my arm. "And I'm so sorry for being selfish this morning. I'm hungover, I'm probably going to barf at some point, and I'm cranky as hell, that's my only defense."

"Don't apologize, I'm not exactly fun to be around with a hangover either. If I'd had even half a clue back then I would have fought for you, for us."

My head popped up. "Oh, Nick. I'm so sorry, I—"

He held up a hand. "No apologies. We were kids, Clara. What do eighteen-year-olds know about life? Jack shit, that's what."

"You have a point. Clearly, I was not my best self at age eighteen. I'm not even my best self right now, for eff's sake."

"Hey, I'm not either." He chuckled. "Don't beat yourself up, baby. It's pointless. I spent my first year at college drunk as hell because all I could think about was missing you. We had no idea what we had with each other. I'm beginning to think we were a classic 'right person, wrong time' scenario. It took a whole lot of trying to cope with more than a decade of shit to make me see what I lost when I let you slip away. You said it yourself last night, remember?"

"Yeah, I wanted to feel it again," I whispered.

"And did you?" The anger was gone, replaced by the sweet Nick I used to know, but he was still just as sexy. Obviously, I was into him again. Still?

"I—"

He pressed a fingertip to my lips. "Don't answer that. You said you weren't ready, and I want to honor your feelings. I'm not here to push you. I'm here to take care of you because you need it, okay?"

"Thank you. I really do feel like hell. I'm never drinking again," I groaned. "Like, I can't believe how much I could put away back in high school and not feel it. It's ridiculous."

"I'm glad you made it through. High school was rough."

"You were a lot of what got me through. I need you to know that."

"Oh Clara, I wish I could have done more—"

"Like you said, we were kids, right?"

"Yeah." He ducked his chin and looked up at me through his lashes. "So, are we okay?"

"For now, I guess. If I didn't drive you away with my hungover ranting."

"I don't know what it says about me, and I don't care, but I think you're hot as fuck right now. The more attitude you throw my way, the more into you I get."

"Maybe you're a little bit crazy too."

"You have no idea." He stood, gathering the remains of our breakfast and putting it all in the bag. "I want you to get back into bed. You need rest." He handed me a huge bottle of water from the bag. "Take this with you and drink as much as you can. Hydration is key."

"You're a bit bossy now, aren't you? Honestly, I find it a turnoff." Typical male, thinking he could tell me what to do. I was not into that.

*Lies! It was hot as hell and that damn smirk on his face told me he knew it.*

"Bullshit. You love it. You need someone like me around to take care of you."

"I can take care of myself," I said in my most derisive tone. "Been doing it for years."

"Of course you can, but that's not what I meant and you know it."

"I don't know any such thing," I muttered.

He stood to leave. "I'll text you later. I'll bring dinner by if you're awake."

"Whatever." I stood too, then sighed. "I mean, thanks, I suppose."

I walked him to the door.

"See you soon, my grumpy little heartbreaker. Go back to bed." He grabbed me by the back of my neck and dropped a kiss to my forehead. "Try not to think about what it would be like if I came up there to tuck you in," he murmured before turning around to leave.

I stuck my tongue out at his retreating back.

"Drink that water," he called with a wave over his shoulder. "All of it. Don't make me come back and force a Gatorade down your throat." The laughter in his voice told me he knew better than to look back.

# CHAPTER 13
# CLARA

*You're the only one who understands me. How did I get so lucky? - Nick*

Days had passed, then a week. Then two-ish more until time had lost all meaning for me other than there were days when I saw him, and days that I didn't.

Days when glimmers of my past with him gave me a smile, and days when it broke my heart all over again. The trouble was, I couldn't seem to predict how seeing him would make me feel.

Some memories were cherished, never to be forgotten; but then there were the kind that hung on no matter how much you wanted to forget them. They existed, clawing at my subconscious, determined to never let me be happy.

Neighborhood chitchat, high school teacher scuttlebutt, and asking about his kids was the name of the game for me now.

Nothing personal.

No feelings allowed, and no more talk about trying to be something we could never be.

And absolutely no more kissing; that was off the table for good.

I had decided to be cordial-neighbor-Clara. It was safe and the right thing to do. I couldn't ignore him anymore; it was rude and he didn't deserve it. Hiding had never really worked, and it was too obvious anyway.

I liked his kids. I even liked him. I'd had to figure out how to make it work and I thought I had it down. Sure, occasionally when his kids were with Morgan, we got caught up in an accidental flirt-fest in the yard. And passing him in the halls at school was as dangerous as it had always been—the longing glances were inevitable. But I always put a quick stop to all of it. I had the sense that no matter what he said, he wasn't quite ready for more with me anyway.

We still had chemistry and shared a lot of memories, but we didn't have to fall victim to them.

But tonight felt particularly hard. The nostalgia was real, and it was driving me to the brink of something terrible.

I was restless. My heart was pounding to the beat of teen-delinquent Clara's angst, and it was all I could do not to run off and hide.

Tonight was homecoming, and for some damn reason I was sitting in the bleachers with my sisters, brothers-in-law, and their kids watching the stupid game.

Did I find it odd to be here, sitting on a bench like an upstanding citizen right above the place where I'd spent almost four years getting wasted with my friends? Yes, I sure as hell did.

Memories of being here while Nick was out on the field doing his thing were chugging like a freight train through my mind. He had been so good; the crowd had loved him, the town had adored him. He'd earned a football scholarship to UT, for eff's sake.

Then there was me, hanging out with Molly and Leo, watching it all, half-drunk in our usual spot. He never knew I was here watching him play—well, except the first time he played as quarterback, but that was it—I had never wanted him to know. How awkward would that have been? The quarterback, the golden boy, wasting his time with a burnout from beneath the bleachers. Nope, no way that could never be . . .

And he was *still* good—and hot, and sexy, and *ARGH!* He was coaching his ass off out there and I couldn't stop staring as he ran up and down the field in that stupid, well-fitting Green Valley High polo and backward baseball cap.

I should be far, far away from here but Gracie had insisted I come tonight, because Willa had insisted that she come. "It's a family thing," Gracie had said.

And when I resisted, she mentioned that Marianne and her two witches would most likely be here and reminded me that I was the only one who knew about their bullshit bullying.

Added to that was the fact that Ruby would be marching with the band and not available to hang out with. And Mari wouldn't be around either; she'd be busy with the pregame and halftime shows. There was no way she could run interference with all she had to do.

How could I say no? I couldn't, and she knew it.

So not only was I here, being tortured alive by memories of my tragic past, but I had a perfect bird's-eye view of Nick stopping and waving to his kids and ex-wife sitting on the bench up front.

Jealousy burned through me like an out-of-control freaking forest fire, and I was ashamed of myself. I had zero right to be jealous of anything, plus he was divorced. Being jealous of an ex made me a nut, but I couldn't seem to stop these feelings.

It was good that they got along. It was even better that they spent time with their kids together. It's what every child from a broken home wants, and I was happy to see it for Sasha and Ethan's sake.

But for me? It made the desire to find my way under the bleachers and hide out almost irresistible. *Ugh.*

I managed to keep my feelings at bay until halftime. My sisters and I headed down to the snack bar to grab popcorn and hot dogs and slushies—football game essentials—while the men stayed to entertain the kids, as they should.

We stood at the edge of the field blending in with the crowd, munching on our snacks and slurping up our drinks as we watched Ruby and the band put on their halftime field show.

Mari was there, running back and forth, making sure everything went off without a hitch. We caught her eye and she stopped for a second for a quick hello before darting off down the field again. Damn, if I had half the energy she did, I'd probably have a heart attack and die.

Gracie grabbed my arm and gritted out, "There she is. It's so hard not to kick her ass now that the freaking boot is gone. Now that I have my balance back, that bitch better watch out." She paused her ranting and closed her eyes. "Oh no, Clara, help me. All my anger management skills are failing me. I need to take a deep breath and chill before I lose my temper. I'm a grown-up. Tell me I'm mature. Tell me I can let it go."

"You're so mature. I'm in awe of your grown-up ways. So, is she up to something? What's going on?" I hissed as she pulled me away from Willa and Sadie. They were so caught up in the game they barely noticed when we stepped to the edge of the stands. We chucked our trash in the can, and I yanked her part way beneath. The echo under here was familiar. My head cleared immediately as I inhaled the smoky mustiness that only years of sneaked cigarettes, mold, and greasy trash could create.

"Didn't you see her take my picture?" She took her phone from her pocket and scrolled through some social media app I didn't recognize—#oldla-dyproblems.

"I didn't notice." Damn, what kind of bodyguard was I? I had to get my head back in the game. I'd gotten complacent; once Marianne spotted me at the school, she'd dialed back on her shenanigans and apparently, I'd become less observant.

"Look." She passed me the phone.

Marianne had edited the pic of Gracie onto a headstone. I read the caption: *How sad is this? Here lies Gracie May Hill. Once the quarterback's girlfriend trying to belong where she never did and never will. And now a pathetic loner hanging around with a bunch of old ladies. Go back to your lavender farm, hillbilly slut.*

"Hillbilly slut?! That little witch! And, hey, I'm not *that* old. Thirty-two is the new, uh, twenty-two, or whatever." It was fine if I made fun of myself for being old, but not if some ridiculous teenage brat did it. It made sense, okay? I handed Gracie back her phone. "God, back in my day we'd just start a damn fight and call it a day. This shit is exhausting." My eyes grew wide with alarm. "Oh my god, do not let Sadie see this or she'll march over there right now and give her a piece of her mind. Or a piece of her hot dog shoved straight into her face." My lips shifted into a sideways grin. "Actually, you could sic Sadie on her, film it, then post it to that app . . ." Sadie was no stranger to causing a scene; she ran out of fucks to give ages ago.

"No." Gracie laughed. "Not tonight. Like, I mostly don't care, it's just annoying is all. She won't let it go." She took a deep breath. "She's so stupid. She never does anything at school anymore, that's why you haven't seen anything. She doesn't want to get in trouble for bullying—there's that zero-tolerance policy." She let out a huge sigh. "I just want to go home. Willa said she was tired. Maybe we can leave."

"Do you really not care? I can't believe that, Gracie. Will you please let me talk to her? I promise I won't make threats or commit any felonies. I'm not like Sadie, I can rein it in. I've had just as much therapy as you."

"No." She let out a laugh. "Thank you though. Look, I finally have all my sisters back in town. I have Ruby and Mari—I mean, Miss Mitchell. And I still have Weston, even though we're broken up for now. I do not give a shit what happens at school or on the internet. She'll get over it eventually. Your job is to prevent me from kicking her ass when I forget to be mature about it. Please?"

I studied her face. She was telling the truth. "I believe you. I'm proud of you, and I'm here to talk to any time you need me. Tell Willa your ankle is bothering you and she'll take you home. I'll wait here. We'll talk more about the Marianne crap later."

Gracie's lips pursed in a knowing look. "I'm onto you, you know."

I gave her my best wide-eyed, innocent look. "I have no idea what you're talking about."

"Yeah, okay. So you're not going to go creeping around down here and end up under Nick's ex like the type of sneaky little eavesdropper all of us Hill sisters have grown up to be? There's something going on between the two of you, I know it."

My head drew back on my neck. "No. I would never—" *It actually wasn't a bad idea . . .*

"Listen, Clara. You're stuck, same as me. Only I'm stuck in school and I can't quit since I need my dumb diploma. You're stuck somewhere in the past, aren't you? It's okay to move on. Letting things go is healthy. Nobody has the power to put you down anymore, and if you're letting someone keep you down, it's on you."

I held one hand up and flattened the other over my heart. "Ouch. Thanks, Dr. Gracie. I'll take that all under advisement." This kid was smarter than me and it kinda freaked me out.

"Think about it. I'm here for you too, you know. I'm going to talk to Willa. I'll see you Monday for school. Or before, if you feel like talking shit over."

"If you're going home, I'm going home too," I lied. "In fact, tell them I'm already gone."

She nodded, that knowing look lighting up her features. She was too mature, too wise for her age, and though I was proud of her, it also made me kind of sad. All of us Hill girls had grown up way too fast.

The temptation to go further under the bleachers was too much. Like the other night with Nick at Sky Lake, I wanted to feel the memories again. I needed a dose of where I had come from so I would remember what I could never have.

I watched Sadie head back up in the stands, then saw Willa pull Gracie into a side hug and call Everett to let him know they were leaving. I smiled as they left arm in arm. Gracie was in good hands with Willa.

Bodyguard duty for the night was complete; my time was my own again. I slipped further beneath the bleachers instead of going home and ditching all the Nick memories like I knew I should.

But I wasn't the only one with the idea. A few kids stood in groups here and there, smoke puffing out of the tops of their little circles.

I squinted into the strips of light that managed to shine through the bleachers. Back in the darkest corner, eyes glued to the field, stood my neighbor, Leonard, knee bent with his foot up against the wall behind him like all the hot bad boys leaned.

What the hell was he doing under here?

"Hiding from Mari?" I guessed.

He jumped about a foot in the air, and I laughed. "What the hell? Is that you, Clara?"

"Yup." I sauntered toward him, feeling better about myself now that I wasn't the only so-called adult under here. Somehow, it made me feel less pathetic. "This was like a second home to me back in high school. I was a bit of a wild child. I thought I'd come down here and reminisce for a few minutes." I poked the edge of his knit hat with a grin. "Nice beanie."

He smiled back. "I know all about you. Your reputation outlived your time here. I was a freshman when you were a senior."

"Aww, then as someone older and wiser, let me give you two pieces of advice. One, don't piss Mari off. She has a bit of a temper."

"What . . . ?"

"Tut-tut, listen."

He rolled his eyes. "You're older, but the wiser thing is questionable. I'm not the only one in the neighborhood who's noticed how you've been dodging Nick lately." He squinted a mock-accusing glare at me. "His ex is sitting right above us with the kids, isn't she? No one will call you an eavesdropping stalker if you're seen talking to your pathetic neighbor down here, right?"

"Touché, my young padawan. Both of our life choices are definitely up for debate."

"Let's hear it. What's number two?"

Damn if I wasn't about to take this sexy nerd-boy under my wing. Would I ever be able to walk away from an underdog? "Start working the nerdy rock-star thing, Leonard. It's hot. I saw you in that caftan the other day, with the pecs and the thighs. Look at you with the glasses and the raggedy old Rush tee and those the sexy arms. You're a tall drink of water, Leonard. Own that shit."

He turned bright red. Nerd, indeed. "I don't know about that," he mumbled. "Also, I prefer to be called Leo."

"Too bad. I already have a friend named Leo and I don't need that kind of confusion in my life, *Leonard*."

"Okay..."

"Glad we got that settled. You like my cousin Mari, don't you?"

He blushed even harder. His expression was agonized. It was obvious he had it bad for her.

"I'll take your red-faced lack of an answer as a yes. You should ask her out." Mari may have sworn off men, but this one was carrying a huge-ass torch for her. He was sweet, and his mom was amazing. I could see good things happening between them, and since I was never one to *not* meddle . . .

His eyes darted nervously back and forth as he twisted his toe in the dirt like something out of a movie. Could he be any cuter? "Uhh . . ."

"I'll accept payment for my sage advice in the form of a clipping from your neon pothos. I covet it, Leonard. You're lucky I haven't snuck over and plantnapped it."

He chuckled and held out his hand. I shook it with a grin. "I accept your terms. And maybe we could trade sometime? I'd love to have an ultra-pink princess philodendron like the one hanging on your porch. No nursery seems to carry them around here."

I nodded as I considered whether or not to let go of my one-sided yard rivalry with him. Could two people exist on a block with equally nice yards?

"Nope, no one does. I got it from some online nursery in Maine. It was half-dead when it arrived at my house. It was touch and go for a few weeks." I bit the bullet; maybe we could end up being friends. "Come over next time you see me outside. We'll have coffee and talk plants."

"Will do, I'd love that. Do me a favor and tell your cousin to keep the band out of my yard. I don't think she gets how—"

"I got you. I'll talk to her. We're plant people, Leonard. It's a state of mind. Like cat ladies without the cats, am I right?" I held out a fist. He bumped it, lips turning up in a sardonic grin.

"No one else gets it," he confirmed.

"We have to stick together." I looked around. "Okay, it's becoming too much for me down here. Nostalgia can be a real kick in the ass. I have to get out of here. Later."

"Hey, wait a second."

I stopped and turned. "Yeah?"

"Nick waits for you to come outside every morning before he leaves for work." He smirked. "Maybe I should tell him to get his ass out to his truck a little bit earlier."

"Are you *sure* you really want to get into my business?" I shook my head, and twisted my lips to the side. "Maybe I'll go find Mari and tell her you're hiding out under here like a creepy little spy kid."

His eyes bulged. "No. Do not do that."

I threw my hands up, palms facing him. "I make no promises. You poked the bear, Leonard. I'm invested now."

"Clara, wait! Let's call another truce."

"Bye-bye, see you on the street!" I wiggled my fingers over my shoulder as I left.

That was weird. Instead of spying like the creepy little freak I was, I'd made a new plant friend.

I popped out from beneath the bleachers in time to see the band march off the field. I watched as they jogged up into the stands with Mari bringing up the rear.

"They sound really good," I stopped her.

"Thanks!" Her smile was infectious as we chatted about her students. I steered the conversation toward the topic of Leonard, and I couldn't help myself. In the spirit of *not* meddling, I told her where he was hiding out. She stomped off in his direction with a determined look on her face.

Sometimes you had to stir the pot.

I was about to turn toward the parking lot gate and get the heck out of here when I was spotted by Nick's son.

Avoiding him was impossible, seeing how he was waving at me with two hands and smiling his little heart out.

Damn, his kids were entirely too sweet. "Hey there, Ethan," I called out. I didn't have it in me to ignore a kid, no matter how much I wanted to hide from his hot dad.

# CHAPTER 14
# NICK

*I kissed the quarterback under the bleachers. Does that make me popular like you? Or is it one of those tree-falling-in-the-woods scenarios? No one saw it, so did it really happen . . . ? - HB*

"Miss Clara, hi!" Ethan waved an arm in the air in greeting before deciding what he wanted for dessert. "Can we have ice cream?" His capacity to fill up on junk food and not vomit was always something to behold. This had to have been his second trip to the concession stand, if not the third. After a dinner of hot dogs and popcorn he was ready for more.

"Absolutely. Anything you want."

"I can't believe Mom is letting him eat all that crap," Sasha chimed in. "You're gonna barf later, Eath."

"Hello? Your father here, also letting him get a treat." I gestured to myself. "I only have a couple minutes before I have to get back to the team."

"You always let us eat crap." Sasha shot me a confused look. "Which is awesome 'cause a kid can't live on healthy stuff alone. Fruit and yogurt are not dessert—that's insanity. But Ethan is on another level tonight."

"Hey, now, it's homecoming. Unless you're playing in the game, it might be a legal requirement to fill up on junk food while you root for your team. Plus, we all know his stomach is made of steel," I joked.

"I guess it's like a special occasion," she pondered. "Well, all I want is a slushie and some cotton candy to put in it." She let go of my hand and ran over to Clara who was standing by the edge of the bleachers looking like a deer caught in the headlights. "Hey, Miss Clara."

"Hey, sweetie." She greeted Sasha while pretending she didn't see me. The two of them had bonded over porch décor and plants over the last few weeks while Clara had been busy icing me out.

Polite conversation and friendly avoidance seemed to be all that was left between us now, and I was done with it. I had been determined not to pressure her, but it was backfiring on me; I hardly ever saw her anymore, no matter how many mornings I sat in my truck like a simp waiting for her to come outside for work.

The progress I'd made at Sky Lake was gone, and I had to start over.

"Come sit with us," Sasha cajoled. "We can make a bet whether Ethan is going to barf after he stuffs himself full of ice cream and whatever else he picks out."

"I'm fine, Sasha," he argued from his place in line. "Mom said I'm a growing boy, and I need dessert."

"Dessert sounds good, y'all," Clara said, backing away. "But, uh, I was about to go home. I have a headache, probably from all the noise. Maybe next time, okay?"

"Sure, maybe we can all go to the next game together, kids. Say bye to Clara."

We made it to the head of the line. I let Ethan and Sasha order while I watched Clara from the corner of my eye as she headed under the bleachers instead of toward the parking lot to leave. I quickly walked the kids back to Morgan and shot a text to my assistant coach. I took a page out of Clara's playbook and told him I had to run to the bathroom and was going to be a bit late coming back. I zipped up my windbreaker to cover up my Green Valley Football shirt, pulled my hat down low, and took off in search of Clara with an odd sense of freedom flowing through my veins.

The feeling that something big was going to happen kept the guilt of ditching the team for a few extra minutes at bay. And while I knew Clara was skittish and I didn't want to push her, the last few weeks made it obvious that I'd have to at least nudge her a bit if I wanted to get anywhere. If we never talked, nothing would ever change.

Dim light flickered through the spaces in the bleachers as the scent of cigarette smoke and fried food from the concession stand filled my nostrils.

As my eyes adjusted, I couldn't help but think about how differently Clara and I had spent our high school years. I'd always had sympathy for what she'd gone through, but being under here somehow made me feel it on a visceral level. You'd have to really want to disappear if you were spending your days under here in this stuffy, graffiti-filled mess.

I made my way to the back corner to find her with her foot pressed against the wall as she listened to the band play "We Will Rock You" in the stands directly above her. She sneezed when stomping overhead sent a flurry of dust down to cover our heads.

"Hey there, heartbreaker. Bless you."

Her eyes squinted, then narrowed. I could feel her sharp gaze boring into me as I approached.

I glanced around the space. There were groups of kids here and there, but they were too busy to notice me, especially right here in this dark corner.

"What are you doing down here?" Her brows drew together in suspicion. "Don't you have a team to be coaching right now? Someone will have definitely seen you walking under here."

"Looking for you. I saw you head under here. Everything okay?"

"Of course it is. I'm fine, I was just, uh, listening to the band play." She shrugged. "It doesn't matter. Shouldn't you get going? The halftime show is almost over, isn't it? Where are the kids?"

I pointed above me. "With Morgan."

"Ahh, okay."

"What's wrong?"

She waved a dismissive hand in the air. "Never mind. It doesn't matter, I'm being ridiculous. I think I will go home now. You should go back to your team, Nick. I'm sure they're wondering where you went."

"Are you . . . are you jealous of Morgan?" The notion was so ridiculous I burst out laughing.

"This isn't funny." She moved to leave but I stopped her with a gentle hand on her arm.

"Morgan is about to be remarried. It's over with her, and has been for years. If I'm being honest, it was over before I even married her. I have no interest in being with her ever again. We spend time with the kids together sometimes and we're cordial. It's good for them to see that their parents don't completely hate each other—"

"That's great, but that isn't it. I—"

"I'm sorry if I hurt your feelings by not seeing you up in the stands. I didn't realize you were here."

She dropped her gaze. "You don't owe me anything, Nick."

"I think I do."

"Stop it."

"We should talk."

"There's that word again."

"Tell me you don't want me as much as I want you, Clara. Make me believe you have nothing to say to me and I'll go away and never bother you again."

"Oh my god, you have to shut up, Nick, please."

"I want to talk to you. I want to be with you—"

Her gaze burned into mine. "You have no idea what you want. You don't know what you're asking for."

"I want another chance—"

"Well, you can't have it. This is too hard. I keep telling you I don't want to talk about the past because it doesn't matter what you say about it. We were young. Kids that age don't have a clue about what they need."

"Clara, we need to get some things cleared up—"

She held up a hand and covered my mouth with a fingertip. "Like I said, this is too hard. Listen, I recently got dumped by a man who jerked me around before deciding he would rather spend his foreseeable future on an oil rig in the middle of the damn ocean surrounded by a bunch of sweaty men rather than stay in Green Valley with me. I'm through with dating, through with men. No more relationships, Nick. I'm finished with getting my heart broken, especially by you. There is no way I could take that again."

I removed her hand and held it against my chest, over my heart. "I won't break your heart, I swear. Do you want me to get on my knees for you?" I sank down in front of her. "I'll do anything to make you give us a chance. I'll even beg you for it."

She grabbed at me, trying to pull me to my feet. "You've lost your mind! Get up, Nick, it's dirty down there."

"I don't care." I reached for her flailing hands, holding them in my own. I needed to make her understand. "I'll get dirty for you. I'll do anything to make you listen to me."

"Fine, I'll listen. But not here. It can't be here—there's too many memories floating around to get lost in."

"Then let me take you somewhere after the game. The kids are going home with Morgan, it's her turn with them. How about you ride home with me, and we can talk at my house. Meet me at the gate when the game is over. Please?"

She sighed. "All right, fine. I'll meet you. I rode with Sadie and Barrett.

You can take me home. We are neighbors, after all. No one will think anything of it if we leave together."

"Promise me you'll be there."

"I promise, okay? You'd better get back out there. The team will be coming out any minute, right?"

"Don't forget you promised," I reiterated, not caring one bit if I came off as desperate, because I was.

Her face softened. "I always keep my promises. Don't worry. I'll be there."

This had to be the longest second half of a game in my life. I searched for her up in the stands every chance I got.

Finally, it was over. We'd won and I couldn't find it in me to care. Playing the bathroom card again, I left the postgame pep talk bullshit to my assistant and once again pulled my hat low and took off to find Clara. She was standing at the gate, off to the side.

We left the stadium and headed to my truck. I helped her into the cab and started the engine.

The lights from the field faded into the distance as I drove toward home. "I think part of you likes hiding out and playing hard to get. You push me away because you wonder if I'll chase you. You don't trust me."

"I don't like it. It's childish," she countered. She huffed out a breath and began rambling. "I don't want to be this way with you. It feels manipulative and I don't mean to do it, but I can't seem to stop myself—"

"Hush, baby, it's okay. I didn't mean that to sound so accusatory." I paused, taking a deep breath of my own. "We have a lot of years to work through, with each other and on our own. Do what you need to do. Do anything, say anything, just don't give up on me. I'm here and I'm not going anywhere."

"Nick, I can't promise you anything right now—"

I turned my head, briefly taking my eyes off the road to gauge her reaction. "I get it. Sometimes I feel the same way. I wonder if you'll come after me if I walk away. But we're different. You and I have different wounds plaguing us, and I know what some of yours are, Clara. Don't forget that."

"I'm so sorry—"

"Don't be sorry. Just don't let this go."

"I don't know what to do anymore," she whispered, the agony in her voice tearing holes in my heart. "I don't know how I should feel. And you don't know where all my wounds lie, Nick. Not anymore. I've acquired a few more over the years."

I took her hand across the console. "That's okay. We have time to figure it out. And if it doesn't work, at least we didn't give up without trying, right? You're so strong—"

"You know what?" She pulled her hand away. "I'm so sick of being told I'm strong. I don't want to be strong anymore. I just want to be normal for once in my damn life."

I pulled into my garage and closed the door behind us. "So be normal then. Or is there something I'm missing? Something you won't forgive me for, no matter how much you say the past doesn't matter? You're hurting, Clara, and I can't fix the problem if you don't tell me what it is. I'm not letting this go anymore—"

"I can't talk about this when it's not even your fault! I don't want to upset you—"

"Do you think I'll leave if you make me angry or hurt my feelings? Is that it?"

"Forget it, Nick. This is why I didn't want to say anything."

"About what? Say anything about the past? Please do, I need to hear it."

"Just drop me off. I can't do this now—"

I decided not to force the issue. It would serve no good to take a hard line when she was in no frame of mind to discuss the past. Reassurance seemed like the better tack to take.

"Clara, I am going nowhere now that I have a chance with you again. Please believe that. We can talk about this right now if you want or we can wait. I don't care if you're tired. I don't care if what you say doesn't even make any sense right now. We can figure out how to fix it together. I'm here and I'm not going anywhere, I promise you."

"But are you really here with me?" She groaned in frustration. "I'm sorry. I'm such a pain about this. I can't help but think—"

"No apologies. Trusting each other after all this time isn't going to be easy. We'll have bumps in the road like any other couple and we'll get through them all. Together."

"I want that. I want to get through this with you." She let out a breath, visibly calming down as she nodded slightly.

I held up a hand. "Do you want to know what I know?"

"Yes, I do. I feel so lost right now, so unsure of everything. But all I can think about is you and how much I don't want to mess this up."

"That's good, baby. I know you're not going anywhere. I know you want to try this with me. The fact that you're so desperate to keep from upsetting me proves it."

"Do you really think this is a good idea?" she whispered into the dark.

I shifted to face her fully. "I know what I feel in this moment, and you do too, don't you? I want to kiss you—right now. I'm dying to know what it would feel like to be with you again after all these years. I can't stop thinking about it. You haunt me, Clara. I've been living with the ghost of you since we ended, and I didn't realize it until you were back in town to stay, living right next door to me, with your bed just two fucking walls away from mine."

"I think about you too." She gave me a side-eye. "Honestly, you're driving me crazy, and it pisses me off."

A familiar sense of awareness surged between us, and I knew for certain she wanted me as much as I wanted her.

I gripped her chin and turned her face to mine.

"Be mad at me if you need to. Run from me, hide from me, yell at me. All I want is to be with you again. Dish it out and I'll take it all. I'd do anything for a chance to be with you again."

"God, Nick, is this real? What are we doing?" She bit her lip as a flush rose over her neck to color her cheeks.

"We need one more time together, at least. For curiosity's sake. For the leftover feelings. Hell, just to get each other off and work out some of this tension between us. Maybe it will make things better—who knows? I don't care how much it will hurt if I have to let you go after. I need to be with you again, even if it's only one last time, just to have some sort of closure."

Having her this close to me was like a drug, lulling me into euphoria. She was on the cusp of saying yes, and I was desperate to hear the word.

"I want you too. I can't lie to you, Nick. I've thought of you so often over the years, more than I want to admit."

I offered her my most charming smile. "I have condoms inside my bedroom."

She threw her head back and laughed. "Presumptuous much?"

My lips turned up at the corner. "More like wishful thinking." The prolonged anticipation was almost unbearable. I ran a hand through my hair as I watched her decide. She was gorgeous, sitting twisted toward me in her seat, chest heaving, lips parted, eyes at half-mast as she thought it over.

"Fuck it. Yes." My heart soared as she reached for me, pulling me close with her hands on my neck as her eyes searched mine. "Yes, to all of it. I've been thinking about you and me together since I saw you sitting in your truck that very first day. I'm done with denying myself what I want."

Like magnets, our lips crashed together. I drank her in—the sweet familiarity of having her mouth on mine again was both nostalgic and brand-new at the same time. I couldn't get enough.

I pulled back, pressing my forehead to hers. "Let's go inside. I want your clothes off."

I got out, racing around the truck to open her door. She jumped into my arms and wrapped herself around me, arms around my neck, legs around my waist. "Hurry," she whispered, nipping at my ear as I took the remaining few steps to my kitchen door.

# CHAPTER 15
# NICK

*It happened. And it will happen again. And from now on, it will happen often and repeatedly. I've had a taste of you, Clara, and I'll never forget it. We can't go back to just being friends now that we've kissed. - Nick*

Once we got inside, the kiss went wild. Blood pounded in my brain and sent my senses reeling before shooting straight to my cock. I pressed her against the door after I kicked it shut, the warm heat between her legs cradling me as I grew impossibly, painfully hard.

"I feel that. Damn, how I missed you," she moaned into my ear. "Take me to bed."

I set her down and offered my hand.

She shook her head and whipped off her tank top, tossing it in my face with a grin before turning to dart toward my staircase, kicking her black, high-heeled cowgirl boots off on the way.

"Game on." Chuckling, I ran after her, kicking off my own shoes and shucking my shirt to toss it over my head as I met her at the base of the stairs. Memories of how we used to be together burst in my mind like fireworks.

Once we'd given up our virginity to each other, we couldn't get enough. All we did was fuck and make plans to sneak off together so we could fuck some more. We were obsessed with each other's bodies and the various ways we could make each other feel good.

We'd lie beneath the stars, in the back of my truck or at the back of her mother's farm on a blanket in one of the lavender fields, making love and making plans. We talked about how lucky we were to have each other, and everything we'd do when we had the freedom to make our own choices.

It seemed she was still the wild, uninhibited girl I used to know and love; it was just hidden beneath years of hurt and disappointment—same as me.

"Baby, wait for me," I called out. "Slow down, we have all night . . ."

"Forget slow, I made up my mind. I want you." She'd already tossed her bra down the stairs by the time I caught up to her.

I wasn't going to debate her further. "Okay, then these jeans need to be off." I hooked my fingers into her belt loops and hauled her close until those perfect, rosy-tipped tits of hers flattened against my chest. I felt her nipples pebble against me, and I groaned against her mouth before placing a kiss there.

"You first." With a flick of her fingers, she undid my jeans and reached inside to free my cock, rubbing her thumb across the tip and making me groan. "Do you taste as good as I remember?"

"God, Clara, I wanted to—"

"You'll get what you want, Nick. Don't you worry about that." Her knees hit the floor in front of me and a huge smile unfurled across her face right before she darted her tongue out to lick the tip of my cock.

"My god, baby. You'll make me finish before we even get started. I'm halfway there already." Before she could get a chance to take me fully into her mouth, I lifted her up with my hands beneath her arms. "You're coming first. I'll be down for the count the second you get those pretty red lips on me."

"If you insist." She kicked off her jeans, stepping out of them to leave her in nothing but a black lacy thong, the sight of which almost made my eyes pop out of my head.

A hot ache grew in my throat as I took her in. "Fuck, Clara. You're even more beautiful than I remembered. I can't believe I'm touching you again. I can't believe you're really here." My hands slid across her hips before one hand slipped to the small of her back while the other caressed up her spine and cupped the back of her neck. I pulled her back into me and kissed the top of her head. "I used to dream of you, Clara," I whispered, my breath ruffling the waves of silken blond against my neck. "There were so many nights I'd lie in bed thinking about you, wondering where you were, if you were okay, and if you missed me as much as I was missing you."

"I did miss you." She pulled back, her mouth curving with tenderness as she wrapped her arms around my neck and gazed up at me. "I'd cry myself to sleep sometimes over you, Nick. No one ever made me feel the way you did."

She reached for my hand on her neck and placed it in the center of her chest, over her heart. "You're the only one who ever got in here, where it truly matters. I know that now. I've only ever felt like this with you."

My chest filled with feelings I'd long since thought were gone forever. "I could fall for you again. Hell, I think I already have . . ."

Smiling to herself, she ran her hands into my hair, giving it a tug. "Kiss me."

My thoughts filtered back to our very first kiss and the way it had felt to finally feel like I had somewhere to belong again after my dad died and my family turned to shit.

The memory remained pure, unsullied by the hurt from losing her or the passage of time as years and distance had piled up between us.

We'd started off with a sweet, spontaneous kiss at the edge of the bleachers where she'd hidden out to watch me play in my first home game as Green Valley High's quarterback. And now, here we were, together in *my* home. And I couldn't help but think that this is where we had always belonged.

I sealed my lips to hers. She was so soft with her sweet little whimpers and sexy little moans. I swallowed them down to keep with the rest of the memories of the way we used to be together. It had been years since I'd felt like this —wanted for who I really was and not for what someone wished I would be.

She was like heaven in my arms. She was everything I'd ever wanted.

*How had I forgotten how this felt?*

*How had I managed to live without her for all this time?*

I was beyond hard for her. I needed her right now more than I had ever needed anything in my entire life. The primal urge to shove inside her body and insist that she was mine—only mine, always mine—was almost impossible to fight.

My hands roamed over her ass, behind her thighs. I lifted her up, smiling when she wrapped her legs around my waist, and I felt her hot, wet heat press tight against my abs as I walked us down the hall.

My room was dark as pitch. Blindly, I reached out to flick the light on. I had to see her. I needed all my senses filled with nothing but her.

When I reached the edge of my bed, I set her down, dropped to one knee in order to slide that sexy-as-hell thong down her thighs, and licked my lips.

"Do *you* taste as good as I remember, baby?"

She inhaled sharply as I sank to my knees in front of her. "Nick . . ."

"That sound you always made when you come? I crave it, Clara. I need to hear it." I raked my eyes up the length of her body, smiling when her knees went weak, and she collapsed to sit on the edge of the bed.

"Oh god." Her voice trembled.

I took her ankles in my hands to lift her feet to the bed, spreading her legs wide as I gently encouraged her to lie on her back. Without wasting any time, I entered her with two fingers and sucked her pretty little clit into my mouth with a long, slow pull.

I licked and nibbled my way over her slick pink skin as I curved my fingers up inside to find that spot I knew would undo her, pumping them in and out until she was shoving her hips into my face and moaning out loud.

"You've always been my girl, haven't you?" I removed my fingers, tapping on her swollen clit for emphasis before entering her with my tongue. She was delicious, even better than I remembered. She was nothing but salty, sweet perfection and I would never have enough of her.

"Yes, yes, yes . . . ," she chanted as I flattened my tongue to glide it up to her clit.

I wrapped one palm around my dick and placed the other on her hip to pin her down on the mattress so I could focus on making her come. I was hard as stone, and it was becoming painful. I needed to get inside her.

With a low scream, she burst apart. Her thighs clamped on my ears as her toes curled into the mattress and she reached low to grab hold of my hair. "I want you now. Right now, Nick."

She scooted up the bed and I fumbled in my bedside table for a condom.

My head was a mess; I wasn't on earth anymore. I was somewhere in the clouds, surrounded by vivid memories both old and new. Being with her had always been an out-of-body experience and this moment was no exception.

I sheathed myself then crawled up her body, savoring the soft perfection of her skin as I kissed and licked my way to her mouth to take it in a searing kiss. My cock nudged her opening, and we moaned in unison at the sensation of finally being close like this again.

I slid in a couple inches, stretching her open and gasping against the smooth skin of her neck as she squeezed me tight. "You feel too good to be real, baby. I can't believe I'm inside you again." I took both her wrists in one hand and pushed them into the bed above her head as I sank into her inch by slow inch.

She gasped. "Oh god, I forgot how big you are. It almost hurts."

I ground myself against her and groaned in her ear, "You can take it, baby. Just like you used to." I was deep inside her, finally back where I'd always needed to be, and I never wanted to stop.

All I wanted to do was lose my mind, lose myself inside her, and let everything else in my life fade away until it was just the two of us again.

I slowed down and shifted back onto one arm so I could reach down between us and circle her clit with my thumb, smiling when her neck arched back, and she tightened in a rippling wave around me.

"Am I hurting you?" I paused so I could search her eyes. "I can stop, or we can slow down."

Her head shook side to side as she wrapped her legs around my back. "No, don't you dare stop. I love how you feel—keep going."

I pulled out and drove back in. "Like this?"

Her throaty groan was so hot my cock pulsed inside her. "God, yes, give me more. This is unreal, like a dream. Make me feel it tomorrow, so I have no chance of ever forgetting you . . ."

I moved up to support myself on my forearms and went harder, fucking into her with rough, almost brutal strokes, making sure to grind into her clit after each thrust.

"You were made to take all of me, weren't you? Look at us. Fuck, Clara, tell me you remember how perfectly we fit."

"Yes, I remember. I've always remembered everything."

"You were made for me. We were made for each other."

"It's like we're two parts of one whole." Her voice was a breathy moan against my neck. "Like we've always belonged together." Her nails dug into my back, then slid to my ass to pull me deeper inside of her. "Please, Nick, I want more . . ."

Our foreheads pressed together as our eyes locked, and we panted into each other's mouths, lips meeting in breathless kisses each time I sank deep.

"Nick . . . ," she murmured. "God, Nick, I'm gonna—" She wrapped her arms around my back, pulling me closer, her legs tightening around my waist and back arching as she came around my cock in fluttering little pulses.

Heat blazed at the base of my spine, radiating through my body like a series of lightning bolts until I went over the edge with a shuddering gasp, filling the condom and wondering if I was still alive.

Like every other time I'd been with her, I'd gone out of my head, lost to the sensations only she could ever give me. She was the only woman who had ever made me lose control like this.

I lifted my head to watch her beautiful face as she regained her senses. "We're not finished yet." I pulled out, smiling when she gifted me with a little whine at the loss.

"I wanted to keep you inside," she murmured. "Just for a little bit longer—"

"Hush, baby, I need more. I want the sight of you undone like this embedded in my mind. Emblazoned so deep within my psyche that I'll never forget how it feels to make you let go for me. If this is my only chance, I'm making the most of it. Spread your legs for me."

Without hesitation she lifted her knees to her sides. I slid down her body, biting my lip as her slick wet arousal painted my abs and chest on the way. "I will never get enough of this," I growled into her inner thigh. "I can't believe I survived without you for this long."

She was sensitive so I took it easy on her, soothing her with soft licks and swirls of my tongue until she planted her feet on the bed and lifted her hips, shoving her pussy in my face with a demanding moan.

"Please . . ."

I looked up the length of her body, one hand fisting the sheets, head thrashing side to side as her back arched and her rosy-tipped nipples turned into hard little peaks as she pinched one between her fingertips.

I stopped. "Look at me," I demanded. "I need to see it happen."

She let her legs drop to the sides and met my eyes as she rose to her elbows on the bed, watching me as I licked my lips and pressed my chin to her clit.

"My god, Nick. You're gonna kill me tonight, aren't you?"

I shook my head as I sucked her clit back into my mouth and moved my tongue against her with relentless little flicks until she went wild, pulling back from my mouth and bucking her hips as she shoved a hand between her legs to spread herself apart with her fingers and send herself over the edge. I watched as she flew into pieces beneath me, gorgeous and wild.

I remembered this. The two of us together and uninhibited, shamelessly exploring each other's bodies as we learned what would drive each other crazy. We were so fucking in love back then, and had all the trust in the world.

I wanted it back—I didn't care what I had to do to get it.

She'd trust me again. It was only a matter of time.

"Let me hold you." I wiped my mouth with the back of my hand and moved up the bed to gather her in my arms.

"Mm-hmm." Her head came to rest on my chest. She was boneless, completely relaxed against me. "You killed me. I knew it," she mumbled into my pec. "I'm dead."

My soft laugh ruffled her hair as it spilled across my chest. "Nah, you'll recover. Then we'll do it again."

We drifted off to sleep together, waking up when the early morning light shone through my window. I'd forgotten to pull the blackout curtains closed.

She stretched, shifting in my arms to face me. "I should go home, right? It's almost morning. We have to keep this a secret, don't we? The kids . . ."

"Damn it. Yes. Morgan and I have an agreement—"

A brief look of hurt crossed her face before she hid it. "I understand. It makes sense." She moved to get up, but I stopped her.

"I fucking hate this. Listen to me before you go. Will you? Please."

"I'm listening, I promise. I'm not trying to run off or escape, I—"

I placed a fingertip to her lips. "I know, baby. We're not going backward again. This isn't a push-pull thing between us anymore, okay? I'm in this for real and I think you are too."

"I don't want to pull away. I don't want to run from you anymore. But I'm not going to lie to you either. The thought of being together again freaks me out a little, Nick, and I'm not sure I'm ready to go all in just yet. Can we have a push-*pause* thing if I need it?"

"Absolutely. As long as we're honest with each other, everything will be fine."

I slipped into a pair of pajama pants and gave her one of my T-shirts to wear home. We gathered her clothes on the way to the front door, but I wasn't ready to let her go.

I yanked her into me, banding an arm around her hips and winding my fist into her hair to bring her lips to mine. "I wish you could stay, but they'll be home in just an hour or so . . ."

Her hands cradled my face. "It'll be okay, baby. I'm not going anywhere." She laughed. "I mean, I'm going home, but I'm with you, Nick. I promise."

"Text me when you get inside." I let go of her and opened the door, sighing when she stepped across the threshold onto the porch. It was stupid, but I felt like I was losing her all over again.

"Why does everything have to feel so right when you kiss me?" She turned back to ask.

"You know why, don't you?"

She bit her lip and nodded.

I reached out and grabbed the back of her neck to pull her in for one more kiss. "You're mine, Clara."

"I think maybe I always have been."

I watched as she crossed our yards and made it onto her porch to go inside.

The *ping* of my text notification made me smile as I headed back up to bed.

# CHAPTER 16
# CLARA

*Whenever I see you at your locker, I wish I could kiss you. - Nick*

I sat down at Clay Meadows's desk—senior honors English and Shakespeare—and stared out the window on the other side of the room. I did not have the energy to deal with this job today and I wanted to go home. The rain pounded in a relentless beat, almost in time with the pounding in my head. We were supposed to have a thunderstorm and I was dreading it; thunder and lightning scared me, and always had.

I wished I could quit and go back to my plants, my podcasts, and my *Rear Window*-ing. But I couldn't, not yet. Not until I was sure this thing with Gracie and her bully bitch trio was over and done with once and for all. I might stick it out for the rest of the school year, just to be sure.

But Gracie hardly needed me here anymore. Her ankle was healed, and Marianne had become too smart to target her again at school. The infamous cafeteria Snack Pack incident had been a one-timer. Once she caught sight of me on campus and realized what I was there for, she had gone into stealth mode.

Unfortunately, Gracie wouldn't let me do any of what I was best at to get her out of the online situation, so my hands were tied there. I was not allowed to create fake social media accounts for return bullying and counter rumors.

She wouldn't even let me call Marianne's mother and put a stop to it the adult way. She was convinced they would just move on.

All this passivity was unlike the Gracie I knew. I blamed Everett's influence, possibly Willa's too. They were just too good. They were wonderful examples of healthy adults in a successful and loving relationship—which I grudgingly had to admit was probably for the best. She was better living with them than a hot mess like me. Despite my years of therapy, I was still a disaster in way too many ways to count.

I'd had to resort to glaring at Marianne and her little friend group in the hallways to let them know I was still onto them and their wicked ways. It was frustrating, and boring, and not at all what I had signed up for. I wanted to thwart them and be the big sister hero, dang it. I wanted to make Gracie feel okay about being on campus without Weston and was pissed that I couldn't.

But what had been on my mind the most over the last week or so was homecoming and what Nick and I had done that night in his bed.

I wasn't hiding out, but I wasn't putting myself out there either. There were too many feelings between us now to deny them so I had asked him for a pause, which I felt had to be one of my more brilliant ideas. There would be no more pulling away or keeping my feelings to myself. Being honest was the right thing to do. I still needed time to sort myself out.

My endless years of therapy had not prepared me to have Nick back in my life. Probably because ever since him, I'd only been using half of my heart. I knew now the other half had been a shriveled up little shell of itself, sitting dormant and useless in my chest cavity. Him being back had awakened parts of me I'd put to sleep a long time ago, and I wasn't ready to feel this much. It scared me. I worried for the both of us. The last thing I wanted to was hurt him or be hurt.

In retrospect, having sex with him so soon was probably a mistake. And though I didn't regret it, it put my heart on the line even more than it had been before. I also wanted to do it again immediately.

None of the heat between us had dissipated over the years, but more than that, I still craved the way he made me feel—like I mattered, like I was special, like I was an important part of his life and he wanted to keep me in it. But we had to keep things a secret for the sake of his kids. I understood it, but it felt a little too reminiscent of our past and therefore still bothered me. I wasn't some random woman he'd started dating, dang it.

I had to get my head on straight or I'd end up being the one to hurt him. I would do anything to avoid that.

"I hate this." My voice was a pitiful little whine. All I wanted was to go to sleep but I knew I wouldn't be able to, not with my hair and shirt a stinky mess.

He stood. "Take my hands. Stand up."

He made quick work of getting me undressed and helping me into the tub where, true to his word, he washed my hair, got me cleaned up, then wrapped me in a towel. Then he led me to my room and helped me sit on the edge of my bed as he dug through my dresser for pajamas.

I blinked, trying not to get caught watching him like an insipid, love-addled fool. I was almost grateful for the hot tears filling my eyes, as they forced me to finally look away from him. I wiped them with the corner of the towel before he could see me in such an emotional state.

Since him, no one in my life had treated me with such selfless tenderness. My sisters and I took care of each other, but with them it was usually us finding our way through our shared problems—it was empathy, it was commiseration, it was us leaning on each other to make it through. Nick was different; with him I felt like I could let myself go and he could handle whatever I may need.

Our eyes met and I silently vowed that I would make him feel exactly as safe and comfortable as he was making me feel. Whenever he needed me, I would be there for him. I froze when I realized that was what our entire past relationship had been based on; we'd always been there for each other. Until it had ended.

"Lift your arms, baby." His eyes burned with a faraway look, and I gasped when I realized what he'd found.

"Nick, I—"

His voice was incredulous. "You kept it."

I lifted my arms as he slid one of his old high school football jerseys over my head. "Umm . . ." I couldn't form words. I was burning with fever, over-come with memories, and struck speechless by the love shining in his eyes.

"After all these years, you still have it."

"I couldn't get rid of it, I—"

"Shh, lie down." His gentle palm cupped my cheek as he pushed me back and tucked me in, pulling my quilt up to my chin and dropping a kiss to my forehead. "I'm going to run to my house and grab some things. Your medicine cabinet is sorely lacking. We'll talk more about everything when you feel better."

"Okay," I murmured, my eyelids heavy with exhaustion.

"But Clara? I have to say one thing before you crash."

"Yes?"

"Seeing you in that shirt again means the world. Knowing that you kept it is everything to me. You have to know that." I nodded, unable to fight against my eyelids closing.

It was dark when I woke. The weather had not improved but my stomach had.

Blindly, I reached into the dark for the lamp at my bedside table to turn it on, smiling when I found a bottle of water and two Tylenol sitting in my tiny butterfly jewelry tray.

"How are you feeling?" Nick's deep voice rumbling across my room sent a shiver up my spine.

"You stayed."

"Of course I did. I would never leave you like this."

I paused and took stock of my body. "I think my stomach is better, it's just sore now."

"I have chicken soup I can heat up when you're ready and I brought over some necessities—crackers, non-moldy bread for toast, applesauce, Gatorade. You need to keep your pantry full, sweetheart. What if I wasn't here to take care of you? Dehydration is a real concern when you're throwing up."

"I know. I just—" My voice was small. "Sadie used to do all that stuff. I usually just order in or pick something up whenever I leave the house."

Thunder crashed in the distance, and I jumped. Growing up hadn't gotten rid of my fear of thunderstorms, no matter how many times my mother had told me it would.

"Still?" *He remembered.* We'd gotten stuck in a thunderstorm one of the nights we'd snuck off to Sky Lake. We ended up huddled on the floor of his truck until the storm faded away. How we had both fit down there was a mystery for the ages.

I nodded. "Will you stay with me? I'm too sick to sleep in my closet. I don't want to be alone."

"Oh, baby." I lifted the covers, and he slid in behind me, spooning me up against the big wall of his chest. "Shh, I'm here . . ."

"You're so warm." I snuggled backward, and he hugged me tighter.

He whispered into my hair, "Go back to sleep," then kissed the crown of my head. "I'll be here as long as you need me to be."

It wasn't even lunch yet and I was already over this entire day. My head had been aching since I woke up and my stomach was a roiling mess of nerves.

Clay's classroom was right next door to Nick's, and it had been driving me to distraction since I got here. Thankfully, I'd made it to my prep period and the kids were at band or PE or art or wherever. The point was they were gone, and I could finally have a moment to myself. I felt so wretched I was tempted to lie on the floor and take a damn nap. Instead I let my head drop to the desk as my hands went to my agonized stomach.

What the hell was wrong with me? I couldn't be pregnant. It had only been a week since homecoming and in addition to the condom we used, I was on the pill.

Maybe I'd caught something. I did work every day surrounded by a bunch of germy kids. Granted, teens were big kids, but they were still a mess.

A cold sweat broke out over my upper lip and along my hairline as shimmering white filled the edges of my vision and a wave of nausea washed over me, turning my stomach into a pulsating knot.

*Shit.*

This was not nerves. I was about to barf.

Something was definitely going around campus. I didn't know if it was the stomach flu or a bad cold, or another dang virus sent straight up from hell. I'd marked at least a third of the kids absent today, damn it.

*Can you get a sub for a sub?*

Frantically, I looked around for something to puke in. There was no time to get to the bathroom and I refused to vomit in my new Chanel tote—no freaking way.

There was nothing in here, not even a garbage can. I made a mental note to complain about that as I ran to the window, threw it open, and leaned out, bent at the waist over the edge. Thankfully I was on the first floor, and everything went into the bushes below.

I located a box of tissues and wiped my mouth as I turned around and sank to the floor, panting and gasping and hoping that the feeling I would toss my cookies again would pass so I could get the hell out of here and crawl into bed with a barf bowl. Or maybe just lapse into a coma on my bathmat so I could be near the toilet.

*This was so dang gross.*

"Are you okay?" I looked up to find Ruby, Gracie's bestie, hovering above me, eyes lit up with concern. "We heard everything. What can I do?"

"I'm sick. I just threw up out the freaking window. I swear I'm dying." My stomach rolled. "Oh god . . ."

"You must have caught that stomach virus that has been going around. You need to go home. I'll pop next door and let Mr. Easton know. We can all go over there with his class until the office finds someone to cover you." She gestured behind her. "We've done it before whenever there hasn't been a substitute available right away." I looked over her shoulder to find the rest of Mr. Meadows's class staring at me.

I narrowed my eyes, letting them drift across each one of their germ-riddled faces. Which one of these little fuckers had gotten me sick? I should have known better . . .

"I'd help you up, but I have two AP tests tomorrow and I can't miss them." She reached for the huge tub of hand sanitizer on the bookshelf next to me and squirted a healthy dollop into her palm. "Marianne, come help Miss Hill up and walk her to her car, will you? You don't have anything important happening this week. Or ever, now that I'm thinking on it. Getting good grades obviously isn't your thing and that's okay. I mean, we're not all cut out to be honor students, right?" If I wasn't feeling like such shit, I would have laughed.

Given the way she was speaking to Marianne, Ruby was clearly not as clueless as Gracie thought she was.

"Yuck. Ugh, fine." Marianne wasn't happy about it, but she immediately came over to do as Ruby asked and reached a hand down to me.

I took it, my curiosity piqued at how this was playing out, but I put a pin in it to contemplate later. Right now, I had to concentrate on not accidentally giving her payback for the way she's been treating Gracie by way of spewing what I'd had for breakfast all over the front of her pretty pink sweater.

"Let's go next door, y'all," Ruby directed the rest of the kids.

"Thanks," I told her as I let Marianne take my arm. I was wobbly on my feet but clearheaded. I'd be okay to drive.

"Not a problem. Get some rest."

Marianne scuttled off the second I unlocked my car door. I made it home in time to cut the engine, flail my way out of my car, and throw up in my recycling bin.

Without bothering to click the garage door closed, I stumbled into the kitchen through the interior entrance and found my way to my living room floor. I managed to yank the throw blanket from the arm of the sofa and curled into the fetal position by the edge of the fireplace.

Sleep was all I could think about. A little nap was all I needed, then I'd be fine. Right? *Please be right . . .*

I kicked off my pumps and tucked my knees tight to my chest with a moan.

I was not fine. I was the opposite of fine.

Thunder rumbled in the distance, followed by a crash of lightning and I flinched. When it rained, it poured—literally. But I was too sick to be scared of the storm so I stayed where I was.

Tears filled my eyes as another stomach cramp sent me spiraling. I didn't want to move. In fact, I wondered if I could even get up if I wanted to. *Oh well*. My floors were wood and would be easier to clean than carpet when this was all over.

*I should have a barf bowl in every room*, I decided as I groaned into the floor and tried to slow my breathing. Why did I only think of shit like this when it was too late to do anything about it?

I hadn't been this sick in years and I was pretty sure I'd gotten vomit in my hair when I hurled into my recycling bin. A quick sniff told me I had, and that it was on my shirt too.

Whatever. At least I was home where I could cry in my living room and feel sorry for myself in peace. I was alone with no one around to care if I smelled like puke.

*How sad was I?*

I wiped my hair as best I could with the throw blanket then tossed it into the fireplace. No way was I doing that kind of laundry.

"Clara, baby, where are you?"

Oh.

My goodness.

It was Nick. He'd probably come in through my unlocked garage. Either that or he'd climbed up to my balcony again to rescue me just like freakin' Romeo.

I buried my face in my arms. Since I didn't have enough strength in my body left to care what I smelled like, I figured hiding was the right thing to do.

*Couldn't I just die in peace?*

"In the living room." My voice was a weak mewl.

"Ruby told me you were sick. Pindich and his secretary are covering the classes." He bent and scooped me into the cradle of his arms as if I weighed nothing. "Let's get you tucked into bed, sweetheart."

"No, I barfed in my hair, Nick. I smell so gross."

He inhaled and drew his head back to look at me with gentle eyes. "No worries. We'll get you cleaned up first."

My voice was barely a whisper when I said, "You don't have to do this. I'll be okay. Go home, save yourself from my germs. You don't want to catch this."

"Hush, baby. You're sick, let me take care of you."

I gave up and relaxed, sinking into the warmth of his arms as he carried me to my bathroom. I couldn't help but notice how my head fit perfectly into the hollow between his shoulder and neck, like I was made to be right here, cared for by him, loved by him, taken care of by him. *Damn it.*

"Okay." My emotions whirled and skidded along with the sudden recurrence of the churning nausea in my gut. "Oh god, put me down."

Ever so gently, he set me on my feet in front of the toilet, bending to lift the lid as I knelt in front of it.

But nothing.

I sat back and leaned against the tub as my stomach seized and my head throbbed. I knew I was burning up with a fever when a flash of heat seared my temples and another cold sweat covered my body. I sat shivering as I fought against bursting into tears.

The back of his hand went to my brow. "You have a fever. Where is your thermometer?"

I flopped a hand in the direction of my medicine cabinet. I had no idea if I still had one in there or not. Sadie had been the one to stock my house with all the necessities that adults were supposed to have. She probably took it when she moved out.

"The kids?" I mumbled as I caught a case of the chills and shivered.

"With Morgan. I'm here for the duration, Clara. I won't leave you alone."

"M'kay. Thank you." I flopped to my side, pulling down a towel to use as a blanket. "I'll stay right here and go to sleep."

"Do you think you can manage sitting in the tub? I can wash your hair for you, then put you to bed."

I felt a bit ridiculous, but I wanted to say yes. The smell was making me gag.

"I'll return the favor if I get you sick."

"Nah, I never get sick. You owe me a date now, that's what I want. Dinner, movie, a walk in the park—I don't care as long as we make plans and do something together. Like we never could before. A real date." He leaned over me to get the hot water started.

"Fine, I'll buy you that steak at The Front Porch we talked about. Oh god, no more talk about food right now. Get out!" I shrieked as I shot to my knees and lost the rest of my breakfast in the toilet.

But he did not get out; he knelt at my side and pulled my hair back. "I got you. You'll be okay," he soothed. He was good at this. He must have had a lot of practice with Ethan and Sasha, or maybe Morgan when she was pregnant.

I nodded and drooped against his side.

# CHAPTER 17
# NICK



One of my strongest, most stubborn beliefs was that I could will what I wanted into existence. I would simply work every angle, analyze each problem, and zero in on my goal until I got my way. The only time it hadn't worked was with Clara, and I blamed my youth for the failure. Deep down I'd always believed I'd be with her again, but something still nagged at me.

Our *pause* had ended after she got sick, but that didn't mean I could see her whenever I wanted. I was serious about her; there was no doubt in my mind regarding where I wanted us to end up. She was it for me and she always had been.

But even though I knew she was serious about me too, she was still cagey about saying the words out loud. She was still resistant to talking things over. I knew she was scared and holding on to hurts from our shared past. I suspected she had hurts and secrets from after we'd broken up too, so I held tight to the notion that we had time. Time, freedom, and proximity. Those things, along with our undeniable chemistry, meant we would eventually be okay.

No matter how much I wanted to, I couldn't tell Sasha and Ethan about us yet, not until I was one hundred percent sure we wouldn't end up in another pause. I didn't want to put them through any uncertainty. They'd taken the divorce hard, and I couldn't do that to them again, especially since they'd grown so fond of Clara.

She was on my mind all the time. In fact, she'd been the only thing on my mind since we'd slept together. The rest of my life was falling through the cracks. The house was a mess, I had papers piling up to grade, and my lawn was getting out of control. Figuring out what to cook for dinner was usually a no-brainer, but not tonight. I was staring into the fridge with sightless eyes, like a living embodiment of the cliché of a clueless man.

"Dad! There's blood everywhere! I'm dying!" Sasha's frantic shriek shot me straight back into reality.

*What the hell?*

I flew up the stairs and down the hall to her bedroom where I found her frantically rummaging through her dresser, tossing clothes behind herself. "What? Blood everywhere? Sasha, sweetheart, what's happening. What's going on—?"

A breathless Ethan came running in behind me. "It's not *everywhere*, Dad. I checked. It's just in her underwear in the garbage can in the bathroom. She got her period."

"Go away, Ethan!" she screamed at him. "Leave me alone! Get out!"

"Oh. *Ohhh.* Oh my god," I heaved out a relieved sigh as I connected the dots and realized what was happening. "Sasha, honey. You're not dying, I promise you. You started your period. I thought your mom told you about that. Didn't she? You had that talk with her, right?"

She stopped throwing clothes and turned around. Her tear-streaked cheeks broke my heart. "My period? She said I'd be a teenager first. I'm not even twelve yet." She sighed deeply, though she was still trembling. "So, I'm not going to die? Are you sure? Every time I went to the bathroom there was blood, and it feels—I don't even know. I kept throwing them away and hoping it would stop."

I pulled her in for a hug. "No, honey. You are not going to die. This is totally normal. You just started your period, that's it. I mean, it's a big deal, but not one that will kill you, I swear."

She threw her arms around me and burst into fresh tears. "I don't have any of the pads and whatever else Mom said she'd buy for me. I was looking for all my old pajama pants to put on. Mom said we'd go shopping together and buy all the things I'd need but she's on a plane right now! We can't even call her until tomorrow. I don't have anything, Dad. Blood is going to get every-where if I leave the bathroom. I'm going to ruin the whole entire house. How will I sit down or go to sleep in my bed? Should I sleep in the bathtub tonight—?"

"No, you do not have to sleep in the bathtub." I rubbed my hand in soothing strokes across her back. "Shh, Sasha, honey, it's okay. Listen to me." I took her by the shoulders and looked her dead in the eye. She was panicking, and I had to make her believe that I could handle this. "I got you, Sash. You will be fine. I'll go see if Clara has stuff you can use for now. Then later I'll go to the store and get you whatever else you need. Everything will be okay, I promise you."

She wiped a hand across one check and sniffled. "Okay, but I don't know how to use any of it. Mom said she'd show me when I started."

"There has to be instructions on the box, right? I will help you. Why don't you go take a shower and clean up and I'll go next door and see if Clara has anything we can borrow. Maybe she can come over and stay with y'all while I go down to the Piggly Wiggly and grab whatever else you'll need. Sound good?"

She nodded. "Yeah, I'm fine now that I know I'm not gonna die. I saw the blood and it scared me. I didn't even think."

I pulled her in for another hug. "Go on and take a long, hot shower and when you're done, I'll help you figure everything out. Sound good?"

"Yeah, Daddy."

I followed her into the hallway where Ethan and I locked eyes as she headed into the bathroom and closed the door. "That was intense," he finally said after we heard the water start.

"You're telling me." My hand went to the back of my neck as I took a breath and calmed my racing heart. She'd scared the shit out of me with all that screaming.

"I'm going to clean up her room for her," he announced. "She was stressed the hell out. And I feel bad. I didn't mean to embarrass her. I thought—I don't know what I thought. But I was worried when she said she was dying."

"That's nice of you, bud."

He grimaced. "Yeah, like, I'd probably flip out too if I went to the bathroom and found a bunch of blood in my underwear, you know?"

My lips twitched in amusement. "I imagine that would be very alarming," I agreed. "I'm going to head next door. Be right back."

"Okay, Dad. I'll get all this crap picked up, no problem."

"You're a sweet kid, Eath."

"Sometimes. Don't tell anyone," he grumbled.

I huffed a laugh and made my way over to Clara's house.

"Hey there, neighbor." She was on the porch with her ever-present mug of coffee sitting on the railing and that same podcast sounding out its motivational quotes through her open front window.

"It's cold out today," I remarked.

"Are we really talking about the weather?" She laughed. "I thought we'd moved past that."

"It was the topic du jour the other night, if I recall correctly."

"Ahh, yes. The thunderstorm. I appreciate your company and big strong arms. Sleeping in my closet is never ideal. What brings you over?"

"Uh, I need your help with Sasha. Morgan is out of town."

"Maybe you should hire a nanny to help you out. I hear all the single dads are doing it." Her mouth twitched at the corners and her eyes sparkled with amusement as she teased me.

"Now why would I do that when I have a gorgeous blond heartbreaker like you living right next door?" I reached over and touched her nose with a fingertip.

"You make a good point. What can I do for y'all?"

"It seems like she's started her period, her first one. Morgan is out of town, on a plane right now, in fact. I wondered if you had any, um, supplies? And would you sit with the kids while I pick up some more? I don't like leaving them alone. Ethan's not the best when it comes to making good choices—he's still a bit impulsive."

She stared at me for a second, mouth slightly open as a spark of some indefinable emotion flickered across her face. Then her eyes softened on mine and she broke into a sweet, tender smile. "I don't mind at all. You're a good dad, Nick."

"Thanks." This scenario was the perfect opportunity to bring her closer to my kids without the pressure of letting them know we were dating or getting back together, or whatever it was we were doing. We still hadn't labeled it. "Would you stay and have dinner with us tonight too?"

Her eyes lit up. "Are you sure about that?"

"Absolutely. We don't have to say a word about me and you. Just a neighborly dinner, right?" I winked.

"Oh." The light left her eyes and I frowned. "Of course. What a great idea. And I have pads inside. I might not have food in my kitchen, but I have always those." She made a joke to cover her obvious disappointment and I couldn't help but think I'd put my foot in my mouth, big time.

"I appreciate this. Clara? Are you okay?"

"Of course I am. I'm fine. I'm glad I can help her. I'll grab everything and meet you at your place." She turned and ran inside, slamming the door behind herself before I could question her further, so I got up and went home, leaving the door open for her to come in.

I arrived in time to hear the water shut off. "I'm back," I called. "Clara's coming over."

Sasha, in her bathrobe, popped her head around the corner at the top of the stairs. "Thank god."

"Like I said, I got you, honey."

"Hi, Sasha." Clara stepped through the open front door behind me and held up a grocery bag. "I brought you some pads. Think of them like puzzle stickers. They fit right into your undies."

"Oh! That's all I have to do? Stick it there?"

"Yep. Easy-peasy, lemon-squeezy."

Sasha ran down and grabbed the bag. "Thank you. Will you be here if I can't do it and need help?"

"Sure thing. Here, let me show you one before you go upstairs." Clara dug into the bag and demonstrated what to do.

Sasha beamed up at her. "I can do that!"

"You sure can." Clara beamed right back.

We watched Sasha run up the stairs with the bag.

"I appreciate this more than I can say."

"No problem at all. She's a sweet girl and I'm glad I was here to help her."

"So, listen. Real quick." I opened my notes app on my phone where I kept a list of products Sasha might need and handed it to her. "I researched this a while back so I'd be prepared, just in case. But it's just too much. How do y'all ever decide what to buy? What would an almost twelve-year-old girl want to use? I had hoped to run this by Morgan but never got the chance."

Her lips turned up at the corners. "What I gave her was pretty basic. She can keep the rest and if she likes it, just keep buying it."

"Hey, Miss Clara! Are you staying for dinner with us?" Ethan asked as he bounded into the living room. "I put all her clothes in the hamper," he informed me.

"But they were clean, Eath." I ran a hand over my beard, trying to keep my cool. "She pulled them straight out of her dresser. We both saw her do it."

He shrugged. "I'm gonna go play Fortnite with Makenna. Cook something good so Clara will stay. Later."

"Yeah, okay, later. Thanks, I guess." I shook my head, exasperated. "Damn, I fucking hate laundry," I grumbled and grinned when she burst out laughing. "Knowing him, it's all mixed up now."

"Poor baby. Did he say Makenna? As in Wyatt Monroe's daughter, Makenna?"

"That's the one. He's got it pretty bad for her."

"Well, isn't that interesting?"

"Forget about them. Forget about the laundry. Forget about everything." I stepped closer to her. "I got it pretty bad for you, you know."

"That's even more interesting. We should talk about it after dinner."

"Talk? *You?*"

"Yeah, perhaps. Sometimes I'm into communication, like when I'm not spying on the neighbors or running from giant killer bugs." She shrugged her shoulders.

"Ah, I see. I have to catch you in the right mood, is that it?"

She pursed her lips, pretending to think it over. "Hmm, something like that."

"I want to kiss you right now," I growled. My heart rate skyrocketed at the thought of getting my hands on her again.

Soft fingertips moved to my forearm as she leaned in to whisper, "And I would very much like to be kissed by you."

I took her hands in mine and walked her backward toward the kitchen, winking when I caught her eyes again. "Let's go make dinner."

"Is that what the kids are calling it these days?" Her gentle laughter rippled through the air, and I wanted nothing more than to hear it in my home forever.

"Come with me, baby. We can steal a minute or two together before reality strikes."

"Reality is not my favorite thing. I much prefer dreamy late nights and dramatic balcony rescues. Although, I could do without the throwing up and bugs. Thunderstorms can eff off too."

I pulled her into the pantry and closed the door behind us. Without hesitation, she stepped into my open arms, reaching up to pull my face to hers. My tongue traced the soft fullness of her lips as she melted into me, and we lost ourselves in each other.

She broke the kiss. "Let's not learn the hard way that your kids are onto us," she whispered. "Getting busted in a pantry would be a rookie move, don't you think? We're better than that, Nick."

I reclaimed her lips for one last kiss before answering. "I don't know about Ethan, but Sasha is definitely suspicious of my feelings toward you. Or maybe she just likes you a lot. She tells me to ask you out all the time." Clara's eyes were soft, sparkling with contentment, and her lips were swollen from my kisses. I didn't want to leave the pantry.

"And what do you tell her?"

"I change the subject and she rolls her eyes and laughs at me."

"She's a clever girl. So, what's for dinner?"

I reached for a package of noodles over her shoulder. "Some sort of pasta? A salad? I'll check the fridge for ingredients."

"I'd offer to help you, but I don't cook." Her teasing voice made me smile. "However, I'll be excellent company while you cook. I excel at drinking wine and making witty repartee. Clean-up duty is my go-to kitchen strength, and I *might* be able to make a salad, but we'll have to see what you got."

"That all sounds like heaven to me." A ripple of excitement shot through me even though what we were doing was normal, mundane even.

The fact that she was here with me and the kids gave me hope.

Our past had been encroaching less and less into our present interactions and I couldn't help but feel like we were now on the path to starting a future together.

I found the ingredients for a quick pasta and salad.

She set the table and we shared a bottle of wine while I cooked.

Dinner was full of talk about school and Green Valley's upcoming Fall Festival. Sasha was doing better. She was comfortable and relaxed, and I was thankful Clara was here to help me.

# CHAPTER 18
# NICK

*One day, Clara, we'll leave this place and have it all. In the open. Where no one can hurt us. - Nick*

It was bedtime. Clara and I were in the kitchen listening as the kids moved around upstairs getting ready for bed.

"Stay for a drink?" I asked after the kids had gone silent. She didn't answer, but her face spoke for her.

I pulled her into my arms and kissed her. Having her close like this, in my house, made my senses spin. I wanted more than I could have right now, and it was frustrating.

"They won't get up? What about Sasha? It's her first time with her period. Do you think she'll be okay?"

"If they get up, we'll be in the living room. The neighbor thing seems to be a good cover. For now, anyway."

"I'd love to stay for a bit. Tonight was nice."

We headed into the living room to talk. I knew I couldn't take her upstairs. She couldn't stay the night with me, no matter how much I wanted her to. I needed more of a commitment from her and less uncertainty about our future before I brought it up to the kids.

Clara and I sat on opposite ends of the couch. "Do you mind if we talk about Sasha? I want to make sure I'm doing the right things for her. Morgan is out of town, but even if she wasn't, I don't relish the thought of talking about this with her."

"I get it, and I think it's wonderful you want to support your daughter. Sure, ask me anything. I don't mind. I'm glad you're so open about it and not grossed out. It will mean a lot to her."

I slid my eyes to hers. "Any man grossed out by a period doesn't deserve to call himself a man."

"I mean, yeah." She shrugged one shoulder up. "It's a huge part of life."

"Does she need chocolate? Is that a real thing? What about Midol?" I drove my hands into my hair and pressed my palms against my eyes. "God, Clara, she still wants Squishmallows for her birthday and she just got her period. I want to hug her and make her feel okay again. It was so much easier when she was little. What else should I do for her. Any ideas?"

"I know I said I'd help. But actually, I—I have no ideas, Nick. No one ever . . ." She shook her head and looked out into the dark outside my front window. "Uh, my sisters and I had to—like, our mother sat us down and explained it to us all at once. Just the one time. Willa was only six, she flipped out completely at the thought of bleeding." Her gaze was faraway. "Anyway, Momma would buy a shitload of supplies every month and put them in the bathroom. We were okay," she quickly added when she caught sight of my horrified look. "We figured it out. Well, mostly Sadie did because she was first, then she helped the rest of us."

"Oh, baby. Come here." I pulled her into my arms. "I'm so sorry."

She was stiff in my arms. "What? I'm fine."

"I didn't mean to bring up bad memories for you. You deserved better— you all did. I'm sorry your mom didn't take the time to explain it all and ease any fears y'all had."

"Oh my god, Nick." She pulled out of my arms and leaned back. "You have to stop. You're being far too sweet and understanding. It's making it too hard to resist you."

"Good, don't resist me." I pulled her back into my side and kissed her temple. "The last thing I want is resistance. What's going on? Talk to me."

"I don't know what to say to you half the time." She tucked her cheek in my chest to hide. "The closer we get, the more I get scared that I'll lose you all over again. It's irrational and stupid and I feel like an idiot, but I can't make it stop."

"You're not an idiot—"

"Thank you for saying that, but I'm being difficult, I know I am. I've heard it before, so many times, and I don't mean to be this way—"

I pulled back so I could look her in the eye. "Wait a minute, stop. Clara, who told you that you're difficult? We need to get into this so I can fix it. I don't want anything standing in our way, okay? Tell me who it was. Better yet, give me an address and I'll show him what the word *difficult* really means."

She patted my chest and offered me a weak smile. "No, I'm okay. I swear."

"You're entitled to your feelings, Clara. You feel what you feel. I feel what I feel. Then we work it out. That's how relationships should work, remember?"

"Um, I mean . . ."

"I just want to understand you."

"Get in line. That's my number one goal too, hence my many years of therapy."

I sifted a hand through her hair, brushing the soft strands over her shoulder. "I wish you could trust me again. I wish—god, I wish so many things. It's pointless to list them all." She took my hand in both of hers, bringing it up to her lips to kiss the back.

"I understand, really, I do. But even I don't trust myself. You should run while you still have a chance."

I leaned my forehead against hers and whispered, "I don't have a chance, not anymore. I'm gone for you again, heartbreaker."

"Oh, Nick. I'm trying." She closed her eyes. "I promise I am."

"Maybe you can go to the Fall Festival with me and the kids. We can keep it casual, neighborly. You can get to know the kids better with zero pressure." It was a longshot, but why not ask? What could it hurt?

Clara was great with Sasha and Ethan, and I wanted them to end up feeling close to her. My mother's remarriage ruined my family, and I wanted better for my kids.

"I would love to . . ."

"But . . . ?" My skeptical look made her laugh.

"My mom has had a booth there every year since the farm got successful. Gracie and I are on duty with her for this one. You can bring them by and visit me, though. I would love that."

"Am I allowed to ask if you're okay with working with your mom? If you don't want to talk about it, say the word."

"Yes, of course you're allowed. This year will be the first time I'll be okay with being there with her." She looked more at ease talking about her mom than I'd ever seen. "She's getting help, Nick. Being around her doesn't feel like pretending or playacting family life anymore, if that makes any sense at all. I mean, it feels like we have an actual shot at being a real family."

My eyebrows shot up. "That's amazing." I was so glad to hear it. Clara deserved to have her mother's genuine affection.

"She acknowledged how badly she treated us when we were growing up and apologized for it. She even offered insight into what was going on in her life and why she was so angry all the time. I mean, it's getting better and better, but it's still—never mind. It's just a bunch of old insecurities I'm dealing with."

"Hey. You can tell me."

"I don't quite know how to be fully at ease around her when I can't completely trust her yet. I constantly question everything." Her voice was fragile; *she* was fragile.

My heart lurched in my chest, but I had to hold myself back instead of holding her like I wanted to. The urge to pull her close so I could try to absorb her pain was achingly familiar. This was the Clara I remembered, and I wanted her back.

I wanted her *mine*.

I wanted all the fucking years we'd wasted gone so I could follow my instincts instead of fighting against them while I waited for her to trust me again.

We used to talk about ourselves and our lives at home all the time. We'd worked out our problems together; she'd been my best friend. The mouthy, defiant Clara was definitely part of her personality and always had been, but it felt like she hid behind it now to protect herself. It made me sad because I could tell it was hard for her to open up like this with me now.

"Is she giving you a hard time?"

"No, she says she understands." She paused, gathering her thoughts. "But it's the opposite of how she's always been, so it feels weird. It almost makes it harder to accept the changes she's making."

"All you can do take it day by day. Kind of what we need to do with each other too, right?"

She pulled back and quirked an eyebrow in my direction. "Are you really this patient?"

"When it comes to you, I am. Well, I'm trying to be. But I have to admit something—I'm exhausted. I can't sleep anymore."

Her worried gaze scanned my face. "What's wrong? I hope you know you can talk to me too, about anything."

"I want you back in my bed. Now that I know what it's like to fall asleep with you, it's all I can think about when I close my eyes. And then I start missing you."

"Nick, I miss you too."

"We'll get there. Count on it."

# CHAPTER 19
# CLARA

*It's supposed to rain tonight. You come to me. - HB*

Confession: I had a recliner in my walk-in closet, and I hid out in there whenever the weather got bad, like right now. I was mostly okay as long as I had a book to distract myself with. I startled easily and each clap of thunder had me jolting in fear, but as long as I stayed in here, surrounded by four walls and zero windows, I'd live through it.

Thunder crashed in the distance and I snuggled further beneath the quilt I'd buried myself under. The lights went out, leaving my Kindle and flameless candles as my only illumination.

Crash after crash had my heart racing until my book was no longer enough to prevent me from freaking out. I set it aside and covered my face with the blanket. I could be brave. It was just a little bit of rain.

*Think of something else. Anything else. Think of Nick.*

The school year was flying by. August to November had poofed away in a blink of an eye, and it was already almost Thanksgiving. I was coming to realize that nothing in the past truly mattered, because all of it had led me to right here. I was falling for Nick even harder than I'd fallen for him the first time.

Seeing him be such a wonderful dad to his children was healing wounds I never even knew I'd had. I'd forgotten what it had been like with my father around. He'd been the buffer between us and our mother, and it had broken me and my sisters when he left.

Years of therapy had tried to tell me that I could heal my own heart and that not every man would turn out like my father and leave me behind. But my experiences throughout the years had told me otherwise, and deep down, I hadn't believed it was possible to find happiness—until now.

Being with Nick this time around was something new.

He was steadily blowing every issue I had out of the water one by one, and I trusted him more as each day went by.

Sasha and Ethan were the luckiest kids in the entire world.

*Could I be that lucky too?*

Loud banging on the French doors of my balcony almost sent my jumpy ass flying to the ceiling and I lost my grip on any bravado I'd been clinging to.

*What the hell?*

Would a serial killer knock?

What about that big-ass bug? Was it back for revenge?

"Clara! Open up. I tried ringing your bell and texting you. It's Nick!"

*It seems like maybe I* could *be that lucky. Holy crap.*

Tossing my blanket to the side, I made it to the door and threw it open. "You're all wet. What are you doing up here?"

"I knew you'd be scared. Were you in the closet?" His lips turned up in a grin. But not the making-fun-of-me kind; this grin was the Clara-is-cute kind. The type of grin that would lead to something if I wasn't having a thunderstorm-induced, on-the-verge-of-a-panic-attack episode.

"*Pfft.* No," I scoffed, letting out a relieved sigh when the lights came back on.

He looked past me, his eyebrows raised when he spotted my recliner and blankets in the closet. "Hmm, right, okay. So we're pretending that adorable little closet hidey-hole doesn't exist?"

"I don't know what you're talking about. It's perfectly normal to keep a chair in the closet. I sit there when I put on my shoes."

"Of course, how silly of me. I'll have to get a chair for my closet. The edge of the bed is such a poor choice when it comes to putting on shoes," he teased. He stepped closer and began to rub his hands up and down my arms. "So, I dropped the kids off at Morgan's and I thought you might be nervous over here all alone. I decided to stop by and check on you."

"So you climbed up to my balcony in the pouring rain just to check on me?" That was the takeaway. Everything else he'd said flew by the wayside, even the teasing. My heart—and my lady bits—swooned.

He shrugged at this like it was no big deal. "Well, yeah."

"Gotcha." This man had no idea. I looked up at him from hooded eyelids and purred, "Take your clothes off and get in my bed. We're having sex right now."

He laughed, but it didn't stop him from throwing his jacket across the room and yanking his shirt over his head. "I have zero problems with that. We can head to my place after for dinner if you want. I was going to suggest it before, but you've got me all worked up now and I'm not hungry anymore."

I pressed myself against his body and wrapped my arms around his neck. "No need. We can stay here. I have leftover spaghetti so dinner is covered. Everett made it, not me," I clarified. "You'll love it."

His hand slipped between my legs, curving around as he pulled me close. "You know what I love to eat more?"

I inhaled a sharp breath. "Oh god. Some things never change, do they?"

He shook his head and slipped his other hand under the front of my silk nightgown to enter me with a finger. "Once I got a taste of you again . . ."

"Far be it for me to stop you from taking your fill."

He drew his hand out, sucking his finger into his mouth with a dirty grin. "I'll never let you get away. You know that don't you? You have me addicted all over again."

All I could do was nod as he grabbed my hips, digging his fingers into my ass as he walked me toward my bed.

Thunder crashed and I jumped out of his arms with a squeal. "Oh my god!"

He paused, searching my face. "Maybe now isn't the time for this."

"No, no, no. Let's get that straight right now. It's always the time to go down on me."

Another jolt of thunder struck with a huge boom—this time it was closer— and I hurled myself back into his arms and bumped my forehead against his chin.

"It's okay, I got you, baby, shh."

"I'm so sorry!" I pulled away to kiss his chin, then pepper little kisses to his cheeks and lips. "Did I hurt you? On second thought, maybe you have a point about now not being the time. I don't want to injure this gorgeous face any further, especially with my vagina. I'd feel so guilty if I broke your jaw or banged you up." I looked at him with wide eyes. "Seriously, what would you tell the kids?"

"New plan," he declared with a grin. "It's blanket-fort and living-room-picnic time. Let's go downstairs, throw on a movie, and heat up that spaghetti."

"Like a grown-up slumber party?"

"Sure," he answered, the laughter in his tone making me smile. "If that's what you want to call it."

"How fun! My god, I love you," I blurted. My cheeks heated. I was on fire, and I figured it likely I'd spontaneously combust and drop dead.

If I was honest with myself, I'd admit it was the truth. But letting it out unplanned like I had was not only mortifying but made me acutely aware that I'd said it first—again. I'd said it first when we were together back in high school, too. "Oh my god. I—"

"Clara, I love you too." His voice was low, a sexy velvet murmur. I watched, mesmerized, as his eyes darkened with emotion.

"Just like that?" I breathed.

"Just like that," he confirmed, as if it hadn't taken fifteen-ish years and us moving mountains of hurt to the side to get here.

"Okay," I whispered. "So we're in love again."

He placed his palm in the center of my chest and mine on his. "The love has always been right here, Clara. It just took a minute for us to grow up and make it ours again."

"It makes so much sense when you say it like that. We didn't know what we had. How could we? But now we know."

"Now we know, and we'll never let it get away again. Damn, Clara. Sasha and Ethan are going to love you so much. I can't wait to tell them."

My heart felt full to bursting. "I'll love them too, like they were my own children. I swear I will."

"I know you will, baby. Let's plan a dinner next week to tell them about us."

"How about next weekend, after the Fall Festival?"

"That sounds perfect to me. It's Morgan's weekend. You and I can have dinner together after the festival and discuss how much to tell them about us. But I already know they're going to love this. They talk about you all the time."

"My heart is about to crack wide open. I don't know if I can take this."

He stepped close and wrapped me in his arms. I could feel his heart thudding against mine and all of a sudden, I didn't care about the storm outside; all I could think about was him.

Thunder struck in the distance, hard enough to knock the power out again, and I flinched. Okay, so maybe I cared a little bit, but that didn't mean I didn't need to immediately show him with my body exactly how I felt about him.

The power flickered back on, and I let out a relieved sigh. "So, thunder-storms are still a no for me—"

"Obviously." His eyebrows raised as his eyes lit up with laughter.

"You'll have to be on top."

His eyebrows shot to his hairline as he stifled a laugh. "I see. We're doing this. You sure?"

My anxiety about the storm combined with the emotional overload of the moment had me rambling. "No oral." I shook my head. "There are just too many ways I could hurt you. Flinching and jumping are a legit concern. And the weather is being way too unpredictable tonight."

"Your reasoning is sound." He nodded once as his eyes twinkled into mine. "Neither one of us needs an unexplainable injury."

"We need a game plan. This is your area of expertise, isn't it, Coach Easton?"

"It is, normally." His voice dropped low. "But the thought of being inside you again has taken over my entire brain and I can't think right now."

My breath caught in my throat. "Oh really?"

He nudged me backward until I had no choice but to fall on my bed. "Yes really." He put a knee to the bed and slipped a hand beneath my neck. I gasped as he gently pressed his thumb to the base of my throat. "Don't move." His growly whisper disappeared into my mouth as he kissed me hard. "If you're good, I'll let you ride me on that recliner in the closet. You won't be thinking about the weather if I keep you occupied."

"'Kay . . ." I held as still as possible as he stood, dragging his hand down the center of my body from my neck to the hem of my nightgown. He was already shirtless and the sight of his rippling abs, that broad wall of a chest, and his wide shoulders standing above me like that almost blew my mind.

"Your choice of pajamas is appreciated by the way," he murmured. Pale pink silk slid up my legs, tickling my skin along with the tips of his fingers. "You're gorgeous."

Thunder crashed in the distance and my back arched off the bed. "Oh god . . ."

"Shh, I got you. No more playing around, come on." He pulled me to my feet and guided me to the closet, walking us backward until he dropped into my recliner and pulled me to straddle his lap, my knees to the seat. "Shit, do you have any condoms?" He squeezed my ass in his big palms and took a nip at my neck. I shivered and lost my train of thought.

"Huh?"

"Condoms, baby. Got some?"

"Yes, I do." I scurried to my feet. "Take your pants off, I'll be right back."

I came back, strip of condoms in hand, to find him naked, manspreading in my chair like he owned the damn thing. My jaw dropped a little bit as I tried to decide where to begin. I mean, he'd found a towel to sit on; if I hadn't loved him before, I sure as heck did now. It was my favorite chair.

But forget about the freaking chair.

I hadn't had a chance yet to get a good, naked look at him. And damn.

*Damn.*

Most of our time together in the past—heck, the present, too—had been hurried, furtive, frantic . . .

Sneaking around lately had been heady, tortuous fun, but it hadn't given me the chance to fully appreciate all that was Nicholas Andrew Easton. And *damn*, he was fine.

His skin was a deep golden tan, probably from playing shirtless football outside with his friends so often.

His chest was broad, tapering down to a set of six-pack abs that had me biting my lip and itching to get my hands on him. I knew from all the touching and snuggling we'd done, our pool time, and observing how his Green Valley High polo fit him every Friday he was toned and strong, but seeing him on full display right here for my eyes only was an entirely different experience.

"You're a beautiful man," I stated.

"Thank you. You're more beautiful than anything I've ever seen."

"Nick . . . ," I breathed.

"Get over here, baby." He fisted his hard cock, holding it steady as his eyes burned into mine. "Don't make me wait anymore. I feel like I've spent my life waiting for you, wanting you, missing you. I need you now, Clara."

Warmth surged through me and pooled between my legs as I tossed him the strip of condoms and slid out of my nightgown.

"Do we need these?" He waved the condoms in the air. "I get a physical every year, so no worries there. I'm okay with it if you are."

"Same. I'm good, and I'm on the pill." I slipped out of my panties, kicking them off as I strode toward him. Bending at the waist, I trailed my hands up and over the smattering of dark hair covering his chest, resting them on his shoulders as I put one knee on the chair, then the other.

My legs were already shaking. I was empty and aching and desperate for him.

The heat in his gaze burned bright as I lowered myself, sinking down inch by inch until I was stretched full of him.

His jaw clenched tight as he sank his teeth into his lower lip to stifle a groan.

With heavy-lidded eyes, he watched me move over him like I might disappear, like I was part of a dream he was deep in the middle of, like he couldn't get enough. Maybe he was as afraid of losing me as I was of losing him.

His hands slid from my hips to rest on my ribs with his thumbs idly stroking my nipples. He was lazy and languid as he let me take control and I loved it. "Kiss me, baby."

I hissed out a breath and did as he asked, riding him slow and taking him deep as his tongue swept against mine, swirling in a slow circle before he sucked my lower lip into his mouth with a growly moan.

He was beautiful like this, with his neck arched back and that sharp jawline on full display.

"Faster, Clara. Go harder, make us both come." He bucked his hips for emphasis, making me squeal in delight as he surged up into me. One hand trailed down to find my clit while the other pinched and pulled at my nipple. "You feel so good. Don't stop. My god, baby, please don't stop."

I panted as I dropped forward to kiss his mouth. "Hold on." The smoldering flame in his eyes lit me on fire too, blazing a path that led straight between my legs. He put his hands on the arms of the chair, bracing himself so I could ride him hard, and I grinned. "That's right, Nick. Don't let go of that chair."

I slid a hand between my legs, spreading myself wide as I bounced up and down, grinding myself against him with a twisty little swivel of my hips each time I bottomed out.

"Damn, look at you. Look at us." His dark eyes roamed over me as I took him. "You're so fucking beautiful like this, so wet, so fucking hot."

It was empowering, the way he watched me, the way he was coming apart beneath me. He was mine and I was his and we were going over the edge together.

His body was strung tight with the need to release. His hands on the chair had moved to my hips, digging into my flesh as he encouraged me to go harder, to move faster. "Please, baby, please . . ." His deep groan sent another wave of hot pleasure through me as I arched back and squeezed him tight. The fluttering waves of my orgasm sent me flying as he thrust up and pulled me down hard. He came along with me, letting out a groan as he released.

"My god, Nick," I gasped as we broke apart together. I fell forward to lie on his chest, struggling to catch my breath and come back down to earth. "I want to fall asleep like this, right here in my closet, straddling your lap, filled full of you. But the dual threats of a UTI and my lower back going out could make that a problem in the morning."

He stood, lifting me as he got to his feet, his hands beneath my ass, and carried me into the bedroom. "I can't sleep sitting up either."

He put a knee to the bed and let me fall backward. I scrambled under the covers and patted the bed for him to join me.

"This is amazing." I took stock of my body and how deliciously languid I felt. "I never consented to all these feelings," I joked. "I don't know how to feel this good. My legs are still shaking."

"But will you consent to me waking you up with my mouth between these pretty thighs of yours in the middle of the night?"

"Only if you consent to me grabbing your hair, clamping your head between my legs, and grinding against your face like a maniac." I grinned as his smile got lazy. "Sleep Clara has vivid dreams on occasion," I explained. "You'd be making one of them come true."

"I consent to all of that. Please do it."

I held up a finger. "Okay, but—"

"If you close your legs or push me away, that means no."

"Good man. You get it. I have to ask you something. It's been on my mind since we started sleeping together again."

"Ask me anything. Get over here." He pulled me into his arms and wrapped me tight.

"How were you always so, um, *good* at it?" I looked up, my chin on his chest so I could see his face.

"At what?" he asked, the picture of innocence.

I closed my eyes. "You're gonna make me say it?"

"Of course." He smirked. "My ego needs stroking just like any other man's."

"*Ugh!* Fine. Every time we were together, you made me come. Even the first time. How?"

His grin spread slowly across his face. "Ahh, yes. If I recall correctly, you thought you died the first time I got you off. That I'd murdered you with a finger bang." His eyes were lazy on mine, seductive, sexy as hell, and totally smug. He'd earned the right to be smug, so I didn't protest.

"Yeah, not gonna lie, I was fairly certain you'd sent me straight up to heaven. It wasn't until later on that I, uh . . ."

"Missed me and my special gifts?" He stuck his tongue out, waggling it obscenely. "Realized that I had ruined you for all others with my constant need to eat you out?"

"You were kind of obsessed with it."

"I was kind of obsessed with *you*." He slid a hand between my legs, stroking me softly, intimately. "This pretty pussy of yours was just a sweet bonus."

I swatted him on the arm with a laugh and threw a leg over his hip to give him better access at the same time. "Come on, be serious. How did you start off knowing where everything was and what to do with it? God, Nick." I gasped as a shudder shot through me.

I bit my lip as he began to swirl his fingers around my clit in earnest.

"Come for me again, then I'll tell you whatever you want to know."

"'Kay . . ."

"Remember when I got you off for the first time, just like this? In the front seat of my truck, with that little jean skirt pulled up to your waist, panties pushed to the side, and those perfect tits of yours out, all red and rosy from my mouth. You bit your lip just like you're doing right now. Do you remember that, baby?"

"Yes, I remember." I was panting so hard I could barely get the words out. "Don't stop, please, Nick."

"You're so fucking sexy." This Nick was a little bit arrogant; he knew he was going to make me explode all over his hand and he loved it. It was as maddening as it was hot. "I can feel you getting tight around my fingers. Are you gonna come for me like a good girl, just like you did in my truck all those years ago?"

"Mm-hmm." My hips writhed against him in time with his pumping fingers. "You're killing me."

"You fucking love it, don't you?" he growled. "You're my girl again, aren't you, baby? Mine to take care of. It's my job to make you feel good, isn't it?"

"Oh god . . .."

"Say it. Tell me you're mine and I'll let you come."

"I'm yours."

He withdrew his hand and swatted it against my ass. I gasped. "That's not what I wanted to hear."

"I'm your girl. I'm your girl, Nick. Please . . ." He drove into me with two fingers while pressing his thumb hard against me.

I let go with a loud, shuddering moan. "What happened to you? You used to be so sweet," I gasped.

Hot eyes met mine as a wicked grin slid across his mouth. "I just made you come—and pretty spectacularly, I might add. That seems pretty sweet to me."

"It is," I conceded. "I'll admit it—I like this new Nick."

He laughed in response and tucked me into his side again. "Ask me anything now. I'm feeling pretty fucking relaxed."

"So, how were you so good at it? I mean, our first time together didn't even hurt, not one bit."

"You know I was an early reader?" I nodded again his chest, grinning at the unexpected beginning of his explanation. "My dad always used to say if you can read, you can figure out anything you're interested in. Information is everywhere."

"Oh my word, Nick." I stifled a giggle at the direction this was going in.

"After we talked about taking things to the next level, I did my research. I wanted to make you feel good and I really didn't want to hurt you. I'd heard some things from guys on the team—crying, blood, pain, regrets—and I didn't want any of that. I couldn't stand the thought of hurting you, and I knew I'd want to do it again." His lips tipped up at the corner. "And I also knew I was bigger than average."

"You are an awesome nerd with a huge, respectful dick, and I love it."

Slowly, seductively, his gaze slid up and over my body sprawled against his as he continued, "So yeah, I went to the library, like any horny nerd would do."

He winked and it was all I could do not to jump him again and fuck his brains out. "I love this."

"Side note, you should have seen the look on Bethany Winston's face when she saw the stack of books I brought up to the counter the week before our first time: *The Joy of Sex, The Kama Sutra, Gray's Anatomy,* and a few more that I can't remember the titles of."

"Oh my god, you're such a good man. Watching porn didn't even cross your mind? I love that."

"I wish I didn't have to shatter that illusion." He chuckled. "Porn was interesting and quite useful sometimes—especially for the moments when I couldn't be with you." He mimed jacking off with a sheepish grin. "What can I say? I was a teenager."

"Of course. Whatever was I thinking?"

"But seriously, it left out some of the best parts, like the stuff we'd already done—all the kissing and touching, how we used to just hold each other in the back of my truck and look at the stars—"

"*Look at the stars.* Is that what you call what we did back there? Best euphemism ever. A lot of fooling around back there is what we did. I have no memories of stars in the sky but plenty when it comes to you and the stars you made me see."

"Right?" He squeezed me tight and kissed my temple. "But seriously, for me? Before all the fooling around—and even sometimes during it—what I loved the most was the simple feeling of having my hands on your skin and how happy I felt when you were close to me." His hands ran slowly up and down my back as he spoke, sending goosebumps and tingles all along my spine.

"I loved it too."

"It was essential, anticipatory, and thrilling to be able to put just a fingertip on you and watch you shiver. Porn didn't get into any of that stuff, at least not the kind I found online. But once I swiped a few of my mother's romance novels, I knew I'd struck gold."

"Romance novels, huh? I love it. I love *you*. You made everything special and wonderful and . . . your ex-wife is your ex because why? She must be crazy."

"Ahh, she was pissed that I never gave in to my mother's demands. Which involved country clubs, smarmy ass-kissing, and taking a job with my stepfather. A teacher's salary was not what she'd anticipated when she spotted me on campus and found out who I was related to."

"Oh, Nick. I'm so sorry—"

"I was drunk a lot back then, trying to forget about you. I was easy pickings for someone like her. She's not all bad—she's a great mom and, for the most part, we get along now. But she wasn't you, and I was never really happy being married to her."

"Well, I have plenty of my own money, I don't need yours. All I'm after is your body, your sweet personality, and your genius brain. Oh, and your massive dick and astounding oral skills. I want those too."

He burst out laughing. "Well, it's all yours. I'm yours."

"And I'm yours."

"Speaking of oral skills . . ." He slid a hand up my thigh with a wicked grin. "How about a little taste before we go downstairs? I think the thunderstorm is over."

# CHAPTER 20
# CLARA

*You're the best friend I've ever had, Clara. I never want to lose you. - Nick*

Fall in Green Valley was always beautiful and to celebrate the bounty there was an entire festival for it every year. It had started out as a tiny festival set up at the edge of town and had grown over the years to include something for everyone to enjoy. There were booths run by local business, carnival rides and games, food of every kind imaginable, and a charity dunk tank run by the Green Valley High PTA—those ladies had big plans, or so I'd heard. Pindich was the number one target, followed by everyone's favorite substitute teacher—not me, of course. All the ladies were dying to see Court in a wet T-shirt. They were in the process of guilting him into the tank right now. Between wet-teacher beefcake and the possibility of a Pin Dick drowning, the PTA was going to raise a bunch of money for new uniforms or equipment or whatever—honestly, I didn't care that much. I was only subbing at the high school for Gracie's sake.

Speaking of . . . Gracie and I would be working with our mother at the Lavender Hill booth and this year, for the first time ever, I didn't dread it.

Like she'd done the past few years, Momma had recreated the Lavender Hill farm stand right here at the festival. It was a mini stable, complete with big bushels of lavender—both fresh and dried—set in the front, and along the counter and displayed on a shelf behind us were all the things she made up at the farm: herbs, jams, tea, sachets, honey from her bees, to name a few. If it could be labeled as *farm fresh* and crafty, she made it and sold it. She was going to make a fortune here today. This year she'd even added a QR code for her website so she could take online orders.

"This is something else," I remarked as I took it all in.

"The QR code was my idea," Gracie informed me as she sorted lavender wands and crowns into neat piles.

"She's a little entrepreneur, isn't she?" Momma beamed with pride. She'd come so far since she started seeing her therapist. It was only a couple years ago she'd grounded Gracie for taking on jobs outside of the farm. "She has you to thank for that, doesn't she?"

"Uh, yeah. I guess so," I muttered. I let my eyes drift across the festival; I was not in the best head space today. The idea of being around this many people was daunting. I squinted, trying to make out someone in the distance. Was that Malcolm?

"That's the dick from your old office, isn't it?" Gracie hissed in my ear. "What the hell is he doing here?"

I nodded as I zeroed in on him buying a bunch of cotton candy at a booth across the way from ours.

Momma was oblivious, sorting through tea bags with her back turned. "Well, I'm proud of you too, Clara. I'm sorry I didn't tell you before. I'm sorry for a lot—"

"It's okay," I said as I refocused on her. "You don't have to keep saying you're sorry."

She turned. "If you want me to stop, I will." Her smile was soft. "But when things come up that remind me of my mistakes it's hard not to."

Our eyes met. "I think I understand. On second thought, it might be a good thing. As long as it makes you feel better too."

I was still shaken by the Malcolm sighting, but I remembered his mother lived in Green Valley somewhere and relaxed a bit. Why would he be here for me?

"Don't worry about me, sugar. How are you? You look tired."

"I've been going through some things—"

"She just spotted her old co-worker who sexually harassed her," Gracie told her. I gave her a hard glare that told her exactly how I felt about her divulging this information to our mother. "What? Maybe she can find him and destroy him mentally or something."

"Is he giving you trouble? You can always come stay at the farm with me and my shotgun." Threatening to shoot a fool was always her default reaction. It made me laugh. It also kind of made me wonder if she'd ever done it; her temper used to be horrible.

I waved a hand in dismissal. "No, it's fine. I just spotted him near the cotton candy is all. He has family in the area, I'm not worried about him. He didn't see me."

"Oh! Maybe I should have gone to her about Marianne and the bully bitch trio," Gracie joked. "Problem solved on first day of school. *Boom!*"

"Marianne?" She turned from the counter to face Gracie. "Marianne Tanner?"

"That's the one," Gracie confirmed. Her eyes went wide. "Wait, don't shoot her. Be reasonable. How advanced are you in your therapy? Like, my anger management class has me pretty Zen about all this—most of the time, anyway."

"I won't shoot her. But I can't guarantee a reasonable reaction yet," she teased. "I may need more therapy for that. Listen, I'll talk to her mother next time she comes to the farm to get her sleepy tea and lavender pillow spray. Marianne won't bother you anymore if I threaten to cut her mother off. She likes her sleep. She's forever droning on and on about it whenever we stop to have a chat. And there's no need to mention the fact that she's been seen swapping spit with a man who is decidedly *not* her husband. One of those little tidbits ought to be enough for her to get her daughter under control. I'll start with the first and if Marianne is still bothering you, I'll move to the second. I guess I have learned something from therapy," she joked. "The old me would have gone scorched earth."

"Hell yeah!" Gracie pointed in the distance. "Now do Mr. Neal. He's over there getting a funnel cake, the stupid, cranky, old grouch."

My mom stopped and turned. "Do you mean Geoffrey Neal?"

"Uh, yeah . . ." Gracie and I exchanged a look.

"Do you know him?" I asked, dying of curiosity given we didn't know much about our mother's past. "How? Tell us?"

"I dumped him during my senior year of high school to date your father," she informed us. "He didn't take it very well. It's debatable who would have been the better choice, isn't it?" She rolled her eyes. "Is he giving you trouble?"

"Only since forever, and I guess now we know why," I answered. "It started in high school and again when I moved into my house down the street from him. He's meaner than a damn snake. He used to call us hillbilly trash.

He slut-shamed Sadie out of the library for getting pregnant by her dumbass ex, for eff's sake."

"He's still a total asshole," Gracie confirmed. "Everyone hates him. I had to start stealing books instead of checking them out because he wouldn't stop asking me if I could actually read."

"Gracie!" I chided. "I'll buy you all the books you want. Don't steal."

"No need." She rolled her eyes at me. "I bring them back when I'm done. I just don't let him scan them into the system. I don't need to put up with his shit, and I like the idea of him looking around for missing books and wondering where they went."

"Well, that's okay then." I hugged her into my side. "I can respect that."

Momma interrupted, smiling at the two of us. "You've been working at the school, Clara. Is he still bothering you?"

I looked at her with my eyebrows raised and nodded. "Yeah, but I feel a bit better about it now that I know that you broke his tiny, shriveled little heart," I teased.

Her mouth tilted up at the corners, though it was not quite a smile. It was actually a little scary. "I'll take care of him too."

"I like this new you." I beamed at her. "It's like you're using your powers for good now."

"Well, I have a lot to make up for with y'all. I should have been protecting you all these years, and I'm glad I have the chance to do it now. And as for Geoffrey, it looks like he's getting into the dunk tank. I always did have good aim . . ." She grabbed a few bucks from the lock box and stomped off to dunk our common enemy.

"This new mom is awesome." Gracie grinned at me. "I'm still staying with Willa and Everett though. I don't—I don't even want to say it out loud."

"It's hard to trust the changes in her and that's okay," I deduced. "Dr. Simon agrees. Do not feel bad about it. Momma wouldn't even want you to feel bad, okay?"

"You're right, she wouldn't. She even said so herself. You should listen to Dr. Simon more, by the way," she added under her breath.

"What are you talking about?"

"You're getting hit with a lot of shit right now and you're gonna get buried under it if you don't start asking for help. You can't do everything on your own and you have to talk about your problems."

I gaped at her. "What the hell, Gracie? How—?"

"Why are y'all so surprised when I figure you out?" she retorted. "Hello? You've been paying for my therapy since I was ten, Clara. It stands to reason I'd be better at sorting shit out than you are. I've had more practice, and arguably, I'm less fucked up than you, Willa, and Sadie. Momma has been getting her shit together and I'm still a kid. The rest of y'all grew up like that and spent a lot of your adult years dealing with it too." My eyes must have glazed over a little because she waved her hand in my face. "Hello?"

I shook my head to clear it. "Ouch. I mean it makes sense, but still—freaking ouch."

"You just got dumped by that idiot Chris, and he hurt your feelings no matter how much you say he didn't. Sadie and the boys moved out, and Mr. Easton moved in next door—*Hello past? It's me, Clara. Don't punch me in the face too hard,*" she sing-songed. "Malcolm, the perverted co-worker from hell, is here in town and most likely he'll end up being a dick to you at some point, because dickheads gonna dick, am I right? What else is going on?" She gave me a once-over. "Are you on your period? Ha! You got sick awhile back, didn't you? Your body is betraying you and you're on track for a major stress-related freak-out."

"Yeah, and? I've been taking care of myself for years on my own. I'm fine. Or at least I will be fine. This too shall pass, and all that crap. Right? And how do you know about Nick and me?"

"Oh my god! Please for once in my life give me some credit. Don't you know better by now than to question how I know stuff? I'm practically omniscient, but even if I wasn't, the two of you could not be more obvious. You two are always casting longing gazes into each other's sappy faces and a person would have to be a moron not to see all the sexual tension spilling out all over the school and throughout the neighborhood. Give me a damn break, Clara."

"Okay, okay. Fine, you got me. I'm a mess, I need at least ten naps, and I've been neglecting my yard, which sucks because that's my main stress reliever. Maybe you can come over and help me weed." I shot her at toothy grin and a mock salute. "I bow down to your observational skills, okay?"

She laughed. "I'm not talking about that kind of help, but I'll help you weed if you want me too. Bet I can get you to spill your guts too."

My text notification pinged in my pocket. "It's Leonard. Mari is sick in her car, and he wants me to check on her while he deals with the band."

She rolled her eyes. "Talk about another stressed-out head case . . . ," she muttered.

"Nice, Gracie. I'm going to see if she's okay. The band is about to start playing soon and he's worried about her. You got the booth?"

"Yeah, I got the booth. Bring me back some deep-fried whatevers and a huge lemonade. I'm not picky and I'm ready to get food wasted. I want to spend the rest of the day riding a sugar high and relaxing with my thoughts."

"You got it." I waved goodbye and headed for the parking lot.

I passed the dunk tank and stopped to watch as my mother proceeded to dunk Mr. Neal while simultaneously cussing him out and lecturing him about letting bygones be bygones. I dropped a kiss to her cheek on my way to check on Mari.

"Miss Clara!" I spun to find Sasha waving at me. She was with Morgan, Ethan, Nick, *and Malcolm.*

I froze and tried not to gape at them like a fish stuck in a tank. Trapped inside the glass and at the mercy of everyone outside of it.

*Shit.*

*What the hell was going on?*

Malcolm's steely eyes narrowed on me as I greeted Sasha while at the same time trying not to make it obvious how horrified I was to see him here with them.

"This is Clara, my neighbor. She's also a substitute teacher at the school," Nick introduced me to a trying-to-send-me-messages-with-his-eyes Malcolm.

Nick was quite impersonal with the introduction, and it stung more than I cared to admit.

I knew he was dropping them off with Morgan today, but I didn't know he'd planned on staying here to hang out with them.

"Hey there, Clara." Morgan took my hand as she looked me up and down. "I'm waiting for your RSVP. Still coming to the wedding with Nick?"

"She is," he answered for me.

"This is Malcolm, Morgan's fiancé." Nick gestured to Malcolm and my brain short-circuited as I took his hand to shake it. *Her fiancé?*

From now on I'd have to start communicating from the afterlife, because I think I just died.

"Nice to meet you," I muttered. "Kids, I'd love to stay and chat with you, maybe go on a ride or something, but I'm in a rush. I have to go check on a sick friend."

*Thank you, Mari. I'm sorry you're sick, but you've just become the perfect excuse to get the hell out of here.*

We'd planned to tell the kids about us at some point after the festival, but Nick didn't have to be so distant. He hadn't even met my eyes, and his smile was barely there. He could at least pretend to be my friend in public, right? I rubbed a circle over my chest and took a step back. I had to get out of here; nothing good was about to happen, I could tell.

I turned tail and left, practically running to the parking lot to find Mari. It was hard not to look over my shoulder like a paranoid freak to make sure that asshole Malcolm wasn't following me.

I wanted to get in my car and leave but I had to work the booth with Momma and Gracie. *Damn it.*

I found Mari in her car, asleep. I knocked on the window and she startled awake; she waved and started mumbling. Poor Mari looked terrible but alive. I snapped a pic and sent it to Leonard, then made my way back to the booth, stealth mode, stopping at all the fried treat stands on the way.

By the time I'd made it back to Gracie, I'd stress eaten half of what I'd bought and was about to recreate my stomach-flu-induced, technicolor yawn from the other day all over the pavement.

"Here you go. Whatever you do, do not eat as much as I did on the way back here."

"Uh, okay? I'll pace myself. You look like you are about to lose your shit —or toss your cookies." Gracie snickered. "What happened? Too much food, or did you see an enemy? Between the two of us, we have so many here. How scandalous and exciting are we?"

"Where's Momma?" All that talk about not shooting anyone would go right out the window when she found out how freaked out I was over Malcolm.

"She saw Marianne and her mother over by the tilt-a-whirl. She's busy doling out pieces of her mind over there."

"Are you okay with that?"

"I don't even care anymore. As long as Marianne leaves me alone, I'm fine. It's also kind of nice to have my actual mother handling a problem for me. What a novel idea, right?"

I reached across the counter and hugged her. "I'm so sorry, Gracie. But also, it's good she's helping now. I wish I knew the right thing to say about this." With a family as screwed up as ours, triggers were everywhere. I'm glad I was here for this one.

"You say plenty of the right things and you always have. I'm sorry I didn't go to her in the beginning. You're a substitute teacher because of me, for eff's sake. Like, what the hell?" She huffed a laugh.

"Hey. No apologies. I'm spending a lot of time with you every day because you came to me, and I love it. Please look at it that way."

"I have the best big sisters in the entire world. Give me a funnel cake before I start crying like an idiot." She snatched one of the bags from my hand

and dug around inside. "I'm already missing Weston today. We came to this stupid festival together last year."

"I'm so sorry about Weston, sweetheart. It's okay to cry sometimes, Gracie." I bumped her shoulder conspiratorially. "Let it out. Crying Hill sister sightings are not unusual around Green Valley, no one will blink an eye."

She wiped her eyes, laughed, and took a bite of her treat. "You got that right." She took a deep breath. "I think I'm okay now. Saying it out loud made me feel better. Funny how that works, isn't it?" she mused with her eyebrows up.

"Ugh, fine, you're right. I have news, too—the unbelievable, horrifying kind. Malcolm is engaged to Nick's ex. How do you like them apples? I can't even process this right now."

"No," she gasped. "What are you going to do?"

"I have no idea. Crawl under a rock? Check myself into a hospital somewhere in Timbuktu for mental exhaustion? Take up permanent residence in my closet?" I threw my arms in the air in exasperation. "What the hell, Gracie? I'm freaking out."

"I know. Go get some popcorn and tell Momma all about it. She's in a fixin' kind of mood today. I say let her take care of him."

I burst into hysterical laughter. "I almost want to. But no, what I really want to do is go home and think. I don't want to see him."

"Go home, I've got this. Don't worry about me. I'll be right here with my fried Snickers and funnel cakes, living my best life." She stabbed a straw into her lemonade and took a huge sip. "I'm fine now. See?"

"Are you sure?"

"Totally. Momma is here and we've been talking, I'm fine. But don't go home and be alone because that's dumb. Go see Molly at the inn or find Sadie or Willa. You'll just wear a track in your floor pacing and ranting if you're by yourself."

She waved me off as a few customers approached.

"Thank you! I'm leaving."

"Take a nap later, it'll help! And maybe some Tums!" she hollered as I ran off.

I found Malcolm at my car waiting for me because, *of course.* "I assumed you'd be leaving soon," he said. "You looked shocked when we were introduced."

"What do you want Malcolm?" I sucked it up and gave him my best don't-fuck-with-me smile—the one with a lot of teeth that said I'd be more than happy to show him all the moves I learned in self-defense class. Or maybe I should just break his fucking nose again and call it a day.

"It was unexpected, running into you here like this, Miss Hill. A bit out of our usual context, wasn't it?"

"Yes, what an unpleasant surprise."

"Of course you will not say one word."

"One word? About . . . ?"

He ground his teeth together and looked away with a frustrated huff. "About *nothing*, obviously. That's the entire point."

"Ohhh, I get it. You mean that time when you *didn't* grab me and force me into your office to grind your tiny little hard-on into my stomach while you tried to convince me that getting on my knees and blowing you was the only way I'd ever make partner? You mean all that *nothing*? Or are you talking about the time when I *didn't* knee you in the crotch and break your nose? It's a bit crooked now, isn't it, you dirty little pig?"

"You know better than to mention any of that to anyone, don't you, Miss Hill?" His smug smile infuriated me. "Isn't that why you haven't escalated your complaints against me? Secrets between colleagues are better off kept under wraps, don't you think? Especially when one of the colleagues has secrets of her own."

I was so over this guy and all his crap. "Are you attempting to threaten me with something? A little bit of friendly blackmail, perhaps? Spit it out, Malcolm. I'm not interested in playing anymore of your pathetic games. Does your daddy know what you get up to at his law firm?"

"I would never *threaten* you, *Lavender Lane*," he sneered. "I'm an attorney, I know better than to waste my time making idle threats. I always have proof."

I was at a loss for words, but my face must have given me away. This went beyond shocked; I was mortified, horrified, and also tempted to get into my car and run his ass over—problem solved. He couldn't tell anyone anything if he was dead. Good lord, was I turning into my mother? *Argh!*

*How did he know?*

"To answer your unspoken question, private detectives can be expensive but quite worth it, don't you think?"

I didn't answer; I was still too stunned to say a word.

"I see I've made my point, so I'll go. I'm leaving. I told Morgan I had a headache, but I have work to do at the office anyway. This dies here, between the two of us. Keep your mouth shut and I will too."

He was a creep.

He was a sexual harasser.

And he would become Sasha's stepfather if I didn't say something. The very thought of him being anywhere near her made me sick to my stomach.

Damn him.

And damn Nick, too. At the very least, I deserved an introduction as a friend. Maybe I'd reconsider having dinner with him tonight. In this mood, it would do more harm than good to be with him.

# CHAPTER 21
# NICK



I was running behind schedule. Instead of dropping off the kids with Morgan in the parking lot, I'd had to drag them all around that damn festival trying to find her, and I had the feeling I'd somehow pissed Clara off when I'd introduced her to Morgan's douchey fiancé.

Making small talk with Morgan was never my idea of a good time, and adding in her fiancé? No thank you. It had wrecked my mood.

To be fair, I had no reason to dislike Malcolm; he just gave me a dirtbag vibe. But bad vibes weren't enough to act like a dick to him, and the kids had no complaints, so I always kept things cool and cordial whenever I was around him which, luckily, was not often.

I pulled my phone from my pocket and sent Clara a text to apologize for acting like a grouchy ass at the festival.

After leaving the kids with Morgan, I'd stopped at the Piggly Wiggly for wine and dinner ingredients. How the place was that busy when half the town was at the festival was beyond me.

I was late for my football game, still had to get the steaks in the marinade, and now someone was banging on my damn door.

My brother's voice rang out. "Hey, Nick. I know you're in there. It's Sam, open up!"

I stalked to the front door determined to get rid of him. I was in no mood for whatever family bullshit he was most likely coming to harangue me with. I'd done my familial duties for the day in dropping off the kids with Morgan, but now I was running late. I was supposed to be at the Smoky Mountain Inn in a few minutes for football and I needed it. I was tense, and a good game always helped me unwind—that, or a long nap. Honestly, I was torn between the two.

Clara and I were having dinner together tonight, and I was exhausted. I wanted to play some ball, come home and shower, have dinner with Clara, then spend the rest of the night buried inside of her—in that order. Sam and his bullshit did not fit into my plans for the day.

I threw open the door. "I don't have time for this—"

He looked like shit. Messy, unkempt. Not at all like the polished, impeccable man he'd become after taking the job with our stepfather.

"We have to talk." He shoved around me and headed for the kitchen. "I need a drink—" He spotted the grocery bags, the bottle of wine on the counter, the candles and cloth napkins piled on the stacked plates ready to be set on the table. "Am I interrupting something? Are you getting ready for a date?"

"I think that's obvious," I ground out.

"You're seeing someone? Is she here? Mom is going to lose her shit. She's obsessed with the idea of you remarrying Morgan. She won't listen to reason."

"That's not my problem, Sam. What do you want?"

"I was supposed to come here and drag you to the Bandit Lake house to make nice with the family, but I'm here to apologize to you."

"For what? I don't have time for—"

"For a lot of things, Nick. So many things. Ivy and I are divorcing. She took the kids to her parents' place to stay and I—"

"I'm sorry. But—"

"I've been thinking a lot about Dad lately. I've been going over all the mistakes I've made since he died and I—" He wandered back to the living room and sat down hard on my couch as a sob shook his shoulders.

I sat next to him and patted his back. "Hey, it'll be okay." When we were kids, I would have hugged him, but we didn't have that kind of relationship anymore. "Divorce isn't the end of the world. I should know, right?"

"I quit working for Phil." Our stepfather was a decent person and we got along okay, even though our basic life philosophies didn't quite mesh. Our mother was the real problem in the family.

I decided to take a few minutes to talk to Sam, then get rid of him.

"How did he take it?" I asked.

"He was disappointed, but he understood. Mom, on the other hand, was horrified and completely furious with me. Apparently, I'm destroying our family."

"You know that's not true."

My phone went off with a text message. Clara's name flashed on the screen before I snatched it off the coffee table.

"I have to answer this. I'm sorry."

"Clara? Hill?" My reaction must have given something away because he went pale. "Fuck . . ." He breathed and dropped his face into his palms.

My eyes narrowed as I set the phone down. "Yes, Clara Hill. Why?"

He ran his hands into his hair and looked up at me with panicked eyes. "Shit, Nick. What has she told you? Where should I start?"

"Told me what? What are you talking about?"

"The day after y'all graduated. The morning at the bus station."

Now I was the one to turn pale. I sank back into the couch completely drained as my mind spun, trying to put the pieces together.

He knew about the bus station. He knew about her? How?

*What else did he know?*

"She's told me practically nothing," I told him. "In fact, she goes out of her way *not* to talk about it. How do you even know about that? What the hell is going on?"

He met my eyes. "Mom found a bunch of notes stuffed in your backpack— love notes and plans to run off together—from Clara to you. I came back for your graduation and to stay for the summer, remember?" I nodded. "When I got home, she was in a rage. She threatened to cut me off, to stop paying my tuition and never speak to me again, if I didn't give Clara a note saying you were choosing college over her and make her believe it." His shoulders dropped. "I shouldn't have done it. In fact, I almost didn't, but she threatened to do the same to you too. So I gave in."

"What the fuck? Why didn't you tell me?"

"She told me to keep quiet and I—with Dad gone, the thought of losing Mom too was—I couldn't stand the thought of it. I thought I had to hold together what was left of our family. Are you back with her now?"

My head was spinning. "I'm trying to be."

"Mom's plan was stupid. I figured the two of you would end up talking, have a laugh, and figure out the note was bullshit. Did you find her and talk?"

"No, I—I should have. But I—it broke my heart when I thought she changed her mind about me. I couldn't face her."

"When you didn't get back with her, I thought you'd be okay. That it wasn't that serious between the two of you." He studied my face. "You weren't okay, were you?"

"No. No, I wasn't okay. Not at all." The words left me in a defeated breath.

"We were all so fucked up after Dad died." He sighed heavily as his voice filled with anguish. "Everything felt like the end of the world, didn't it? Like nothing good would ever happen again. It was hard to believe in anything."

"Yeah, she left, and god, it hurt, but it also felt like it was inevitable, like I had been waiting for it to happen the entire time I was with her. I guess that's why I gave up and let her go. I thought she'd be better off without me always having to keep our relationship hidden from Mom. I felt like I was letting Clara down."

"I'm so fucking sorry. What can I do? Would it help if I talked to Clara and told her the truth?"

I was angry—no, furious—with my mother. She'd cost me my relationship with the love of my life. But I understood why Sam had done it and reminded myself he was just as much a victim of her in this situation as Clara and I were. Our mother had never been an easy person to deal with, especially not after our dad died. She'd constantly been on the verge of a breakdown, and neither one of us had wanted to upset her.

We'd barely even begun to grieve our father before things began to change, pulling us in opposing directions. Sam had done everything our mother asked of him while I'd fought against it, clinging to the memory of our father and all that he'd taught us growing up.

"No. Now that I know what happened, it explains a lot." I let out a deep sigh.

"I'm so sorry, Nick. And Mom? What are you going to do?"

"What would be the point of doing anything?" I half yelled, my exasperation flowing through the room. "She only hears what she wants to hear. It kills me to say it, but I don't know who she is anymore." My head fell back on my shoulders, and I closed my eyes. "I haven't since Dad died."

"She was never the same after, no matter how hard I tried to make it so. I've been going along with what she's wanted for years, Nick. I went to the college she chose, I married who she told me to, took the job with Phil—but nothing is ever good enough for her." He threw his hands in the air. "I've reached my breaking point. She's never going to change and I'm too exhausted to keep trying to fix our family. I bought a place in town, and I found a new job, one I got on my own." I'd never heard my brother as contrite as when he said, "I miss my brother, Nick. I was hoping we could get back to how we were before."

I hated to see him struggling but was glad he'd finally wised up. And I missed him too. "It will be okay, Sam. We can try. You, me, and our kids."

"You don't hate me for this?"

"No. I'm not happy about any of it, not at all, but I get it. This is all on her. I wish I could understand where she was coming from, but I don't think I ever will."

"You won't, so don't even try to figure her out. I've stayed close to her all these years, and I still don't get it. It's not about Phil, he's great. She just lost herself after Dad died—lost her way, lost her values, lost her fucking mind? I don't know. I don't blame you for cutting her off like you did. I only wish I had done it, too, sooner."

The distance between me and my mother was never an easy thing to deal with, even though I knew it was for the best. "I didn't want to."

"I know that. But you're arguably better off for it."

I shrugged. "Maybe, but it doesn't make it hurt any less."

"I know it doesn't, and I'm so damn sorry. I'll go. You should talk to Clara, let her know how you feel about her. Tell her everything. And please tell her I'm sorry."

"That was actually the plan. We were going to talk over dinner."

"Shit." He winced. "I'm sorry I intruded."

I waved off his apology for the interruption. "No, it's okay. I know everything now, and that's a good thing. She's been holding something back. It was so long ago I thought that maybe it didn't matter if we never brought it up, but I think it's been the key all along."

He stood and gave me an unexpected hug. "If you change your mind and want me to talk to her, I will. I will do anything in my power to make this right."

"Thanks, Sam." I hugged him back.

"I don't deserve your thanks, not when I'm such a huge part of what messed this up for y'all."

"Look, it was Mom. She knows what buttons to push. She's not above using manipulation to get her way with us, and she never has been. I don't blame you for this." His hesitance in believing me was clear in his expression. "I mean it. Do I wish you'd come to me? Of course I do. But I understand why you didn't. We're going to be okay."

He slapped my upper back and headed for the front door. "I'll call you," he said when he reached the foyer and turned back. "Maybe we can get the kids together sometime, act like a real family for a change. How about Thanksgiving? No more phony bullshit. No more Bandit Lake and the country club. No more catered dinners and thousand-dollar bottles of wine. I want to dig out Dad's stuffing recipe. I want to bake Grandma's pies again. I want to burn a fucking turkey and be like we used to be in that tiny little trailer. Can we try?"

"I'd like that a lot."

He grinned at me. "Me too. Remember what Dad always used to say?"

I shook my head, my lips turning up in a sad smile. "He used to say a lot of things."

He stopped, hand lingering on the doorknob as his expression grew serious. "Sometimes you lose at the wrong time so you can win at the right time. Maybe now is supposed to be your time with her, Nick."

"Maybe it's our time too," I said with all the hope in my heart. "He held our family together. Now it's up to us."

"Love you, brother."

"I love you too. See you on Thanksgiving." I threw my hands out wide. "Right here."

"Count on it."

An idea struck. Why did we have to wait until Thanksgiving to start reconnecting? "Hey, hold up. I'm supposed to play ball with the Monroes and a few other guys up at the Smoky Mountain Inn. Want to come with?"

His eyes lit up. "That sounds better than moping around my empty house. Thanks, man."

This was it—things were changing for the better. I was going to get my brother back, and I knew in my heart now was my time with Clara. Now that I knew what had happened to break us up, I could start doing the work to repair the damage.

# CHAPTER 22
# CLARA

*I'm sorry, Clara. I can't go with you. I have to put my focus on college. My dad would have wanted that. I can't do this face to face. I'd never be able to leave you. - Nick*

The Fall Festival faded into the distance as I drove home.

I'd decided to tell Nick everything; I had no other choice. There was no way to keep it to myself now that Malcolm was in the picture. I would never be able to live with myself if Morgan actually ended up married to that asshole.

A quick text from Nick after I pulled into my driveway told me the kids were with Morgan at the festival and they were fine, and Malcolm had gone home to Knoxville "with a headache" exactly like he'd told me he would do.

I had time. I could plan the best way to tell Nick. But I was still beyond angry.

*This was my secret.*

It was one thing in my life that would not hurt anyone if I kept it to myself forever, and goddamn Malcolm for putting me in this position.

The entitlement of mediocre men would never cease to amaze me. I was a threat to him at that law firm. His father had founded it, and after little Malcolm had graduated from law school, his daddy hired him. He'd had to "earn" his partnership by working there, but there was never any doubt he'd get the position.

I'd earned my position every step of the way. My record was better than his, and I was on the cusp of eclipsing his dumb ass by becoming a partner alongside him. But *nooo*, he couldn't have that, could he?

He needed to have all the power and prestige for himself, and god forbid he be forced to share it with a mere woman. So he chose to belittle me. To turn me into a sex object put there for his own enjoyment, because in his mind, I was nothing.

Gracie was right. I shouldn't be alone right now. The temptation to rage-flail around my house, throwing things and stomping around like a toddler having a tantrum, was far too real.

I backed out of my driveway and headed toward the Smoky Mountain Inn. Being alone was stupid when I was in this mood.

I'd tell Molly and Leo everything. It could be sort of like a test run before I had to tell Nick. I could also let go and freak out a little bit too. Leo would feed me, and Molly would smother me with hugs, and everything would feel okay. *Probably.* Maybe Garrett would be there too. He was always good for a laugh, and I needed a laugh because *what the hell was happening to my life right now?*

Sadie's van was in a spot up front when I arrived. Perfect. I could tell the three of them. Now I'd get food, hugs, *and* Sadie would come up with at least a hundred crazy ideas for revenge.

They were all sitting on the huge enclosed front porch sipping lemonade and sharing a plate of cookies when I rounded the corner and made it to the front entrance.

Willa was there, too. I smiled at her, and she waved me over. "We're here to get our nails done," she called to me. "Want to join us?"

Molly nudged her. "Oh no, something's wrong." She scanned my face, then looked me up and down, probably checking for injuries. "You look . . . ," she began. "I don't even know. Is your life flashing before your eyes right now, Clara? You look like you've seen a ghost or something."

"What's happening, sweetie?" Leo rushed toward me to help me up the front stairs. He could always tell when I was too upset to function.

Sadie joined him at my other side and took my hand. "What's going on?"

"Malcolm" was all I could manage to say.

"That prick!" Sadie hollered. "Is it time? I've been saving up all my tuna fish cans. They're in a sealed-up tote in the Bandit Lake garage. I am fully prepared to bribe his housekeeper to stash them throughout his house—think of the smell! We'll call that a soft opening before we get to the good stuff—"

"No, Sadie." God, I loved how fierce she could be, especially when it was on my behalf. "I mean, maybe? But not yet."

"Okay, fine. Hear me out. We tell Momma and let *her* take care of him. She's always threatening to shoot someone. I say we let her."

Though I loved the idea of watching my mom shoot Malcolm right in the butt, I knew I couldn't condone it. "No, we finally have a chance with her. I don't want to have to visit her in prison."

"Fine. Point taken. I'll come up with something else—"

"Do not listen to your nutball sister." Leo guided me to a chair, and I sat down hard with a plop.

It was so pretty here. The inn backed up to the Great Smoky Mountains National Park. I let my eyes wander up into the misty mountains in the distance as I tried to clear my mind of all the garbage floating around inside it so I could focus on the problem at hand.

Years' worth of feelings butted up against each other just like those old hills and trees, spreading up and down and every which way until I'd lost all train of thought. I was stuck somewhere deep in the recesses of my mind thinking of everything I had done wrong to lead me to this place right now.

"Have some lemonade." Molly slid a cold glass into my hand, then gently closed my fingers around it. "Take a sip now, go on. You'll feel better."

In another universe, somewhere in another time, I was simply sitting on a porch with my friends and nothing bad had ever happened to me. Oh, how I wish I could be there right now . . .

I sipped at the lemonade and slowly came back to myself. I blinked and looked around, finding them staring at me in expectation. They wanted to grill me but were holding back.

I couldn't even object, because I'd done the same thing to them every time I'd had the sense they were troubled about something. Funny how it wasn't quite as fun when the shoe was on the other foot. Despite my reason for being here, being the center of attention was not my favorite thing.

"What's going on?" Leo finally asked. "Your mood is bleaker than I've ever seen."

Malcolm weighed heavily on my mind. Being forced to tell Nick about how I'd paid my way through college and law school weighed even heavier. Suddenly, I didn't feel like talking anymore. I felt like curling up into a ball and forgetting my entire life.

"Earth to Clara." Molly waved a hand in front of my face. "It's okay, you know. You can talk to us. We are fully stocked with hugs, comfort, cookies, milk, booze, more of that kick-ass lemonade, and whatever else you need. Plus, none of us are judgy. Not only have we all made our share of mistakes, but we love you."

"What did you say?" I came out of my bitter reverie with a jolt. "I'm sorry."

"Is this about Nick?" Molly asked.

"Huh? Yes. Well, kind of, but mostly no. Not really."

"That made total sense," Willa cracked.

My head flopped forward and I let out a deep sigh. "I'm sorry. I don't even know where to begin with this."

"One thing at a time." Leo patted my leg and offered me a cookie.

"Thanks." I stuffed half of it in my mouth while contemplating how to begin. After chewing and swallowing, I finally said, "Malcolm is trying to blackmail me."

They all knew about Malcolm and why I'd left my job but none of them— no one at all—had any idea that I'd stripped to pay my way through college.

"What could you have possibly done that's worthy of blackmail? None of us are going to think less of you, whatever it is," Leo soothed. "We've known you forever, Clara. You're safe with us. Just get it out and let us help you."

I took a deep breath. In, then out.

*Time to rip off the Band-Aid.*

"I never planned to ever tell anyone about this. And I dread telling Nick. He's not like anyone else I've ever dated—he's the real deal. I mean, Chris wasn't a real boyfriend. He was just a hot mistake I kept making over and over until he got sick of me and took off. Like, brooding is hot, but it isn't a real personality trait. I was so stupid about him, about all the men I dated when I really think about it. For years, I chose men I could never truly be happy with because—"

"Because deep down, you never let go of Nick, of loving him and holding on to the possibility of being with him again someday," Sadie deduced. "If you were with someone easily dumpable, you could move on fast."

It felt odd to sit here having a normal conversation with my sisters and friends while my entire life crumbled around me piece by piece.

"You can tell us anything. You've lived your life, Clara. You took it by the reins and look how far you've come." Sadie took my hand with an encouraging smile. "Nothing can be *that* bad, right?"

"She has a point," Leo chimed in. "It's better to regret what you did rather than what you were too afraid to try. Unless it's murder or something, of course." He pointed at me. "Don't kill people."

I rolled my eyes. "Fine, Leo, I guess I won't run off and murder Malcolm." I cracked a joke to try to get some of this tension out of my chest.

"Attagirl." He clinked his lemonade glass to mine.

"So, what's the big secret?" Sadie prodded. "Let us help you."

"Um, so, remember when I told you I was a waitress? Back in Nashville, I mean. When I was in college."

"Yeah, at the Sizzler," Sadie confirmed with a nod.

I closed my eyes and rolled my lips between my teeth, then blew out a big breath. "I was not a waitress at the Sizzler, Sadie." Step one of the confession was done. One more step to go.

"Ohhhhh snap!" Molly's eyes got huge. "What did you do? Is that what he's coming after you with?"

"You can't make the kind of money I made waiting tables at the Sizzler," I added pointedly.

*Was I hoping they'd just guess?*

"No, you cannot," Willa confirmed. "I've been waiting tables for years and I can't afford to dress like you, have a car like yours, or a big ol' house like yours . . ." Willa's eyes went on a trip from my eyes to my toes then back up again. "Oh. Ohhh. Dude. Not gonna lie, I considered doing it a time or two after my divorce, but I was too shy. Being broke sucks so bad. Good for you. This explains the pole class you taught at Stripped, doesn't it?"

My lips slid up into a half smile. She had figured it out.

For some reason I couldn't bring myself to say the words out loud. *I was a stripper.*

"Wait, hold up. What are we all *ohhing* for?" Sadie questioned. "I don't get it. Are you saying . . . ?"

"She was a stripper, sugar plum," Leo answered for me. "With all that T and A and those killer dance moves, well, it explains a lot. Law school is expensive and little miss Clara over there doesn't have any student loans to speak of, do you, sweetie?"

I couldn't help but crack a smile. "No, I do not."

"Oh my lord. Why did I never think of doin' that?" Sadie frowned. "If Momma blessed us with anything, it was her boobs. I could have cleaned the frick up! Hot stripper mom Sadie—think about that! I would have kicked ass at it. Okay, back to you. You did clean up, didn't you? Willa said it—look at that huge house, the BMW, all those Louis Vuitton purses and fancy shoes. You minored in finance, right?"

I nodded.

"What was your stripper name?" Molly asked. Her tone implied she was intrigued and not disgusted by me. "Will you teach me some moves?"

To clarify, there was nothing wrong with stripping—for other people. I still carried huge amounts of the shame my mother had heaped on me growing up and I couldn't seem to let it all go.

"Lavender Lane." They were making this almost fun, but it shouldn't be, *should it?*

"You named yourself after the farm!" Sadie hooted. "I love it!"

I was in shock. "This is going to come out after I tell Nick about Malcolm, and I'm mortified," I reminded them. "Why aren't y'all disappointed in me?"

"Why would you be mortified?" Willa questioned. "And why would we be disappointed in you? Look what you've accomplished."

"Hell no, Clara." Sadie stood and poked a finger in my face. "Do not be ashamed of what you did to survive. Be proud of it, damn it." She had gone from joking with the rest of them to righteous indignation. "Do you think any of the women down at the Pink Pony should be mortified? Should Hannah Townsen be ashamed of herself? Hell no! She took care of her sick momma by stripping, everyone knows that. Should any of the women you worked with in Nashville be mortified? Fuck no, they shouldn't, and neither should you. In fact, I wish I would have done it myself. They shouldn't be embarrassed, and neither should you. Right, Clara? Are you ashamed of yourself? Are you really?"

I stood up to pace the porch. "No, I'm not ashamed of it, not at all, not really. But it's not that simple for me, okay?" I tried to gather my thoughts so I could explain what I meant. "There's nothing wrong with stripping. Not one thing. It's a perfectly acceptable profession. It's artistic. It's athletic. It was fun. It can even be beautiful sometimes—"

"So, it's okay for them to do it and not for you?" Sadie scoffed. "Explain that to me, because I do not understand where you are coming from."

"It's more complicated than that. Don't you remember all the shitty things everyone said about us over the years? Hillbilly trash? Worthless, slut, dumb, and *good for nothing but a piece of ass*. Even Willa with her scholarship to that private school heard all the same shit. And I proved everybody right, didn't I? I turned out exactly how people said I would."

"You did no such thing! You supported yourself. You even supported me for a while too, you dang ol' dingbat. You put yourself through college and law school and bought a damn house in town for us all to live in when I couldn't afford to take care of my boys on my own. Damn it, Clara. You saved my life. You did that. *You*, my beautiful, smart, determined, ambitious, brilliant sister."

"And hey, you live in the nicest house on your block, and I know you paid for it outright. You never have to work again, do you?" Molly asked.

"No," I grudgingly admitted. "I could retire right now if I wanted to. I was more interested in finance than law. Dabbling in the stock market is a fun hobby—that, and working in my yard. Becoming an attorney seemed more outwardly impressive, I guess." I flopped back on the couch as what we were all saying sank in. "Oh god, my whole entire thought process is so fucked. I think I may have a problem."

I looked up to find them all staring at me like it was obvious.

"You did all these things because deep down you think you're not good enough," Sadie stated. "The big house, the BMW . . . because if you're dressed in more expensive clothes than everyone in town and your purse is worth more than the average house payment then nobody would dare call you a hillbilly, or a slut, or bring up how Daddy left Momma high and dry to raise a bunch of raggedy little girls."

Well, crap. When you put it like that . . . "You might have a point—"

"Hell yes I have a point, and it's a good one." Once Sadie started on a rant, it was hard to stop it, so I closed my mouth and let her go on. "You did all that so you could shut them up by threatening to sue them with your expensive law degree, or kick 'em in the shins with a Louboutin, or maybe whoop them upside the head with that little Fendi bag I've been coveting, am I right?"

"Yeah. I think subconsciously I had to know what I was doing," I admitted. "Like, deep down, I know I don't need all that stuff, but it makes me feel better to have it. You want the Fendi? You can have it."

"Listen," Willa cut in. "Even if you don't need those things, you earned that money and there's nothing wrong with spending it however you see fit."

"Your mother was the same way," Molly pointed out. "She cared a lot about what people thought of her. Her reputation is impeccable. Only people who cared to look closer knew about what was really going on with y'all."

"She was determined," Sadie agreed. "She built up the farm and created her own little empire up there. You've built a solid reputation for yourself too, Clara." Her voice softened, and I knew I wasn't going to want to hear what she said next. "But unfortunately, sugar plum, it's a house of cards. The outside means nothing if you don't believe in yourself."

"Dang it, Sadie." Tears filled my eyes. "That was too real. Was I this mean to you when you had your thing happening with Barrett?"

Her eyes shifted to the side and a sardonic half smile quirked up the right side of her face. "I almost don't wanna answer you, but yes you were, and I'll be grateful forever for it. What kind of sisters are we if we don't call each other out on our bullshit?"

I sniffled back the tears threatening to fall. "That's fair and you're right. Maybe someday I'll appreciate this and not want to cry."

"We all have triggers," Willa pointed out. "You wanted approval, didn't you? From Momma, from people in town? And maybe even from Nick?"

"Not him. Nick never treated me like I wasn't good enough. But his family turned into a bunch of snobs after his mom remarried, and I guess I had hoped they'd accept me someday. Or maybe I'm wrong—we kept our entire relationship a secret, didn't we?" The tears finally spilled down my cheeks, and I brushed them away. "And it wasn't my idea. Maybe I should forget about him. This is too hard. Especially when I can't seem to let anything go"

"It's always bothered you, hasn't it?" she murmured. "That you could never be open about being with him."

"Yeah." My whispered admission felt like a betrayal. And it wasn't fair to Nick since I had never spoken up about it. How could he fix a problem he never knew existed?

"Well, you *are* good enough, no matter what. Even if you weren't dripping in designer stuff and living in that big-ass house, you're good enough, Clara," Leo insisted. "I wish you would believe in yourself like we do. You deserve to be happy. You've sure as hell earned it after all these years taking care of everyone except yourself."

My heart wanted to believe what he was saying. "I guess so."

"Whatever blame you're placing on yourself, whatever grief for the past you're holding on to? Try to let it go. Forgive yourself, forgive him, and go get what you want. You're more than good enough," Willa added. "It's hard to let go of the past—believe me, I know. But it will be worth it once you're on the other side."

"Forgiving myself won't take away the pain if I lose him again," I argued.

"If you give up and let him get away, years from now you'll remember this moment and you'll wish you had put your heart out there again," Sadie insisted. "You'll wonder if he really was the one for you and you'll think, *What if?* Don't stop now. Tell him everything, including how you feel about keeping your relationship a secret."

"What if I tell him and get my heart broken again? How will I be able to take it? It almost destroyed me the first time."

"If he breaks your heart, then he doesn't deserve it. And this time you won't be alone with it, sugar," Leo soothed. "We will be here for you every step of the way."

"Go out there and do some main character shit." Sadie nudged me toward the door. "Go on now, talk to him."

"Fine. I have to talk to him, if only to tell him about Malcolm, for the sake of his kids. They don't deserve to get stuck with a stepfather like him. But all I want for myself is peace, and I don't know if I'll ever be able to have it when I'm in a relationship."

"Oh, Clara, no—" Sadie started.

I cut her off. "I want to feel good about myself. I need to be settled and secure and not constantly wondering when something will go wrong. Like . . ." I struggled to find the right words to explain how I felt, which was hard since I didn't completely understand it myself. "Nothing in life is perfect, I know that. But do you ever doubt Barrett, Sadie?" She bit her lip and looked away. "Molly, do you ever wonder if Garrett is going to leave you? If something happens, do you know Everett is going to stay and work shit out with you, Willa? And Leo, you know Landon is with you forever. You two are the gold standard."

Molly hugged me into her side. "I'm so sorry you feel like this. As the biggest mess of this group, I might be the only one here who completely gets how you feel right now," she joked. "But even I think you should try. Nick is a great guy, Clara. He comes out here all the time to play football with Garrett and the guys. I wish I had known what he meant to you. I wish I could have helped somehow."

My voice felt small and shaky. "I just want someone who will stay with me, you know? Because I'll stay. I'll try until there's nothing left—it's what I do. But I don't know if I can take losing him again."

"You deserve to have that, Clara," she insisted. "I've known Nick for years —the adult Nick, not the memory you've been carrying around with you. Even though you have this huge past together, you're still getting to know each other again. He won't judge you for this. I honestly believe everything will be okay."

"I wish I did too. Why am I so afraid?"

"Because this is huge and, like you said before, it's the real deal. It's potentially the rest of your life on the line. Plus, a bunch of crap you've been burying is hitting you all at once. Don't give up. You'll get through this." She took my hands and gave them a squeeze.

I stood and went to the window overlooking the vast expanse of lawn in back of the inn. Nick was out there playing football with his friends. Maybe they were right, and I should go talk to him.

*Could it really be that easy?*

I watched him catch the ball then toss it to someone. I took a step back and to the side to move out of view when I saw his brother run across the lawn to catch it.

Over the last few months, I'd forced the memory of that day at the bus station out of my mind. I'd truly believed the past had no bearing on my future with Nick. But seeing Sam brought back how much it hurt.

He was the one who met me that night to give me the note from Nick telling me he had to choose college over me. I'd understood. It had been the smart choice. He had earned a full scholarship to UT and I had nothing, so I accepted his decision without a fight and went on with my life so I wouldn't hold him back.

Funny how the mind of a teenager can be so fatalistic. Like we couldn't have worked something out, or even communicated over the years at some point? By the time I had realized how stupid I'd been it was too late.

I couldn't deal with this right now.

But I would soon for the sake of his kids, and because I loved him, and because no matter how scared and angry I felt right now, I didn't want to lose him.

I needed a minute to process my feelings and figure out the best way to tell him.

I needed a *pause*. A small one, just for a few hours, until dinner tonight.

"I'm going home," I told them. "I have to be alone for a little while." I turned back to the window. "Look at them. Out there playing football without a damn care in the world, never having to worry about being slut-shamed for their life choices or turned into a sex object for some horny asshole's amusement."

"Maybe you should stay here with us," Sadie suggested. "Or maybe I can go home with you? I don't think you should be alone right now."

"I'm fine, Sadie. I swear I am. But I'm way too clumsy to be around all this fragile masculinity right now. I'm afraid of what might come out of my mouth if I try to talk to him right now. But I promise I'll think about every-thing that y'all said."

"Okay, honey. I'm just a phone call away. Always. We all are." She pulled me into a hug. "Please call me later. I'm worried about you," she added under her breath.

"I'll call, I promise. I'll be fine. I'm just so angry right now. Not at him, he didn't do anything—" I ran my hands into my hair as I spun around looking for my purse. I had to get out of here.

"Here you go." Willa thrust my bag at me. I took it and dug through it for my keys. "You have every right to feel angry," she whispered, pulling me into the foyer and gesturing for Sadie to follow. "When guilt tries to creep in with it, do not let it. This entire situation is horrid and unfair."

"I'm already feeling guilty. I should go out there right now but—"

"Hush, it won't hurt anything to wait," Sadie soothed. "Malcolm slithered off back to wherever he came from, right? He doesn't live with them."

"You're right, he probably wouldn't do anything to really hurt them anyway. That's the entire point of keeping me quiet, isn't it? And I'm such an angry mess, I can't think straight."

She wrapped an arm around me, and Willa joined her on the other side, pulling me tighter until I ended up squished in the middle of a three-way sister hug. Which, considering I was about to lose my dang mind, was the perfect place to be.

"We're supposed to have dinner together at his place later," I mumbled into Sadie's shoulder. "How am I supposed to do this? I'm exhausted. I mean, god forbid I get to keep anything to myself, right?"

"We're coming home with you," Willa declared. "We all know better than to try to deal with things alone by now, don't we? No running. No hiding. We need each other."

"Damn right," Sadie agreed. "Let's go. We'll stop at the Piggly Wiggly on the way to your place, because I know your fridge is empty. Those cookies were delicious, but they won't hold me over until I get back home. And you'll need something later too."

We said our goodbyes and headed out to Sadie's minivan.

I let out a huge sigh, knowing they'd be giving me so much shit. "My kitchen is not empty anymore. Nick convinced me to keep my house stocked when I was sick . . ."

"Oh, he convinced you, did he? You mean that time when he left work to rush to your side and hold your hair back when you were puking, carry you to bed, make you chicken soup, and take care of you when you were sick because he's in love with you? You mean that time? That's when he convinced you?" Sadie's grin told me she was going to go off and I couldn't blame her. I'd done the same thing to her several times when she was falling for Barrett.

I rolled my eyes and bit back a smile. "Yeah. And?"

"So you, Miss Clara Jean Hill, the woman who subsists on coffee, angst, and whatever food her loved ones happen to bring by, went to the Piggly

Wiggly and bought yourself some groceries." She gave Willa an exaggerated eyebrow waggle in the rearview mirror. "Clara, you're frustrated now, and you have every right to be, but I see good things in your future. Don't you agree, Willa?"

"Yes, I sure do, Sadie." She stuck her fist through the seats and Sadie backward bumped it with a laugh.

"Whatever." I couldn't wipe the begrudging grin off my face as they continued teasing me all the way back to my house.

I deserved more than to be someone's secret. I *was* good enough. They were all right. I deserved to be loved no matter what I'd done in the past.

I had to finally take my therapist's advice and take time to grieve the life I never got to have. The mother I'd never had . . .

And the love I had lost because I was too young to know that it was everything I would ever need.

They stayed long enough to ensure I ate a sandwich and took some medicine for my headache, then they tucked me into bed for a nap and left to bring back my car.

Dinner with Nick later was still on, but I had to pull myself together first—and I would. Because I was my own knight in shining armor, and I deserved to be happy.

# CHAPTER 23

# CLARA

*We'll get through this. We can handle anything that comes our way*
*as long as we have each other. - Nick*

I woke up in the dark to loud pounding at my front door. I'd slept longer than I had planned.

Nick wouldn't bang on my door like that.

When I made it to the base of the stairs, the door flew open, thudding against the wall. Squinting into the dark of my foyer I tried to make out who was standing there. "Malcolm?"

I was disoriented from my nap and still exhausted from my perpetual lack of sleep. Belatedly, I ran my hand up the wall next to me to flick the light on. Taking my eyes off him would not end up good for me. His energy was off; it sent a chill up my spine.

"What did you tell her?" His voice cracked through the silence like a whip.

"Who?"

"Morgan broke off the engagement. She called me a couple hours ago and ended everything with me. What did you tell her?!" he repeated in a crazed shout.

"Malcolm, I haven't said a word to her. I've been here sleeping. I don't know what you're talking about." I fumbled for the light switch again, plunging us into darkness once more as I debated backing up the stairs to find something to hit him with, or lock myself in my bedroom—something, anything to get away from him. He was not here to have a coffee and a chat; I knew that much.

"Get back here!" he snarled.

There was something going on; he was off. I had the feeling he'd follow me then I'd be trapped upstairs without my phone to call the police.

"We have to talk. You're going to fix this for me or—"

"Or what?" I shrieked as I flew down the rest of the stairs, tackling him and taking him down to the hardwood floor. "Help me!" I screamed through the open door. "Help!"

The *thunk* of his head against the doorjamb as he fell was sickening, but it didn't stop him from struggling beneath me.

He took hold of my wrist, but I managed to twist out of his grip and dash into the living room.

He was disoriented but he stood up to follow me further into the house. Flipping my coffee table over to stall him, I made it to the fireplace to get to the poker, but he grabbed me from behind in a bear hug before I could reach it.

"Get off me!" I lurched back, shoving my full weight into him as I twisted and struggled in his grasp. "Get out!" I shrieked. "Let go of me, you asshole!"

"Take your fucking hands off her before I rip you apart."

It was Nick. In two strides, he was there prying Malcolm's arms apart so I could slip free.

"Mind your own goddamned business and get the hell out of here," Malcolm grunted as he stumbled in my direction. Unbelievably, he tried to hit me, but it was weak since he had to break out of Nick's grasp to do it.

Nick missed catching his arm, but I dodged his wild swing. Nick wrapped his arms around Malcolm and I used the opportunity to shift my weight and let loose an uppercut designed to smash Malcolm's smug face in. I didn't knock him out, but it stunned him enough that Nick was able to tighten his grip and walk him back toward the front door and out to the porch.

I met his eyes. "The cops are on the way," he told me. "You're okay. Baby, take a breath."

I did as he said and inhaled a deep breath as I found the light switch by the door and flipped it on to light up my porch and foyer.

Malcolm struggled in Nick's grasp. "You will not file a report. This dies here—"

This asshole's entitlement knew no bounds. "Fuck you, Malcolm. You broke my door and probably trampled through my flower beds. You bet your ass I'm filing a report!"

"Watch yourself, Miss Hill." His voice was a snarling gasp. "Or I might have to give up our little secret."

I whirled on him, waving my pointer finger at him for emphasis as my temper came back online. "I'm going to tell him everything, Malcolm. And I don't care who else finds out what I had to do to put myself through college. Not everyone is born with a silver spoon in their mouth like you were. Some people have to work for what they have, you pathetic, whiny little bitch."

He ground his teeth together and tried to glare me down.

I poked my finger into his chest. "I'm going to sue you until I own everything you have. I'll tie you up in so many legal knots you'll never be free. And I'll do it all by myself, just for fun. Destroying you will be my new hobby. Fighting me in court will cost you *everything*, because you're stupid, Malcolm. Your paralegals did all your real work—we both know that."

"You?" he scoffed. "You're nothing but a stripper whore. No one will believe what you have to say against me." He tried to lunge forward once more, but Nick was taller and stronger and there was no way Malcolm could break his grip. "Who do you think you are?"

"I'm smarter than you," I hissed. "I work harder than you, and I know more than you—that's why you couldn't stand it when I was about to make partner with you. All you are is a spoiled little trust fund baby with an overinflated sense of entitlement and a legacy law degree bought and paid for by your daddy. You should have just kept your fucking mouth shut and left me alone."

"You wouldn't dare—"

"Really?" Now I was the one lunging at him to shove my finger in his face. "Try me and see. What do I have to lose now, you moron? That was my only secret."

He kept quiet.

"He's already lost everything." Nick's deep voice echoed in the charged silence. "Morgan played you at your own game, didn't she?"

"What?" I had no idea what Nick was talking about.

"Morgan is set to inherit millions once she can access her trust fund," Nick explained. "That's partly why my mother is so obsessed with me getting back with her and why Morgan was always after me to take the job with my stepfather. Her problem is she can't get to her money until she's thirty-five. I just got off the phone with her. Her dad dug into you, just like you must have done to Clara. Right, Malcolm? That law firm of yours isn't doing too well, is it?"

He looked at the floor and continued to say nothing as Jackson James and

Wyatt, the sheriff's deputies in town, entered my house and took command of the situation.

In a daze, I followed, watching in disbelief as they led Malcolm outside and read him his rights.

How someone could look so conceited and entitled while being handcuffed and shoved into the back of a deputy sheriff's cruiser was beyond me.

He was huffing and puffing and talking about his father and his connections as if he had a leg to stand on. As if my freaking security cameras didn't exist to capture this entire thing, as if there weren't a crowd of neighbors outside watching the ridiculous aftermath play out.

Wyatt closed the door and pulled me into a hug. "You'll be okay with Nick? Should I call your sisters? An ambulance? Are you hurt?"

"I'll be okay, I'll call them. No ambulance. I'm just shaken up a bit is all. Thanks, Wyatt."

"We'll be in touch. And if you need me, don't hesitate to reach out." He exchanged a look with Nick.

"I got her. Thanks, man."

"Hey." Wyatt turned back. "I'll call Everett to come secure that door for you, okay?"

"Thank you."

As they drove off, Nick pulled me into his arms to lead me back to the house.

"Holy shit, Clara. My life flashed in front of me back there. The thought of not having you in it is intolerable. I can't live without you, not anymore. You know that, right?"

"I was so scared," I whispered as my arms tightened around his waist and the sob I'd been holding back shook me from head to toe.

He squeezed me back. "I'm here, I've got you, and I don't think I'll be able to let go of you anytime soon."

"He broke into my house." My tears stained the front of his shirt, but I couldn't find it in me to care.

"It's okay, baby, we can fix that."

"My therapist is going to make so much more money off me now . . ."

His chest rumbled in a laugh. "Baby, let's get you inside."

# CHAPTER 24
# NICK

*You mean everything to me. I love you, Nick. - Clara*

Malcolm was under arrest. The sight of Wyatt dragging him into his cruiser and hauling him off to the sheriff's station had sent a huge surge of relief through me.

Sasha and Ethan were safe at home with Morgan. She was upset about the breakup, but okay. She'd been after family connections, not love. And thankfully, as such, she hadn't encouraged the kids to become attached to him, so they would be okay too.

Clara sat on her sofa, staring blankly at her broken-in door with big eyes. I tugged a blanket around her shoulders while I set about packing a few of her things so I could take her to my place for the night.

Every ounce of adrenaline had left my body and I wanted nothing more than to collapse right next to her, but I couldn't. Not yet.

She needed me. I stood above her, glass of water in hand. "Drink this. I'm going to take care of you, and you're going to let me."

"Okay." Her voice broke slightly. "Did that really happen?"

"Yes, and we're going to my place. Everett is on his way to fix your door."

"I'm sorry this happened. It's because I keep secrets. I'm not honest—"

Hearing this incredible woman talk badly about herself made my heart sad. "You've been very honest this entire time, baby. Don't be so hard on yourself."

"But Nick, I didn't tell you about Malcolm. I didn't tell you what I did—"

"Stripping?" She nodded, her eyes downcast. "Were you okay? Were you forced?"

Surprised eyes landed on mine. "No, it was fine. It was even fun most of the time. It was burlesque, lots of dancing. It was safe. It was a good place, nice people—"

"That's all I care about. You can tell me about it or keep it to yourself—that information is yours and you decide what to do with it. You did what you had to do, Clara, and I would never judge you, not for anything."

The relief on her face almost broke my heart. I would love this woman, always, no matter what. She beamed at me. "I love you so much, Nick."

"I love you too. Always. Don't ever doubt it."

"I'm ready to listen now, Nick. Let's get everything out in the open. Tell me why you didn't try to find me. Tell me everything I haven't let you say. Tell me you're sorry. Tell me you missed me." Her tone turned pleading, her love and past hurt blending together with her desire to move forward together. "Tell me you were empty without me all these years and make me believe it, Nick. Please . . ."

"You sure you want to do this now?"

"It's the only thing left between us, and I'm ready to have it gone."

I kissed the top of her head and sat next to her. "I think if I loved you less, I might have been able to find you sooner and make things right between us, but you were everything to me." I grabbed her hands in mine. "Losing you burned a hole straight through my heart, and I couldn't face the thought of you rejecting me. I think the loss of my dad and you going off to Nashville got twisted up together and I couldn't cope with it."

"I believe that. I understand, because I felt that way too. And it's not all your fault—I should have come back. I should have found you and demanded to know what changed your mind about me. I should have fought for us, but I was too afraid to lose you, even though you were already lost. I know it doesn't make sense—"

"I've never changed my mind about you," I said softly. I had to tell her about Sam and my mother. "Not now, and not ever. I don't know how I managed without you for all these years. I took one look at you in that parking lot, and I was gone again."

"But what about the note you sent me?" she murmured.

My eyes drifted shut as I struggled to find the right words. "I didn't write the note, Clara. My mother did, and she forced Sam to give it to you." She was stunned. "You waited for me there, didn't you? I can't imagine how much that must have hurt, sitting there all alone. And I never came."

I watched as Clara's eyes welled with fresh tears. "I waited hours for you. Then Sam showed up with the note. I don't know what made me do it, but I bought myself a ticket to Nashville and never looked back. I think the thought of going home to live a life in Green Valley with you not here was too much for me to handle." Clara paused. "But it was more than that. It was my entire life. I didn't want to go back to my mother, and I didn't want to struggle here in Green Valley. I didn't want the judgement."

I nodded in understanding. We shared so many of the same feelings. "I waited for you. The next day I found Sadie to ask her if you were okay and to try and find out where you were."

"Oh my god, what did she do to you?" she scoffed. "Once I'd checked into a hotel, she basically spent the entire night on the phone with me trying to convince me to come back home. I told her everything about us. I was a mess, Nick."

"That explains her reaction. She yelled at me—she told me I'd done enough to you and she wouldn't let me hurt you any further. I figured maybe you thought we'd gone too far, or you weren't ready—"

"Where were you that day? If you didn't change your mind, why didn't you come?"

"My mother. She pulled out photo albums of our family. She promised to make changes, told me she'd accept me being a teacher. I thought I had finally gotten through to her. But it was all a lie. She manipulated me to keep me home, to make me late. I know that now."

"I'm so sorry, Nick."

"In retrospect, it was such a simple thing. Hell, Clara. I thought I'd be late, we'd laugh, then we'd be free. But you were already gone when I got there. Sam showed up at my house earlier today—I'll tell you about that later—and told me everything. But what I can't understand is why you believed that note." I whispered, "Why did you stay away?"

"Because I knew I'd never be good enough for your family and the note only served to prove it. It's always been easier for me to believe the bad things people say about me. And you were like a dream, Nick. So smart, so honorable, so perfect in every way. Most of the time when we were together, I was in disbelief, waiting for you to discover what a huge mistake you were making with me." She shrugged. "I figured that's why you always wanted to keep me a secret."

"I'm so sorry—"

"I called your house and talked to your mom, you know. It was a few days after I'd arrived in Nashville. I was thinking about us and wondering if I should come back." She let out a dry laugh. "She let me know very quickly that I should leave you alone. They'd moved you into an apartment near the college—you had your own place just like you wanted, exactly like we had talked about. You were taken care of and safe and waiting to start football practice. The way she spoke to me made me think she knew, and I was right."

Learning just how much my mother had meddled in my relationship made me even angrier with her. "I wasn't happy, not one bit. I was miserable."

"I know that now. But it hurt, Nick. It made it feel like we'd never existed. I wasn't going to tell you about the things she'd said. I never wanted you to know just in case you could have a relationship with her someday, like I have with my mother." Her face grew serious, her tone hardening. "But if she used your own brother against you and lied to make you late, then she doesn't deserve my silence. It's one more thing she has to atone for."

"I didn't want her to treat you badly—that's why I wanted to keep us a secret. I knew she wouldn't accept us. All I wanted was to be able to tell her, my own damn mother, how I'd found the woman I was going to spend the rest of my life with, how happy you made me, and how you gave me peace after my dad died." My eyes closed, emotion threatening to overcome me. "I loved you so fucking much, Clara. Please believe that. I was trying to protect you, and instead I created this insecurity in you and I'm so, *so* fucking sorry."

"No, you didn't create it. This insecurity is ingrained in me, it's been part of me for as long as I can remember and nothing I have done has ever fully eradicated it."

"You were always good enough. Always. My god, Clara, you were a fucking miracle in my life. I loved you then and I love you now. When I saw you again, I realized almost immediately that I'd never stopped, not for a second." I needed her to understand. "And as for me wanting to hold off telling the kids about us—it isn't like before. It's not the same kind of secret. I wish I would have made you understand where I was coming from when I said it. Can you forgive me for that?"

Her answering smile broke through the emotion of the moment like the sun shining through the clouds after a storm. "Of course I forgive you. I get it now. And I love you too." She leaned in and offered me a sweet, gentle kiss.

"We really fucked up, didn't we?"

"We were kids struggling to get through the worst time in our lives. We were both in so much pain."

"For years, I believed my kids were the only good thing I've ever done in my life. That being their dad was the only thing I managed to do right."

Clara leaned into me, nestling herself against my body. "You know what? We have nothing to forgive each other for. Let's forgive ourselves instead, and just be together. And if we were really honest with ourselves right now, we would realize that we would have never made it back then. How could we have?"

"You're probably right about that. We would have collapsed under the pressure. We're older and I'd like to think a little bit wiser. Let's use this as a new beginning."

"You're right. We're grown. And we're free." She laughed. "And I'm exhausted. Let's go to your place and crawl into bed."

# CHAPTER 25
# CLARA

*I love you. I can't wait to be with you forever. - HB*

This would be the first Christmas in my entire life that I'd wake up and be part of a "normal" family morning. Sadie and the boys had moved in with Barrett before we could have one at my place together and suffice it to say, my childhood Christmas mornings were better left forgotten, even the ones my father had been a part of.

It was Nick's year to have Christmas with the kids and I'd been beyond honored and only mildly freaked out when they'd asked me to stay the night and spend all day with them.

Sasha and Ethan told me their dad had traditions: stuff like homemade cinnamon rolls and eggnog with whipped cream for breakfast, then opening presents one by one while *A Christmas Story* played in the background. Those were some of the things he'd done growing up, and he'd kept that alive for his own kids.

Like me, Nick had four bedrooms. I had crashed on the pull-out bed in his family den which doubled as the guest room. The kids knew we were together. They even knew we had dated in high school, but we chose not to tell them all the fraught details. As far as they were concerned, we liked each other a long time ago and now we did again. We agreed that we wouldn't share a room until we'd been together for a few more months.

I opened my eyes as a sliver of light from the hallway crossed over me. "Hello," I whispered.

"Baby, wake up." It was Nick. "I have something to give you before the kids get out of bed."

I sat up, patting the mattress next to me while I wiggled my eyebrows. "Get in here."

"It's not that, though I like the way you think," he joked as he crossed the room. He didn't join me in the bed. Instead, he knelt at the edge and placed a small velvet box next to my knee.

The breath left my body along with his name in a slow whoosh. "Nick . . ."

"I love you." I opened my mouth to speak but he quieted me with a kiss to my lips. "I have to tell you how much before you say yes."

"Okay, tell me," I whispered. Goosebumps rose over my skin.

"It's timeless, endless, boundless . . . Some people find their way into your heart and never leave. You've never left mine." His hand slid over his heart to rest there. "You've been right here since I met you."

Happy, overjoyed tears filled my eyes, threatening to spill. "I love you so much, Nick."

"You were my first love, my only love. Every memory we've ever made together is part of me. I never, ever forgot you and now that I have you again, I'll never let you go. Clara Jean Hill, will you marry me?"

I beamed at him. "Yes. I will marry you, Nicholas Andrew Easton. Just try to get rid of me."

"Never. Now that you're mine, we're doing all the classics—every normal, cheeseball thing I can think of. We're starting traditions together, Clara."

He opened the box, and I gasped.

"This was my grandmother's ring."

I held out my hand. "It's beautiful." And it was. Round, brilliant, about three carats on a platinum band. It fit me perfectly as he slid it on.

"This makes it official. You're mine forever."

"I'm yours, Nick. Forever and ever, like I've always been. Get up here and hold me." He climbed in next to me and I snuggled back, enjoying the feel of having my future husband's arms wrapped around me.

He took my hand in his and held it out so we could admire the ring.

"Sam brought it over on Thanksgiving," he murmured. "How about next year we celebrate together? You'll love his kids."

I hummed my agreement. "I'd like that. Maybe we could have it at my place."

"*Your* place, huh?" He brushed my hair over my shoulder as he nuzzled my neck, dropping little kisses behind my ear.

"Oh!" Joy bubbled inside me when it hit me that we'd be moving in together. "We're getting married!"

"We sure are, baby." He chuckled.

I wiggled with excitement. "When should we do it?"

"As soon as possible. Tomorrow?"

Images began to play through my head like a movie. "I want a spring wedding in one of the lavender fields, Nick. Now that I've made peace with my mother, I think it will be the perfect place."

The deep rumble of his laugh made me smile. "How about in the field where we had our first time, out behind the barn," he suggested. His voice dropped low as he whispered in my ear, "No one has to know what we did back there."

I turned in his arms to face him. "We can find the exact spot!"

"Have I ever told you I love your dirty mind?" His eyes sparkled with naughty thoughts of his own.

"Shh," I hissed. "Someone's coming."

Sasha poked her head in the door. "Dad?"

"Did he do it yet?" Ethan shouted.

I let out a giggle. "They knew you were going to propose?"

"They did," he confirmed. "I asked them first and they—"

"We said yes!" Sasha shrieked as she burst into the room. "We can't wait 'til you marry our dad!"

Ethan popped his head through the doorway. "We have presents for you too." He was adorably sheepish when he asked, "Can I give mine to you now?"

My heart swelled. "You sure can, sweetie. Come in."

Sasha stage-whispered to Nick, "I brought the one from you too, Dad."

"Oh, but my presents for y'all are out under the tree." I needed to hop up and go get them but—

"This is a new tradition," Nick informed me. "Just for you."

Tears filled my eyes as I looked at the three of them. Their smiles were so sweet, so full of love. "Oh," I squeaked. "Okay, I—"

"It's okay, baby." Nick pulled me into his side. "I got you."

"Dad's goes first." Ethan handed me a small box. Inside was a bracelet with a tiny engagement ring charm dangling from one of the links.

It was gorgeous. "I love it, y'all. Nick, I—don't know what to say . . ." A warm glow lightened my heart as tears ran freely down my cheeks.

Ethan shoved his present toward me. "Now mine." I unwrapped it and discovered a tiny ornament charm with *Our 1st X-mas* engraved on the front with the year on the back.

"Y'all, I—oh my god." I could no longer contain myself. I bawled.

Sasha wiped away her own tears as she passed me a bigger box. Inside was a tiny potted plant and a watering can. "I couldn't decide," she said. "So dad said I could get you both."

"I love them. All of them, and I love all of you too. These are the best gifts I've ever received in my entire life."

I no longer had any words left in my brain to say, so I held my arms out, wiggling my hands for them to come to me so I could hug them.

"I'm going to be the best stepmother ever," I finally managed to squeak out as I kissed their cheeks one by one. "I swear it."

"We know you will, Miss Clara. You're already the best neighbor we've ever had," Ethan said.

"Just Clara, now. Please," I murmured. *Would they call me something step-mother-y in the future?* I couldn't wait to find out.

"You're always so nice to us, Clara," Sasha added. "And you're fun to talk to, and you're also my best plant friend. We can garden together all the time now!"

"And you're funny too, and you always have Dr Pepper." Ethan tried to one-up her, and it was adorable.

"But most of all, you love our dad a lot," Sasha finished. "That's the best part."

"I do. I so do, " I sobbed as I squeezed them close. "I love him more than the whole world and I'm going to love you both that much too, I promise."

Nick pulled all of us into his arms, laughing when we tipped over and fell against him.

"How are we ever going to top this morning?" I mumbled into his chest.

"Wait and see, baby," he told me. "It'll only get better from here."

# CHAPTER 26
# CLARA

*One day I'm going to marry you in the middle of one of these lavender fields,*
*Clara Jean Hill. - Nick*

"**Y**ou made the right choice," Momma whispered to me as she fluffed up my veil in the back. "And I'm honored to be here with all of you right now."

My sisters and I, along with Sasha and Molly, were crammed in my old bedroom at the farm. They were helping me get ready.

Leo was in the kitchen putting the final touches on the food before he'd head down to the wedding site. He and my mother had been bonding and cooking all day. I'd seen the cake; it was adorable, with two tiny houses side by side on top.

It was my wedding day. Nick and I were getting hitched in the exact spot we'd discussed: the one where we'd had our first time.

My dress was a simple silk sheath, strapless and cut on the bias. It was knee-length and trimmed in beaded lace. I was wearing my favorite pale pink cowgirl boots—not only would regular heels sink into the ground outside, but these boots were lucky. I wore them when I had my first time with Nick. No one knew the significance of the location and these boots except for the two of us.

*I guess I have one secret left after all,* I laughed to myself.

My eyes drifted around the room that was almost the same as it had been when I'd left it, like a little time capsule from my past: same twin bed, covered in that old purple quilt Momma had made so long ago; same wooden bureau with the mirror on the back and old books and baubles littering the surface.

I traced a finger down the glass and smiled at what I saw shining back inside its dusty wooden frame. For the first time, I didn't feel the same when I looked in the mirror. I was no longer that lost little girl who'd left this place so many years ago. I'd found myself, and more importantly, I liked what I had discovered.

"I love you, Momma," I said to her reflection at my side.

"I love you too, sugar." She pulled me into a sideways hug and smiled at me in the mirror before saying to the room, "None of you go givin' her a hard time now. I'm going to go check on everything and make sure Leo stops fussin' over that gorgeous cake and doesn't miss the ceremony."

"We won't," Gracie told her. "We think it's the best choice too. It's sweet."

"I think it's brilliant," Sasha announced with a giggle. She was my maid of honor and would be walking with me down the aisle.

Ethan was the best man and he'd be waiting with Nick at the end.

It was like the four of us were creating our own little family today.

I'd never try to usurp Morgan's role as their mother. But I wanted today to be special for the kids too.

"Let's go," Sadie ordered. "Time and preachers wait for no man—or woman. Y'all, I have no idea how that saying actually goes. But the bottom line is we've got a wedding to get started."

"Yes, ma'am." I turned away from the mirror to find them all watching me, with huge smiles lighting up their beautiful faces.

"I'm beyond thrilled for you," Molly declared. "You're gorgeous, but more important, you look happy—truly happy—and it's a sight to behold."

I pulled her into a hug. "I love you, Molls."

She squeezed me back. "Love you too. I'll see you out there."

Willa pulled me into a quick hug of her own. "We love you," she whispered. Come on, Hills, let's move out." Sadie and Gracie followed behind her out the door.

It was just me and Sasha. "Are you ready, sweetheart?"

"I can't wait! We'll have another day for our family to celebrate now—your and Dad's anniversary." She looked up at me with hopeful eyes. "We can add that to our family traditions, right?"

"Darn right, honey. Let's go."

We found our way to the old red barn out behind the house and stopped to take it all in. Lavender, sweetly scented and planted in perfect purple rows, led all the way to the horizon with the Smoky Mountains standing at the end.

Placed in the middle of it all—in the spot Nick and I had, *ahem*, rediscovered a couple weeks back—was a wooden arch covered in pale pink roses and wound with shimmering tulle ribbons that billowed in the breeze.

White chairs filled with family and friends sat in the spaces between the lavender. Everyone turned to look as I flipped the music on and the soft notes of Pachelbel's Canon in D drifted over the flowered field.

Nick spotted us and waved, beckoning us closer, urging us on. I watched the play of emotions cross his face as, hand in hand, Sasha and I moved toward him, step by step heading into the future finally within our reach.

The shadows in my heart were gone. I'd let everything go to shine in the sun.

# EPILOGUE

NICK

*Only nerds and suck-ups go to prom, Nick. Of course I don't want to go.*
*Would you like to do it in a lavender field instead? - HB*

"I s it obnoxious that I'm wearing my wedding dress?" Clara wrinkled her adorable nose as she studied her reflection in the tinted window of the black stretch limousine parked in front of our house.

It was a toss-up as to which of our two houses we'd live in after we got married. My pool and huge backyard had been the deciding factor. She reluctantly agreed to leave her yard and porch behind, and her house was currently up for sale.

"No, you look fucking beautiful." I stepped behind her and dropped a kiss to the back of her neck.

"Thank you. And who says you can only wear your wedding dress once?"

"Certainly not me." I chuckled as I took in the vision standing before me. She was beautiful, though instead of the pale pink cowgirl boots she'd worn on our wedding day, she wore gold, strappy high-heeled shoes. Her hair was piled on top of her head in a sexy bun, and I figured maybe she thought the veil would have been too much to chaperone Green Valley High's senior prom.

"Good. Okay, then is it obnoxious that I rented a stretch limo and made you buy me a corsage?" Her lips twisted up in a grin as she turned to face me.

"No, not at all," Gracie deadpanned. "All of this is totally normal."

I held my fingertips an inch apart. "Maybe a little bit. Tiny," I teased her. "Miniscule."

"*Hmph.* You know what?" She spun in a circle. "I don't even care." Her giggle was adorable and infectious and also unprecedented. Clara Jean Hill was not a giggler, but Clara Easton was, and I loved it.

"You shouldn't care what anyone thinks. You look beautiful, Mrs. Easton, and tonight is going to be fun. Don't listen to them."

"I always knew I liked you, Weston." She reached out and booped his nose with a grin. "And new rule—I want everyone to call me Mrs. Easton all night, even you, Nick."

"You got it, Mrs. Easton." I watched her shiver in pleasure as a huge grin spread across her face and she threw herself into my arms.

"I love you," she declared.

"I love you too . . . Mrs. Easton."

"*Gah!*" She smacked a quick kiss to my lips, and I yanked her closer and laid one on her. Because one quickly smacked kiss from my beautiful wife would never be enough for me.

"Aww, look how cute and happy they are, Weston." Gracie snapped a picture of the two of us with her phone. "I'm going to post about the two old people we ended up on a double date to prom with."

"Ha ha, very funny, Gracie," Clara playfully huffed as she pulled out of my arms.

"Seriously, though. You're beautiful, Clara," Gracie said. "I mean, Mrs. Easton."

"Duh, we're both stunning tonight." She wrapped an arm around Gracie's shoulders. "Take our picture, Westie. This night is one for the books."

He pulled his phone out, smiling to himself as he took their picture. Gracie and Weston had gotten back together after he'd come home from his first year of college.

A Jeep Wrangler pulled up to the curb and Ruby hopped out. "Sorry we're late!" she hollered. "My date just got off a plane, y'all."

"Who's that?" I whispered to Clara as a handsome college-aged dude climbed out of the passenger seat and took Ruby's hand with a besotted smile on his face.

She leaned in and whispered in my ear, "That, dear hubby, is Marianne's older brother. Ruby flew him in from whatever college he goes to."

"No shit?" A smile quirked up the corner of my mouth.

"Nope, zero shit. One must not make the mistake of underestimating that girl, a lesson Gracie and I have learned all too well over the last couple of weeks. That one plays the long game. It's truly devious."

"I don't know about that. It looks like she might like him too."

I'd never been in a limo before. This one was something else; it was too bad we were only a block away from the high school. We pulled up with a flourish. Our limo was at least twice as long as what any kid at this place could get their parents to pay for. Clara had spared no expense.

Strands of twinkling lights and streamers were wrapped on and around every available beam and structure leading the way to the gym.

We'd gone from an immaculately planned and decorated lavender field wedding only days before, to a seventies-themed disco party prom in the Green Valley High School gymnasium—and I couldn't have been happier to be right here. Who needed a honeymoon when you could have all this?

I led my wife out to the middle of the wooden floor, directly beneath the giant rented disco ball where everyone could see us.

"Dance with me, heartbreaker." I took her hand and twirled her in a circle beneath my arm, smiling as her delighted giggle floated in the air with the music. Hands at her waist, I pulled her close until we were face to face. "I mean, Mrs. Easton." My god, she was gorgeous, and I was the luckiest man in the world.

"I will dance with you forever, Mr. Easton . . ."

# ABOUT THE AUTHOR

Nora Everly is a life long reader, writer, and happily ever after junkie. She is a wife and stay-at-home mom to two tiny humans and one fat cat. She lives in Oregon with her family and her overactive imagination.

* * *

**Newsletter:** https://www.noraeverly.com/newsletter-1
**Website:** https://www.noraeverly.com/
**Facebook:** https://www.facebook.com/authornoraeverly
**Goodreads:** https://www.goodreads.com/author/show/19302304.Nora_Everly
**Twitter:** https://twitter.com/NoraEverly
**Instagram:** https://www.instagram.com/nora.everly/

Find Smartypants Romance online:
**Website:** www.smartypantsromance.com
**Facebook**: www.facebook.com/smartypantsromance/
**Goodreads:** www.goodreads.com/smartypantsromance
**Twitter:** @smartypantsrom
**Instagram:** @smartypantsromance

Want more from Nora Everly? Check out her self-published Sweetbriar Hearts series starting with *In My Heart*, available now!

Growing up, Luke and Lily were everything to each other.
He was her rock. She was his reason to live.
Ending up together was inevitable—until it wasn't.

Years later, Lily wants one thing. To spend a quiet summer with her kids settling into their new life in her old hometown.

But her long lost first love, nosy family, and an inept, yet scary stalker won't leave her in peace.

Luke also wants one thing. He wants Lily back.
He's out of the army, recovered from his injuries and wants to reclaim his life.

But Lily isn't ready to trust and Luke won't open up.
Will their second chance at first love be over before it begins?

**Praise for *In My Heart***

★★★★★ "This was my first Nora Everly book. This author writes with passion and flair, managing to capture the reader's imagination, heart and attention. The characters are incredibly multifaceted, engaging and lovable. Nothing gets my nerdy little reading heart revving quite like a second chance Romance and all the conflict, drama, heartache, angst and love that comes along with it." -*Emerald Book Reviews*

★★★★★ "With what I now know is classic Nora Everly, she delivers a sweet story full of delicious heat and some twists that left me rapidly turning the page until the very end!" -*Jes, Goodreads Reviewer*

★★★★★ "Small town, second chance romance is right up my alley and *In My Heart* delivers a deliciously complicated romance invaded from every angle by hurtful memories and nosy well-meaning family members." – *Lisa, Amazon Reviewer*

# ALSO BY NORA EVERLY

**The Sweetbriar Mountain Series:**

<u>In My Heart</u>

<u>Heart Words</u>

<u>From the Heart</u>

<u>Heart to Heart</u>

<u>Change of Heart</u>

**Smartypants Romance:**

<u>Crime and Periodicals</u>

<u>Carpentry and Cocktails</u>

<u>Hotshot and Hospitality</u>

<u>Architecture and Artistry</u>

<u>Passing Notes</u>

**Star Crossed Lovers (As Piper Everly):**

<u>Midnight Clear</u>

# ALSO BY SMARTYPANTS ROMANCE

**Green Valley Chronicles**

**<u>The Love at First Sight Series</u>**

*Baking Me Crazy by Karla Sorensen (#1)*

*Batter of Wits by Karla Sorensen (#2)*

*Steal My Magnolia by Karla Sorensen (#3)*

*Worth the Wait by Karla Sorensen (#4)*

**<u>Fighting For Love Series</u>**

*Stud Muffin by Jiffy Kate (#1)*

*Beef Cake by Jiffy Kate (#2)*

*Eye Candy by Jiffy Kate (#3)*

*Knock Out by Jiffy Kate (#4)*

**<u>The Donner Bakery Series</u>**

*No Whisk, No Reward by Ellie Kay (#1)*

*Dough You Love Me? By Stacy Travis (#2)*

*Tough Cookie by Talia Hunter (#3)*

*Muffin But Trouble by Talia Hunter (#4)*

**<u>Oh Brother! Series</u>**

*Crime and Periodicals by Nora Everly (#1)*

*Carpentry and Cocktails by Nora Everly (#2)*

*Hotshot and Hospitality by Nora Everly (#3)*

*Architecture and Artistry by Nora Everly (#4)*

**<u>Small Town Silver Fox Series</u>**

*Love in Due Time by L.B. Dunbar (#1)*

*Love in Deed by L.B. Dunbar (#2)*

*Love in a Pickle by L.B. Dunbar (#3)*

**<u>The Green Valley Library Series</u>**

*Prose Before Bros by Cathy Yardley (#1)*

*Shelf Awareness by Katie Ashley (#2)*

*Dewey Belong Together by Ann Whynot (#3)*

*Checking You Out by Ann Whynot (#4)*

**<u>Scorned Women's Society Series</u>**

*My Bare Lady by Piper Sheldon (#1)*

*The Treble with Men by Piper Sheldon (#2)*

*The One That I Want by Piper Sheldon (#3)*

*Hopelessly Devoted by Piper Sheldon (#3.5)*

*It Takes a Woman by Piper Sheldon (#4)*

**<u>Park Ranger Series</u>**

*Happy Trail by Daisy Prescott (#1)*

*Stranger Ranger by Daisy Prescott (#2)*

**<u>The Leffersbee Series</u>**

*Been There Done That by Hope Ellis (#1)*

*Before and After You by Hope Ellis (#2)*

**<u>The Higher Learning Series</u>**

*Upsy Daisy by Chelsie Edwards (#1)*

**<u>Green Valley Heroes Series</u>**

*Forrest for the Trees by Kilby Blades (#1)*

*Parks and Provocation by Juliette Cross (#2)*

*Letter Late Than Never by Lauren Connolly (#3)*

*Peaches and Dreams by Juliette Cross (#4)*

*Young Buck by Kilby Blades (#5)*

*Package Makes Perfect by Lauren Connolly (#6)*

**Educated Romance**

**<u>Work For It Series</u>**

*Street Smart by Aly Stiles (#1)*

*Heart Smart by Emma Lee Jayne (#2)*

*Book Smart by Amanda Pennington (#3)*

*Smart Mouth by Emma Lee Jayne (#4)*

*Play Smart by Aly Stiles (#5)*

*Look Smart by Aly Stiles (#6)*

*Smart Move by Amanda Pennington (#7)*

*Stage Smart by Aly Stiles (#8)*

**<u>Lessons Learned Series</u>**

*Under Pressure by Allie Winters (#1)*

*Not Fooling Anyone by Allie Winters (#2)*

*Can't Fight It by Allie Winters (#3)*

*The Vinyl Frontier by Lola West (#4)*

**Out of this World**

**<u>London Ladies Embroidery Series</u>**

*Neanderthal Seeks Duchess by Laney Hatcher (#1)*

*Well Acquainted by Laney Hatcher (#2)*

*Love Matched by Laney Hatcher (#3)*

**<u>Wolf Brothers Series</u>**

*Truth or Wolf by Anne Marsh (#1)*